THE SECRET LETTERS

The

SECRET LETTERS

of

MARILYN MONROE

and

JACQUELINE KENNEDY

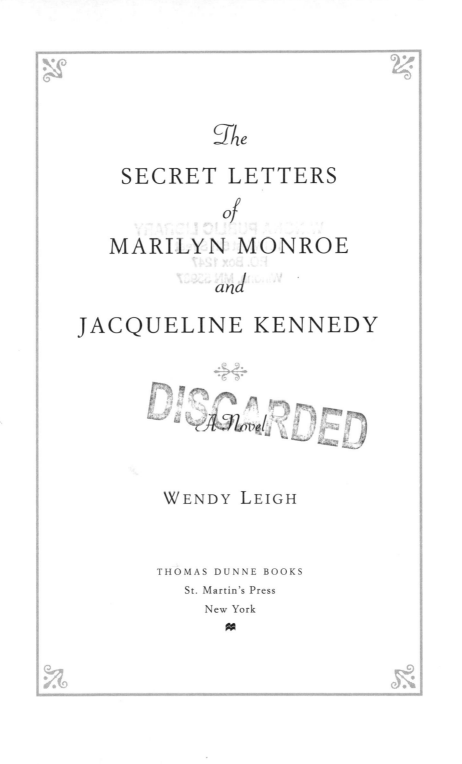

A Novel

WENDY LEIGH

THOMAS DUNNE BOOKS
St. Martin's Press
New York

THOMAS DUNNE BOOKS.
An imprint of St. Martin's Press.

www.stmartins.com

ISBN 0-312-30368-8

First Edition: April 2003

10 9 8 7 6 5 4 3 2 1

To Dr. Erika Padan Freeman

NOTE TO READER

This is a work of fiction. Although many of the events discussed in the letters actually occurred, the letters themselves are the product of the author's imagination. This novel has not been authorized or endorsed by the estates of Marilyn Monroe or Jacqueline Kennedy Onassis.

PATRICE RENOIR
Apartment 1
The Renaissance
1600 La Brea
Hollywood, California 90069

Richard Winchester
Winchester Literistic
17 Sutton Place
New York, New York 10021

June 1, 2002

Dear Mr. Winchester,
Forty years ago I made Marilyn Monroe a sacred promise.
I kept that promise. I waited 40 years, and now I am writing to you.
I was Marilyn's friend and the morning before she died, she gave me
something.
Do you ever come to the Coast?
It will be worth your while.

Best regards,
Patty Renoir

P.S. I read about you in *Variety*.

RICHARD WINCHESTER
Winchester Literistic
17 Sutton Place
New York, New York 10021

Patrice Renoir
Apartment 1
The Renaissance
1600 La Brea
Hollywood, California 90069

July 3, 2002

Dear Ms. Renoir,

Thank you for your letter of June 1. Unfortunately, at the moment
I have no immediate plans to visit California.

However, if you would care to send me your manuscript, I should
be delighted to read it with a view to representation.

Looking forward to hearing from you.

Best regards,
Richard Winchester

PATRICE RENOIR
Apartment 1
The Renaissance
1600 La Brea
Hollywood, California 90069

Richard Winchester
Winchester Literistic
17 Sutton Place
New York, New York 10021

July 10, 2002

Dear Mr. Winchester,

You've got it all wrong. I couldn't write my way out of a paper bag! I didn't write anything. Josephine (whoever she might be) did—for nine years—lots of letters, all to Marilyn, addressed to her alias, "Martha Marshall."* Marilyn wanted it that way. All she said was that the letters came from a friend called Josephine and that they both wanted to keep the letters a secret. I never asked why. I just agreed. You didn't ever say no to Marilyn. At least, I didn't.

So the letters kept coming. Most by mail. Some Marilyn got when

---

* Marilyn relished applying nicknames to friends, lovers, and acquaintances alike and using aliases for herself.

See Susan Strasberg, *Marilyn and Me* (New York: Warner Books, 1992): "Mom was 'Black Bart' in her pointed black sun hats and black muumuu; my father was 'the great white father'; a press representative was 'Sybil' for sibling rivalry; Marlon Brando was 'Carlo'; her friend Norman Rosten was 'Claude' because he looked like Claude Rains. Marilyn's nom de plume for herself was 'Zelda Zonk.'"

3

she was away on a trip, or living in New York, and gave to me to take care of. I kept all the letters in a big maroon and gold Max Factor box I got one Christmas. Never read any of them either. Marilyn knew I wouldn't. She trusted me, you see, because of what I always did for her.

Well, anyways, the day before Marilyn died, a big box arrived for her from Washington. Recognized the writing—as same writing on the Josephine letters. Called Marilyn, still had my phone then, and she came running over, all excited. But when she read the letter that came with the box, she crumpled it up in a ball, flung it across the room and started crying like there was no tomorrow. I'd never seen her cry before. You see, she always saw me just before she was about to see Mr. G, so she was always happy, thrilled because she knew she was going to see him soon.

She cried for about twenty minutes. Cried like a baby. Shook all over. Skin covered in red blotches. Kept popping Nembutal like they was candy.

Never opened the box. Ran out the door. Next thing I knew, she was back, with sealing wax. Helped her seal the Max Factor box and the one from Josephine.

She was still crying. Then she begs me to keep the boxes safe. "Keep them safe, Patty," she says. "But if anything ever happens to me, promise me you won't open them till 40 years after I'm gone." 40 was her age then. "After that," she said, "what's in them belongs to you. But not till then, Patty, not till then. Promise me." So I did.

I'm old now, Mr. Winchester (72 on October 10), and I've got no more pulse left in my legs. Can hardly walk. I don't want to end up in some flophouse in Watts or someplace. I've got no one, you see. Nothing. Only the two boxes, and a letter from a woman called Josephine.

Please come see me before it's too late.

Patty

4

WESTERN UNION TELEGRAM

July 13, 2002

Imperative that you call me collect at
212 758 6211 right away.
Best regards,
Richard Winchester

PATRICE RENOIR
Apartment 1
The Renaissance
1600 La Brea
Hollywood, California 90069

Richard Winchester
Winchester Literistic
17 Sutton Place
New York, New York 10021

July 13, 2002

Dear Mr. Winchester,
    I don't have a phone and I hate pay phones. Besides, I'm scared that the phones are tapped. Marilyn told me so.*

Come to California,

Patty

---

* Re: Marilyn's phones being tapped, see Anthony Summers, *Goddess: The Secret Lives of Marilyn Monroe* (New York: Macmillan, 1985).

VIA FEDERAL EXPRESS

RICHARD WINCHESTER
Winchester Literistic
17 Sutton Place
New York, New York 10021

Patrice Renoir
Apartment 1
The Renaissance
1600 La Brea
Hollywood, California 90069

July 18, 2002

Dear Patty,

I am delighted that I shall, in fact, be in Los Angeles later this month. I'd like to invite you to have dinner with me at the Beverly Wilshire on the evening of July 30. I shall, of course, send a car for you—at eight.

In the meantime, I am most curious about your friendship with Marilyn Monroe, how it came about, what special service you did for her, and the true identity of Mr. G.

By the way, I think it best that you don't discuss our impending meeting (or the letters) with anyone, don't you?

Looking forward to seeing you on July 30 at the Beverly Wilshire.

With warmest regards,
Richard

PATRICE RENOIR
Apartment 1
The Renaissance
1600 La Brea
Hollywood, California 90069

Richard Winchester
Winchester Literistic
17 Sutton Place
New York, New York 10021

July 19, 2002

Dear Richard,

I am glad you are coming to L.A. and will see you for dinner at the Wilshire. But I won't be bringing the boxes. We have to wait until August 4.

Like I said before, I can't write my way out of a paper bag, but I'll try and tell you a little. The rest can wait till we meet.

Here goes. Back then, I was a makeup artist and beauty therapist around Hollywood. People said I looked like Marilyn. Wore my hair silver blonde, had a beauty spot, scarlet lipstick, sharp long red nails, a Stetson, slinky clothes. Didn't really look like her, though. Came from Flatbush, didn't have the style or the oomph. But hearing it made me feel good.

Met Marilyn in 1951, real early in her career, at a party thrown by that S.O.B. Charlie Feldman, her agent. We hit it off immediately. Asked me to come by her house. Told her about my specialty. A Brazilian wax, they call it (though what Brazil's got to do with it I really don't know). Waxing away the hair from all over. From everywhere, if you get my drift. Today, everybody does it (Madonna gets it regular).*

Marilyn hated getting it most the first time, because then she was just trying it out, so nothing would show under her tight dresses. Two days after I first did it to her, she met him. He loved the way she looked down there, so she started having it regular. She did it for him, so no matter how much it hurt—and it does—she loved doing it, because she loved him so much and, loving him like she did, lived to please him.

I never knew his real name. Just that for over eleven years—all the time that I knew her—Marilyn loved him. Whether or not he loved her, I don't know. He sure made her feel loved. She called him Mr. G. One day I asked her who he was. Hard for her to lie to me when I was in the middle of putting wax where I was putting it. But she was no fool, was Marilyn. She didn't exactly tell me to mind my own business, and she did tell me something, but not what I really wanted to know. She said, "G for Gemini, Patty. G for good. Or G for God. Like God, Patty. Like God. The best person in my life."

She told me they met through Charlie Feldman, and that same night Mr. G took her to the Beverly Hills Hotel. When he saw her down there, what I'd done to her, he went wild, she said. Went wild, she said, told her he loved it because it made her look so vulnerable, so available, like a child, all his.

Mr. G did really care for her, I think. Might not have admitted it, but did lots of things, said lots of things that showed her he cared and he did see her over and over, like clockwork.

If you want, I can show you all my appointment books. The minute

---

* See *Miami Herald Tropic Magazine,* 1994 interview with Delia Bernardino, Madonna's beautician.

after she got the call from Mr. G and he told her where and when he wanted to see her, she made an appointment with me. She wasn't shy about getting it done. Not the first time. Not ever. Almost enjoyed it, because whenever I did it, she knew she was about to see him.

Once, though (I think it was November 1960), she bleached it blonde, then waited six weeks before sending for me. Asked me to wax her so it looked like an eagle.* Crazy, but I did.

Anyways, when you read my appointment book, you'll see that I first worked on Marilyn in 1951, at 9400 West Olympic, that grungy hotel she was living in (it was May, I think), then at the Bel-Air (a step up in the world for her), then her apartment 882 North Doheny. After that, at 508 North Palm Drive (she was married to Joe then, but he was out of town and Mr. G came to see her). Then, when she moved to New York, she got me a job at Billy Rose's and I used to see her at the St. Regis (Suite 1105), at the Waldorf Towers (Suite 2728), and at 444 East 57th Street (she was married to that Miller man then, but it was nearly over and Mr. G came around). Then back in L.A. at

---

* A Brazilian wax takes approximately twenty-five minutes, during which all hair is removed from the pubic and ancillary areas by applying warm wax and then removing it, after which the entire area remains baby smooth for over three weeks. At this point, a regrowth occurs and the process needs to be done again. In Marilyn's day, strippers, showgirls, dancers, and call girls routinely underwent Brazilian waxing. According to Patty, Marilyn originally approached her to bleach her pubic hair so that it did not show through some of her more transparent gowns when, as was her wont, she failed to wear underwear. On inspecting the area and noting the sensitivity of Marilyn's skin, Patty advised a Brazilian. Marilyn endured the first treatment and may not have repeated the procedure had she not met Mr. G soon after. Based on his reaction, she continued to have Brazilians throughout most of her career (apart from during much of her marriage to Joe DiMaggio, who did not approve of the process).

In the nineties, Beverly Hills beautician Nance Mitchell specialized in waxing the area into a design (for example, a Mercedes-Benz emblem requested by the mistress of a millionaire who owned a fleet of them).

A woman's willingness to submit to a Brazilian wax for the sole benefit of her lover is often a manifestation of her innate masochism, and a conscious or unconscious submission to him. By transforming herself into a prepubescent child, she is, in effect, putting herself in his power. Marilyn's underlying masochism infuses many of her descriptions of her sexual encounters and will be discussed in greater detail.

10

the Beverly Hills (Bungalow 21), when she was with that Yves Montand. In the end, of course, she had me come to her house on Helena.

She gave me pictures, too, signed ones and I'll show you. "Dear Patty, thank you for being so gentle." "Dearest Patty, wishing you luck in Vegas." (I worked there for a bit, at the Trop with the Lido girls.) Near the end, she gave me a silver cigarette case, engraved with the words "Dear Patty, waxing sentimental . . . you are wonderful!" So was she. I am only doing this because I am desperate and because I know she wouldn't mind anymore.

So that's it, really. Dinner at eight (wasn't that a movie?) at the Wilshire.

Best,
Patty

PATRICE RENOIR
Apartment 1
The Renaissance
1600 La Brea
Hollywood, California 90069

Richard Winchester
Suite 1977
The Beverly Wilshire
Beverly Hills, California 90201

August 1, 2002

Dear Richard,

Thank you for dinner. After, I realized I was wrong. I should have brought you that letter from Josephine, which Marilyn crumpled up and threw on the floor that last day. I worked out that I got to trust you, so I'll tell you what the letter says (don't want to let it out of my hands yet). Here are the words.

July 28, 1962

Martha,

This is the last letter I shall ever write to you. Our correspondence is over. I have retrieved all your letters from Miss S and am herewith returning them to you.

Josephine

I suppose that explains why Marilyn cried so much when she read the letter and got the box from Josephine. But it still doesn't explain who Josephine was, does it? I was thinking, though, that maybe she wasn't really a she at all, that Josephine could have been just another name for Mr. G.*

I guess we'll find out on August 5. See you then.

Best wishes,
Patty

_____

* Patty's failure to intuit the identity of Mr. G, and thus, Josephine, cannot be attributed to lack of intelligence or education (in fact, she graduated from City College with honors, and many of her witty Hollywood bon mots have been frequently quoted—see *Sex, Sin and Salaciousness in Hollywood,* by James Worthington [Honolulu: Baynards Press, 1961]). In subsequent conversations with the publisher of *The Secret Letters,* she made it clear that out of loyalty to Marilyn, she never read any of the letters and consistently willed herself not to speculate regarding the identity of Mr. G or Josephine or the nature of their correspondence.

RICHARD WINCHESTER
Winchester Literistic
17 Sutton Place
New York, New York 10021

Patrice Renoir
Apartment 1
The Renaissance
1600 La Brea
Hollywood, California 90069

August 18, 2002

Dear Patty,

Opening the boxes with you on August 5 was one of the most moving moments of my entire life. I feel privileged that you have entrusted the letters to me.

You will be glad to know that they have now been authenticated by two independent experts. In short, there is no doubt whatsoever that I now have in my possession the secret correspondence between Marilyn Monroe and Jackie Kennedy. Many congratulations!

We can now take steps toward securing a lucrative publication deal. I shall, of course, keep you informed at all times.

Best regards,
Richard

BY MESSENGER

RICHARD WINCHESTER
Winchester Literistic
17 Sutton Place
New York, New York 10021

Thomas Dunne
Thomas Dunne Books
175 Fifth Avenue
New York, New York 10010

August 25, 2002

Dear Tom,

I was delighted to talk to you earlier this morning. You have *Letters* for twenty-four hours, exclusively. I have no doubt whatsoever as to what your answer will be.

This is a once-in-a-lifetime project. And I know that—with your instinct for melding the historical with the commercial, your fabled editorial talents, and your intense acumen for marketing—you are the right publisher for a project which is not only close to my heart but destined to make news throughout the world, and to break all bestseller list records for all time.

Awaiting your offer with anticipation.

Warm regards,
Richard

Thomas Dunne Books
175 Fifth Avenue
New York, New York 10010

Richard Winchester
Winchester Literistic
17 Sutton Place
New York, New York 10021

September 13, 2002

Dear Richard,

When you first hit me with the news that now that the deal is sealed, your client wants nothing more to do with the project, I was somewhat dismayed. However, after much reflection, I realize that her decision may well work to our advantage.

This book is not only a portrait of two icons, but also a slice of American history, of Hollywood history, replete with celebrity gossip, sexual salaciousness, and—to top that—a grand romantic saga. On another level, it is a tale which every wife who has ever worried about her husband having an affair and every mistress who has ever speculated regarding her married lover's wife will want to read. It delves into the eternal triangle, presents a classic cat-and-mouse game between the wife and the mistress, yet at the same time is a portrait of female bonding at a time when the feminist movement was not yet born.

With so many delicious subtexts, I feel that the manuscript needs to be introduced and annotated by a major international figure whose scholarship encompasses American history, Hollywood history, cultural history, and human nature in general. Only one name springs to mind. F. R. Lichtenstein. (I think he's an Ed Victor client.)

Let me know what you think.

Warm regards,
Tom

RICHARD WINCHESTER
Winchester Literistic
17 Sutton Place
New York, New York 10021

Thomas Dunne
Thomas Dunne Books
175 Fifth Avenue
New York, New York 10010

September 28, 2002

Dear Tom,

Brilliant idea! But try explaining to my client. . . . At first, of course,
she had never heard of F.R., so I soft-pedaled it. Then—for someone
who positioned herself as not wanting anything else to do with the
project—she flew into action. I don't know who she called or how
they managed to get it together so fast, but within half an hour, she
got back to me with full chapter and verse on F.R., including his latest
New Yorker essay on—of all people—Jackie.

She wasn't deterred by the five wives (not even the story of how his
last mistress, Lulu von Richthofen, knifed him that Halloween in
Buenos Aires) nor by his cocaine period or his Hollywood shenani-
gans. And, of course, she was impressed (as we knew she would be) by
his Pulitzer. His artistic volte-face in the latter years (he must be 79
now?) also impressed her, his renewed scholarship, the Harvard history fellowship, etc., etc. What nearly scuppered the entire deal,
though, was his *New Yorker* characterization of Jackie (which, as luck
would have it, her source read to my client) as "a venal woman with a

carnal soul." That incensed her. And although I reminded her that out of all the journalists on the sixties beat, F.R. was unique in that he conducted interviews (for *Life*) with both Marilyn and Jackie, none of that cut any ice with her.

Strangely enough, Tom, now that she has released the letters, Patty isn't the least bit protective of Marilyn's memory, yet is virulently protective—not to say reverential—regarding Jackie's. I've explained to her that—as you and I both agree—the letters don't reflect remotely negatively on Jackie. Instead, they show her human side, her struggles, her passions, her love for Jack, and her warmth as a woman. Far from desecrating her memory, I think they consecrate it.

In any event, my client wouldn't allow me to go ahead with F.R. unless I made what she termed as "a sacred promise" that he will not be permitted to make any direct comments on Jackie in the manuscript. I acquiesced, and mollified her further by pledging that we would do our utmost to illuminate the letters by seeking someone close to Jackie to comment on a number of them. I'll get back to you as soon as I have co-opted a suitable candidate.

In the meantime, perhaps you could sound F.R. out?

Warm regards,
Richard

RICHARD WINCHESTER
Winchester Literistic
17 Sutton Place
New York, New York 10021

Thomas Dunne
Thomas Dunne Books
175 Fifth Avenue
New York, New York 10010

October 21, 2002

Dear Tom,

This entire project seems to be born under a lucky star (as opposed to those relatively unlucky stars . . . our heroines). Through an amazing series of coincidences, we have been able to obtain limited access to those pages of Jackie Kennedy's Purple Diary, covering her correspondence with Marilyn.

The Purple Diary has hitherto been in the possession of Evangeline Auchincloss. As chance would have it, Evangeline and my first cousin Poppy Winchester roomed together at Vassar. And once I took the liberty of allowing Poppy to show Evangeline the Secret Letters, she became convinced that she owed it to history—and to Jackie's memory—to allow Jackie's diary comments on her correspondence with Marilyn to be published in tandem with the Secret Letters. The relevant pages will be messengered over to you forthwith.

Warm regards,
Richard

Winchester Literistic
17 Sutton Place
New York, New York 10021

Patrice Renoir
Apartment 1
The Renaissance
1600 La Brea
Hollywood, California 90069

October 30, 2002

Dear Patty,

Just a note to let you know that *The Secret Letters* will be published on April 25, 2003! You are about to make history!

Warmest regards,
Richard

THE LETTERS

EDITOR'S INTRODUCTION

*By F. R. Lichtenstein, Director of the Yale Faculty Vanderbilt Foundation,
Professor Emeritus of Modern Culture and English Literature, Downing College,
Cambridge, and Freud Professor of Psychoanalysis, University of Graz, Austria*

These priceless historical documents first came to light in 1998 when they were released by former Hollywood beautician and Marilyn confidante Patrice Renoir. Shortly before Marilyn's death, Jackie returned her letters. Soon after receiving them, Marilyn bequeathed the entire correspondence between her and Jackie to Renoir.

However, due to legal strictures, the documents cannot be reprinted. Marilyn's letters are written in different colored pens (navy, green, red, purple, orange, silver). The pale pink notepaper is tinged with the scent of violets. The writing is large, expansive, with complex curlicues, flourishes, and many of the *i*'s are dotted with a large circle or a heart. The letters are in good condition, folded just once.

Jackie's letters are written with a navy ink pen on thick cream paper. The corners are generally crumbled and it is clear the letters have been read repeatedly by Marilyn.

Marilyn tended to be a lamentable speller. Following her ear, she habitually made such slips as "definate" and "fantasize." Proper names were her downfall, and she often transposed the *e* and the *i*. But given the public perception of her innate dumb-blondeness, her occasional spelling mistakes have been retained in the text, if only to highlight how rare they were and the fact that, despite her rudimentary education, her strength of mind and purpose spurred her to improve her literacy level. Interestingly enough (and this is most apparent in Marilyn's last long letters), her powers of description and her level of self-knowledge are often more well honed than Jackie's.

These letters chart the course of the friendship between Marilyn and Jackie. In the process, they chronicle the inner lives of two unique, iconoclastic sirens. Friends and enemies, mirror images, fatherless girls, hostages to history, celluloid images, female role models, fashion queens, eternal legends, each living in her own kaleidoscopic universe, unique yet similar, they are two of the most famous and revered women of their time.

Artful seductresses, mistresses of enchantment, like Cleopatra, both Marilyn's and Jackie's charms cloaked sharp intellects. And it is clear that both women—each a female Machiavelli—relished the intellectual challenge inherent in the cat-and-mouse game played out in the Secret Letters.

The hallmark of the letters, which range from Jackie's sharp observations on Washington to Marilyn's revealing Hollywood gossip, is an exchange between both women of intimacies about life, love, loss, their hopes, and their fears. In the process, they also expose the deepest recesses of their hearts. Compared with the multitude of comments made by both women to the press, these letters are doubly interesting in that they graphically reveal subtle aspects of their individual natures.

Both women were prolific correspondents. Jackie's propensity for writing letters is well known. Her most recent biographer, Sarah Bradford, confirmed that Jackie not only relished corresponding with famous people but kept their letters for many years and, just before her death, read a selection to her close friend Nancy Tuckerman.

According to Bradford, "Jackie was sitting before the fire, astrakhan thrown over her lap. On the table beside her were bunches of letters, all neatly bound with ribbons. These were the letters Jackie had received from famous people over the years. Jackie unbound the letters and read some of them to Nancy."

Marilyn, too, was a prolific letter writer, often writing one letter with two or three different pens. According to Marilyn intimate James Haspiel, "Paula Strasberg told me that there existed personal letters written by John F. Kennedy to Marilyn, that Paula and Lee had placed 'into a safe-deposit box, not to be opened for fifty years.'"

The fact that Jack Kennedy risked putting pen to paper to correspond with Marilyn indicates that her response was also worth receiving and that intellectually she was not dramatically inferior to Jack or, indeed, to Jackie.

For as much as Hillary Clinton might hate admitting this about Monica Lewinisky, Eleanor Roosevelt about Missy Le Hand, Queen Alexandra about Lillie Langtry, Lady Nelson about Emma Hamilton, or Jackie about Marilyn, the reality is that despite their intrinsic animosity toward each other, on a deep level, the wife and the mistress generally have far more in common than they might care to admit and could, had fate dealt them different cards, even have been true friends.

The historical value of the letters has been enhanced by the access to Jackie's hitherto unpublished Purple Diary, which was bequeathed by her to her niece Evangeline Auchincloss.

I believe that I owe it to history to make Jackie Kennedy's relevant Purple Diary entries available in tandem with the Secret Letters. For it is my belief that Jackie's diary entries on Marilyn elucidate her state of mind during the correspondence, add dignity and resonance to the Secret Letters, and are thus a fitting memorial to her.

Above all, I would never have lent my name and reputation to this enterprise had I not believed that the documents truthfully reflect Marilyn's and Jackie's mutuality of spirit, their deep intimacy, their similarity of soul, and their unrequited passion for a remarkable man. All of which I believe serves only to add to the final legacy, the historical importance, and the rich beauty of these Secret Letters.

WESTERN UNION TELEGRAM

Bel-Air Hotel

The Office of Senator John F. Kennedy
Washington, D.C.

November 5, 1952

Dearest Jack,

Congratulations on winning the Senate Race. Since we met last year in Hollywood, I've been rooting for you, so I'm glad.*

Love,
Marilyn

---

* "For nearly a decade, his [Kennedy's] regular host on trips to Hollywood had been the prominent agent Charles Feldman. Feldman had represented Marilyn in the early fifties, and two witnesses suggest that Kennedy met Marilyn through him as early as 1951." (Tony Summers, *Goddess*)

Marilyn kept a copy of this (rather indiscreet) greeting with all the subsequent correspondence.

MARILYN MONROE
Apartment 3
882 North Doheny Drive
Beverly Hills, California

Senator and Mrs. John F. Kennedy
1095 North Ocean Boulevard
Palm Beach, Florida

September 13, 1953

Dear Senator and Mrs. Kennedy,

I am so sad that I couldn't accept Ambassador Kennedy's kind invitation to attend your wedding.* I was in Canada, making River of No Return. † *But when I saw your beautiful wedding photographs in the newspaper this morning, they brought tears to my eyes.*

---

* On receipt of this letter, Jackie wrote in her diary, "Quel surprise! A wedding gift from none other than Marilyn Monroe . . . plus a cryptic note. Still, old Joe must know what he's doing. . . . Or wants to do . . . As if the Swanson scenario hadn't been sufficient. . . . Oh, well, les garçons always remain les garçons, don't they? . . ."

In the above diary entry, Jackie is assuming that because Joe Kennedy invited Marilyn to Jack's wedding, she and Joe were having an illicit affair. It is highly likely that Jack inveigled his father into inviting Marilyn to his wedding. As Sarah Bradford noted in *America's Queen* (New York: Viking, 2000): "There was competition between Jack and his father over women: each got a thrill from sleeping where they knew the other had gone before. It was a totally amoral situation. There was something incestuous about the whole family."

† Marilyn's co-star in *River of No Return* was Robert Mitchum, a male star rippling with sex appeal. Yet according to Mitchum, he did not succumb to Marilyn's charms. Instead, he and his cronies took pleasure in teasing her. "One day she yearningly remarked that she hadn't seen her

Mrs. Kennedy, you look just like a movie star, only better, which of course you are.

I wish you joy, happiness, and all that you desire and hope that this little music box will remind you that here in Hollywood, Marilyn Monroe is thinking of you both with love. ‡

Marilyn

---

man Joe in some time, and Mitchum's boisterous stand-in, Tim Wallace, supposedly suggested they take up the slack with 'a round robin.'

"'What's that?' Marilyn asked.

"'You know, you and me and Mitch,' Wallace said, leering.

"'Ooh,' said Marilyn, 'that would kill me!'

"'Well, nobody's died from it yet,' Wallace snickered.

"'Ooh, I bet they have,' Marilyn told him. 'But in the papers they just say . . . the girl died from natural causes. . . . '" (from Lee Server's *Robert Mitchum: Baby I Don't Care* [New York: St. Martin's Press, 2001])

Years later, Marilyn would say wistfully, "Mitchum is one of the most interesting, fascinating men I have ever known."

In one of the many incidences in which Marilyn and Jackie were both attracted to the same man, Jackie also expressed an attraction to Robert Mitchum. "At one point in his career, he wanted Jackie to edit his autobiography and was surprised and flattered when the agent got back a few days later and said Mrs. Onassis would be delighted to do the book with him. Mitchum had always been her favorite movie star, she said to the startled agent, and had always reminded her very much of her own father." (Ibid.)

‡ The music box (listed as number 763 in the catalog of Kennedy/Bouvier wedding gifts lodged at the Rhode Island Bouvier Institute) plays "Falling in Love Again," the song from *The Blue Angel*.

After writing this letter, Marilyn consoled herself by watching the transmission of her television debut, aired on CBS that same evening, a sketch called "Honolulu Trip," with Jack Benny, which she recorded at the Shrine Auditorium a few months previously. According to Jeannie La Riviere (Marilyn, My Best Friend [Honolulu: Baynards Press, 1968]), a starlet she'd befriended at the Fox commissary, the two of them watched the show together. Marilyn appeared mesmerized during her "Bye Bye Baby" number, then said to Jeannie, "Well, if I don't have him, at least I've got this."

Senator and Mrs. John F. Kennedy
1095 North Ocean Boulevard
Palm Beach, Florida

Miss Marilyn Monroe
Apartment 3
882 North Doheny Drive
Beverly Hills, California

October 9, 1953

Dear Miss Monroe,

Thank you for your charming letter and enchanting wedding gift. The Senator and I were extremely touched by your kindness and generosity.

Naturally, we were crushed that you were unable to attend our wedding, but quite understand that your moviemaking commitments must take priority and look forward with eagerness to seeing *River of No Return* as soon as it is released.

With kind regards and many thanks,
Jacqueline Kennedy

In her 1964 memoir of Marilyn, *Forever Blonde* (Düsseldorf: Muller Books, 1981), her voice coach, Vera Romanoff, recalled the events of October 15, 1953, when Marilyn received Jackie's letter: "Marilyn was in the middle of reciting Shakespeare's Sonnet 18, and kept getting the line 'Sometime too hot the eye of heaven shines' wrong, and saying, 'Sometimes too oft the eye of heaven shines,' when the mailman arrived. She ran to the door, as if she had been waiting for a special letter all morning long, and when she saw 'return address, 1095 North Ocean Boulevard,' her eyes lit up and a dreamy look came over her face. Then she tore it open, read it, and went ashen. 'I never thought SHE would reply,' she said, her voice shaking. I looked at her questioningly, and she shook her head."

Senator and Mrs. John F. Kennedy
1095 North Ocean Boulevard
Palm Beach, Florida

Mr. and Mrs. Joe DiMaggio*
The Beverly Hills Hotel
9641 Sunset Boulevard
Beverly Hills, California

January 15, 1954

Dear Mr. and Mrs. DiMaggio,

Please accept our sincere congratulations on the occasion of your marriage. This gift[†] is a small token of our esteem and brings with it our best wishes for your future happiness.

With warm regards,
Senator Kennedy and Jacqueline Kennedy

---

* After Jack failed to respond to Marilyn's letter—with its veiled declaration that she was devastated by his wedding ("When I saw your beautiful wedding photographs in the newspaper this morning, they brought tears to my eyes" and "Marilyn Monroe is thinking of you with love")—she finally accepted Joe DiMaggio's proposal and married him.

[†] Jackie sent Marilyn the gift of a picture frame, a gift she would select for friends and acquaintances with alarming regularity during her White House years. (See Tish Baldrige, *A Lady, First* [New York: Viking, 2001].)

MRS. JOE DiMAGGIO
2150 Beach Street
San Francisco, California

Senator and Mrs. John F. Kennedy
1095 North Ocean Boulevard
Palm Beach, Florida

February 24, 1954

Dear Senator Kennedy and Mrs. Kennedy,
Joe and I were thrilled with the beautiful silver Cartier picture frame. We would love it if you would send us a photograph of yourselves—as neither of us can think of anyone else's picture we would rather have in such a beautiful frame.
Joe had to go to Japan on some baseball business, so we decided to make the trip our honeymoon and go to Korea, where I entertained the troops.* It

---

* In Korea, "Marilyn performed ten shows in snow flurries and sub-zero temperatures, wowing the troops in a skin tight, low-cut purple sequined gown and no underwear—husband Joe was furious when he saw the newsreels. . . . Marilyn recalled what it felt like:
'There were 17,000 soldiers in front of me, and they were all yelling at me at the top of their lungs. I stood smiling at them. . . . Standing in the snowfall facing these yelling soldiers, I felt for the first time in my life no fear of anything. I felt only happy.'" (See Adam Victor, *The Marilyn Encyclopedia* [Woodstock, N.Y.: Overlook Press, 1999].)

Jackie recorded her reaction to Marilyn's letter in her diary: "Another endearing note from Miss—sorry, Mrs.—Marilyn Monroe. Confidences from Mount Olympus! Is the blush fading from marriage to Mr. D so soon? Or do things run deeper with Joe K than we all thought. . . ? Then again, maybe I'm being a touch too cynical? Perhaps she really is sincere, although I do tend to doubt it."

was such a privilege for me and, for the first time in my life, I felt like I was accepted and doing work that mattered. Much better than making movies. I have just finished _No Business Like Show Business_, and the studio wants to rush me right into a real stinker called _Girl in Pink Tights_.

But all I really want now is to be plain Mrs. Joe DiMaggio because Joe is the only man now for me, and to be a good wife. In the end, I'm just another pretty girl, while Joe is immortal—a legend. We want to have six children—at least I do. Joe says he will be happy with one.

Thank you again for the picture frame.

Love,
Marilyn

P.S. Please call me Marilyn, as I feel I already know you.

SENATOR AND MRS. JOHN F. KENNEDY
3321 Dent Place
Washington, D.C.

Mrs. Joe DiMaggio
2150 Beach Street
San Francisco, California

March 6, 1954

Dear Marilyn,

Thank you for your charming letter. It is most kind of you to ask for a photograph of both of us. Here is one taken outside the Kennedy compound in Palm Beach, which I hope you will like.

Your last letter was so enchantingly informal. Consequently, I should like to reply in the same vein; you might find it amusing to learn that when I worked as "Inquiring Fotographer," for the *Washington Times-Herald*,* I regularly asked celebrated Washingtonians the question "If you had a date with Marilyn Monroe, what would you talk about?"

How life has changed since then for both of us! Being married is so much better than dating, isn't it? Especially given that we are both married to such exceptional men.

You will see from our new address that although the Senator and I do not yet have our own home, we are now renting a sweet little

---

* On March 26, 1952, Jackie was given the title of Inquiring Fotographer by the *Washington Times-Herald*. In that role, she asked prominent Washingtonians a brief series of questions and then photographed them.

house in Georgetown. It may be small, but at least it is our own private domain at last.

The Senator and I saw *How to Marry a Millionaire* last week, which we both absolutely adored. He has asked me to convey our congratulations to you upon winning the Most Popular Actress Award and to reiterate that we both think that it would be exceedingly sad were marriage to keep you away from the screen for too long.*

Warm regards,
Jackie

---

* At this point, six months into his marriage to Jackie, Jack may have been feeling restless and, as a result, used the unwitting Jackie to signal to Marilyn. The subtext of the letter—one that he knew Marilyn would divine—is that he wants her to use her career as a means of momentarily escaping from Joe DiMaggio and making it easier for him—Jack—to see her once more.

MRS. JOE DIMAGGIO
2150 Beach Street
San Francisco, California

Senator and Mrs. John F. Kennedy
3321 Dent Place
Washington, D.C.

March 28, 1954

Dear Jackie,

The photograph is lovely. I shall always treasure it. How cute that you asked all those men about me. I'd love to know what they answered, if you have the time to write and tell me.*

Love to you and to the Senator,
Marilyn

---

* In her diary, Jackie wrote, "Letter from MM wanting to know what my interviewees answered when I asked them, 'What would you say to Marilyn Monroe if you went on a date with her?' I am utterly amazed that she would care about something so trivial, given the current magnitude of her career. And to show it. . . . I could never be so open-hearted, nor would I ever wish to be."

SENATOR AND MRS. JOHN F. KENNEDY
3321 Dent Place
Washington, D.C.

Mrs. Joe DiMaggio
2150 Beach Street
San Francisco, California

April 2, 1954

Dear Marilyn,

How very remiss of me not to have gone into details regarding the responses to my question about you. Fortunately, I kept my columns and thus am mailing the relevant ones to you for your amusement. I do hope you will enjoy reading them.

Warm regards,
Jackie

MRS. JOE DiMAGGIO
2150 Beach Street
San Francisco, California

Senator and Mrs. John F. Kennedy
3321 Dent Place
Washington, D.C.

April 10, 1954

Dear Jackie,

Thank you for sending me the columns. I was so glad to get them and they made me laugh a lot. But I wish those polite and friendly answers were closer to what men really said to me on dates, but they couldn't be further from the truth. When I used to date—and it seems like forever ago—men would all say the same stupid things, like "Gee, you've got such lovely white skin," or "You look smaller than in the movies."

It must have been wonderful to have such an important, serious job on a newspaper. I'm only ever on the receiving end of newspaper reporters, and most of them, particularly the women, write about me as if I were some kind of exotick [sic] dumb animal, and not a person at all. Living and working in Washington must be so much better than being in Hollywood and doing what I do. I'd love to know more about your life there, so please write back and tell me about it when you have the time.

Love,
Marilyn

P.S. What did men say to you on dates? I am sure the Senator said some special, clever things to you, not like the men I knew.

---

* Marilyn was clearly so gratified by Jackie's friendly response, and her thoughtful gesture of sending her the columns, that she began the letter in a spontaneous frame of mind, thus manifesting the first indication of how much Jackie's approval and friendship would come to mean to her. It is only when she ended her own letter that Marilyn reminded herself of Jackie's role as Jack's wife and probed as to whether Jack (who never paid her compliments) was in the habit of complimenting Jackie, his wife.

SENATOR AND MRS. JOHN F. KENNEDY
3321 Dent Place
Washington, D.C.

Mrs. Joe DiMaggio
2150 Beach Street
San Francisco, California

April 15, 1954

Dear Marilyn,

How extremely enjoyable our new correspondence is! But I am deeply saddened to learn that men didn't always treat you with the courtesy you so richly deserve.

As for the Senator, he did, indeed, have an enchanting way of talking to me during our dates. He was amusing, witty, and endlessly curious about me. Or so he seemed. I, in turn, was fascinated to hear about his childhood amid such a large family, the Ambassador (who, as I am sure you know, is a unique individual),* and of the time they all spent in England. But no matter what he is speaking about, Jack has an

------

* Here Jackie is slyly alluding to what she believes to be Marilyn's illicit affair with her father-in-law, Joe Kennedy. In reality, Marilyn never met Joe Kennedy. However, had she ever been in his proximity, with her fondness for dominant, controlling men, she would probably have been susceptible to him.

Jackie's own fondness for Joe Kennedy is a matter of record (see Bradford, Klein, Heymann) and she prided herself on being the one woman who was capable of manipulating him. A cousin once said of Jackie's attraction to men who resembled the bootlegger and kingmaker Joseph P. Kennedy, "If Jackie were at the court of Ivan the Terrible, she'd say, 'Ooh, he's been so misunderstood.'"

43

almost hypnotic quality—as if he is peering straight into your heart and mind.* As if he can read your thoughts, which I found both disquieting and somewhat flattering. Being the focus of his attention is rather like burning up in a red-hot beam of light—spellbinding.

I am deeply flattered that you would like to know more about my life in Washington. In comparison to the glittering existence you must lead in Hollywood, mine will sound extremely turgid. At the moment, I am drowning in books on American history† (which I am studying at Georgetown University), and am also trying golf (which I am not crazy about).

As for cooking, most of the time I tear up to a little Greek place that makes wonderful casseroles and bring them home for dinner. Or else Jack takes me out. I signed up for a cooking course because I definitely did not want to be one of those bird-brained housewives who burn everything. The great day dawned when I was to make my first ever supper for Jack. I don't know what went wrong, but I rubbed the potatoes in olive oil, just like the course taught. First, I placed them in the gas oven, then I closed the kitchen door with a sigh of relief, and went into the bedroom to read *Gone With the Wind* (for the fifth time), until the potatoes were done. Next thing I knew, the whole house was full of smoke and the neighbors had called the fire engines!

Jack has just walked in and saw that I am writing to you. He says he would adore meeting you when we come out to California this sum-

---

* Myriad women have breathlessly enthused about Jack Kennedy's charisma. One of many examples: "I was almost hypnotized by the sight of this man. He was such a stunning figure. He didn't have to lift a finger to attract women; they were drawn to him in the battalions, by the brigades. . . ." (Gloria Emerson to Seymour Hersh in *The Dark Side of Camelot* [Boston: Little, Brown, 1997])

† "My brother and Jackie knew everything about the Civil War," Teddy Kennedy recalled. "She had a fantastic desire for historical knowledge, and she was a sponge once she learned it. She caught every nuance." (Sarah Bradford, *America's Queen: A Life of Jacqueline Kennedy Onassis* [New York: Viking Press, 2000])

mer. Naturally, my sentiments are identical and I should find it
enchanting to meet you and Joe if you both happen to be in California when we are.

Warm regards,
Jackie

MRS. JOE DIMAGGIO
2150 Beach Street
San Francisco, California

Senator and Mrs. John F. Kennedy
3321 Dent Place
Washington, D.C.

April 25, 1954

Dear Jackie,

I am so excited that you and the Senator are coming to California. I know that once you get here you won't want to leave, at least that's what most people say. I've missed L.A. so much that I've convinced Joe to let us move back next month and I'm so glad. Because although it is pretty here, and close to the Marina, there is nothing like L.A. I know that you will love it.

I feel as if we know each other so well already and are so similar. Gone With the Wind is one of my favorite books, and I am not great at cooking either.* I do try and cook for Joe—Italian, of course, he insists—but sometimes I long for the days when I was broke, living in a rooming house and

---

* The fact that Marilyn and Jackie both adored *Gone With the Wind* (see Chris Anderson, *Jack and Jackie* [New York: Morrow, 1996], and Colin Clark, *The Prince, the Showgirl and Me* [New York: St. Martin's, 1996]) is indicative of their underlying similarities. Like Scarlett, Marilyn and Jackie were both wilful, self-centered, narcissistic, iron-willed, intensely ambitious, accomplished actresses—in Jackie's case, off-screen.

just eating yogurt mixed with raisins, fresh fruit, and peanuts and not having to cook at all. But men do seem to like us cooking for them, and they get so mad if it doesn't work out exactly the way they want. It doesn't always go well. I tried homemade noodles and the book said wait till they dry, but they didn't. By then the dinner guests arrived, but they still hadn't dried, I gave the guests drink after drink, and in the end dried the noodles with a hair dryer. Never told anyone, because when I did tell people that I washed lettuce leaves with Brillo, they thought I was a weirdo or something. I didn't want them to say that about the noodles because I knew I was right.

Maybe when you come out, you would like to take a tour of the studio, and I can arrange it, though there isn't much to see. Washington must be so much more exciting. History was always one of my favorite subjects at school, and there is so much of it in Washington, but I've never been there, or to Europe either. My movies don't do badly over there, so maybe one day they'll send me for publicity.

Please let me know the dates of your trip so I can look forward to it.

Love to you and the Senator,
Marilyn

·ᐖᑎᕦᐱ·

SENATOR AND MRS. JOHN F. KENNEDY
3321 Dent Place
Washington, D.C.

Mrs. Joe DiMaggio
508 North Palm Drive
Beverly Hills, California

May 15, 1954

Dear Marilyn,

I must apologize for the delay in writing, but we have only recently firmed up the plans for our Californian trip. This will be my first visit since our brief stay there during our honeymoon, and I am wild with excitement and anticipation.

Jack has been so dear and says that as the trip falls during my birthday—at the end of July—he wants to make it one, big gigantic birthday surprise. He has even enlisted his brother-in-law Peter Lawford—perhaps you know him?—as co-conspirator.* He insists that you contact Peter directly—via the studio—and co-ordinate our meeting with him, as I am to be kept in the dark! How very mysterious it all is, and very unlike Jack, too, which makes it all the more intriguing!

---

* British movie actor Peter Lawford was sexually enthralled by both Marilyn and Jackie—as well as being Jack's friend and, some say, pimp. Enamored of Marilyn (although never willing or able to consummate the relationship), he would also go on to have a 1967 dalliance with Jackie during her trip to Hawaii. "I only know that Patricia Kennedy was livid that Peter and Jackie were in Hawaii together. And I do think they had a flirtation. Jackie definitely was sexually attracted to Peter." (Patricia Seaton Lawford quoted in Wendy Leigh, *Prince Charming: The John F. Kennedy, Jr., Story* [New York: Dutton, 1993])

A studio tour would be delightful, thank you for suggesting it. I hope you will not be offended by my request—which I make at the risk of sounding like a soppy fan*—but if Clark Gable is affiliated—is that the right term?—with Twentieth Century-Fox and if you know him, I would adore meeting him, if only briefly. Primarily because of my passion for *Gone With the Wind,* and Rhett, but also because he is a dead ringer for my father, and I have been passionately in love with him since I was just knee-high.† In the eventuality that you can, indeed, arrange a meeting, I promise to be dignified, ladylike and not fling myself at Mr. Gable's feet! I hope my request is not too troublesome, and shall, of course, fully understand if it is too difficult to arrange.

Please give my best to Joe.

Warm regards,
Jackie

---

* Jackie's fascination with Hollywood is a matter of record, and remained strong throughout her life (see Bob Colacello, *Holy Terror: Andy Warhol, Close Up* [New York: HarperCollins, 1990], for her curiosity about Elizabeth Taylor, and *Prince Charming* for her cross-examining her son, John, regarding Madonna).

† Jackie says that she has always been in love with Gable since she was knee-high; however, her unconscious emotions came to the fore when writing this sentence, which reads that she has been passionately in love with her father since she was knee-high. Sarah Bradford noted that Jack Bouvier's obsession with Jackie bordered on the unhealthy and was reciprocated in kind: "But his passion for Jackie (and hers for him) was overriding and semi-incestuous."

Because Marilyn never knew her father, and Jack Bouvier's emotions and behavior toward Jackie (see Klein on the young Jackie's favorite game with her father—guessing which women were his lovers) tended toward the inappropriate, neither woman grew up with the security generally provided by a traditional father. Consequently, Jackie and Marilyn always gravitated toward father figures in their romantic lives. Part of Jack's attraction for both of them (Marilyn was nine years younger than Jack, and Jack was twelve years older than Jackie) lay in his ability to listen intently to their concerns and give stellar advice, which lent him a paternalistic patina and an authority both women found alluring.

MRS. JOE DiMAGGIO
508 North Palm Drive
Beverly Hills, California

Senator and Mrs. John F. Kennedy
3321 Dent Place
Washington, D.C.

May 30, 1954

Dear Jackie,

I was so happy to get your letter. I really wish I knew Clark Gable, but I only met him once, years ago, at Chasen's and he signed my napkin. I think Joe used to play poker with him, but I'm a bit afraid to ask him to arrange an introduction.* Is the Senator a jealous man?† Because Joe goes really crazy if I talk about any other man, and I think he'd flip his lid if I asked him to set up a meeting with Clark. Even if I told him the truth that you, not me, want to meet him, he would still get mad. But maybe one day I'll get to make a movie with Clark, then I'll work it out so you can meet him as well.

---

* Jackie observed in her diary, "Joe D is clearly living up to the stereotypically jealous Italian male. And I've got the feeling that MM isn't the least bit amused. I'm starting to feel a little sorry for her. All that sex appeal, but no stability. A recipe for disaster??"

† Marilyn often complained to beautician and confidante Patty Renoir that no matter how sexually desirable her male leading men, and no matter how strongly she stressed their desirability to Mr. G, he categorically refused to show any signs of jealousy. Thus she is probing to see whether or not he used the identical tactics with Jackie.

I called Mr. Lawford, but I'm not allowed to give anything away, just that your trip will be real fun. I can't wait to meet you and the Senator at last.

Love,
Marilyn

P.S. When I was a little kid in the orphanage, I used to dream all the time that Clark Gable was my real father. I even had his picture next to my bed and always kissed it good night every single night. Isn't it cute that we are both crazy about the same guy?

ᑲᘓᓀᘗᔑ

SENATOR AND MRS. JOHN F. KENNEDY

3321 Dent Place

Washington, D.C.

Mrs. Joe DiMaggio

508 North Palm Drive

Beverly Hills, California

June 15, 1954

Dear Marilyn,

You are so dear to be concerned about my childish whim regarding Mr. Gable. Please do not feel under any obligation whatsoever—for if you had managed to arrange a meeting, I would probably have dissolved into shyness, or run a mile! Apart from the fact that Jack would have been furious, not because of jealousy but because he would have considered it unseemly for a Senator's wife to have a crush on a movie star. All of which leads me to answering your next question.

You asked whether or not Jack is a jealous man. He is jealous when it comes to his mother and how much she adores Teddy—his youngest brother—and also when Ambassador Kennedy talks too much about his eldest son, Joe—who died in the war—and how he was "the pick of the litter"—as you know, that's how the Ambassador talks, but he is so charming that I generally forgive him his frequent linguistic lapses of taste. But when it comes to me, Jack has never exhibited any signs of jealousy. I think he would be quite sanguine about my spending an entire evening with Mr. Gable, and not remotely concerned with the possibility that he might spirit me away to some secret Hollywood mansion and make passionate love to me all night long!

On a more serious note, I think the basis of Jack's lack of jealousy is a deep sense of security, garnered through years of women adoring him—often not from afar. Of course—and I know you won't repeat this to Jack when you finally meet him—I also adore him, but I don't generally tell him so. But I am rambling on and this letter has become a series of incoherent thoughts, I suppose because I feel that I can trust you with my musings, as you do me with yours.

In any event, I can hardly contain my anticipation at meeting you.

Warm regards,
Jackie

Mrs. Joe DiMaggio
508 North Palm Drive
Beverly Hills, California

Mrs. John F. Kennedy
The Bel-Air Hotel
701 Stone Canyon Road
Bel Air, California

July 30, 1954

Dear Jackie,

It was wonderful meeting you and the Senator at last. I think Peter was very clever to pick Charlie Feldman's house for our surprise dinner, what with Charlie being my agent and the Senator being his old friend.*

You are even more beautiful than in your photographs and you make me feel like dieing [sic] my hair brunette. I loved your dress and think that Dior is such a heavenly designer. I also adored the stories you told me about your cheating father.† No one ever told me stories when I was a child—not even

---

* Tony Summers writes that in 1954, Marilyn and Joe rented a house at 508 North Palm Drive, Beverly Hills. Her agent, Charles Feldman, lived across the road. "In the summer of 1954, Jack and Jacqueline Kennedy were invited to Charlie Feldman's for a dinner party and among the guests were Peter and Pat Lawford and Feldman's neighbors, the DiMaggios."

† Jackie may, as was her wont, have talked freely about Jack Bouvier's womanizing. However, it is highly unlikely that she was so blithe regarding his propensity for dallying with men as well—if, indeed, she was ever aware of it.

at bedtime—so I love them even more now. I am sending you a tube of my lipstick, which you liked so much—Revlon Strawberry Pale—so you can try it. I am sure it will look wonderful on you. I am also mailing you a lip brush—because that way you can apply the lipstick more accurately. You asked about my makeup secrets. Well, they aren't anything that special.* I usually use three colors: a dark one to outline my lips, a paler color inside, and a little white or silver dot in the center of my mouth. Then I cover my lips with a thin coat of Vaseline, to make my mouth gleem [sic]. I don't know if you want to do all that, but if ever you do, I hope knowing that is a help.

C. David Heymann in *A Woman Named Jackie* (New York: Birch Lane, 1994) explores the allegation that Black Jack Bouvier might have been bisexual. He cites Charles Schwartz's *Cole Porter: A Biography* (New York: Dial Press, 1977): "Some of Cole's most intense affairs were with men from distinguished families. Cole for instance was reported to have been very much taken at one time with Black Jack Bouvier. 'I'm Just Wild About Jack' Cole is supposed to have written about his very close friend at the height of his relationship with Bouvier." Heymann goes on to say, "Several members of the Bouvier family were aware of a sexual relationship between Black Jack and Cole Porter. One family member confirms—Jack was very bi."

* Here Marilyn is playing modest. In actual fact, her makeup secrets are intricate, and were revealed by her makeup artist, Whitey Snyder.

To make Marilyn up for the movies, Snyder first applied a light base. He highlighted under her eyes and out, over, and across the cheekbones. Next he added toning to the eye shadow, working lightly out toward the hairline, followed by a pencil outline around the eyes; her brows would be pointed slightly to make her forehead look broader, with more toning would be added beneath her cheekbones. Further shadings were added to match costume and lighting. Lipstick colors vary depending on what was needed for a particular scene.

It took Marilyn and Snyder anywhere between one and a half and a full three hours to work the magic that turned her from Norma Jeane into the Marilyn fans wanted and expected.

When doing her own makeup, Marilyn would use a base stick to darken the flesh tones of her face and chest, and then take most of it off, using witch hazel and tissue.

Marilyn washed her face several times a day to prevent clogged pores, took long baths, and made frequent visits to the dentist to make sure that her teeth were in perfect gleaming health.

She also studiously avoided the sun to keep her skin as white as possible.

At various times during her life Marilyn protected her face by smearing it with Vaseline, cold cream, or hormone cream. Partly as a consequence of using hormone creams, by her mid-thirties, Marilyn had a fine down on her cheeks (see Victor).

Most of all, I really wanted to apologize for Joe. At heart, he is a very decent man, but he sometimes goes crazy for no reason and I can't understand why. After all, he was in the middle of a fascinating [sic] conversation with you about Italy, and shouldn't have cared less that I stepped outside for a minute to show the Senator Charlie's new pool house. Joe dragging me away from the party before I could even eat dessert made me feel as if I had committed some kind of crime.

Joe always behaves so unreasonably whenever I am anywhere near another man, even a happily married one like the Senator. At first, I was flattered by his jealousy because it made me feel wanted and needed. Now, though, I feel as if I am in prison. As we were saying over dinner—and I loved our conversation—men are so different, so difficult for us to understand. Yet sometimes we love them just because they are that way.

But I don't love Joe for his jealousy. Or that a lovely evening is ended because Joe suddenly goes crazy with jealousy, which he shouldn't be feeling or showing. I feel like someday doing something he really can be jealous of!!!

But I have never cheated on Joe, I can promise you that. I have been faithful from the moment of our marriage and shall be faithful to him till the day I die, if I can. I have to be completely in love before I can be faithful forever. Joe is a decent man, of course, only he does seem set on isolating me. He never wants me to see any of my movie colony friends—although you can't really blame him that much, because some of them are real creeps—or my other friends either. Even when strangers applaud me, like in Korea, when the crowds went wild, Joe just hates it. He threatened to divorce me, even though we were still on our honeymoon. But I am sure things will get better because I would rather be Joe's wife than just a love potion to the world. . . .

I was so glad you wanted to know about all the stars I've met. At dinner, I was dying to tell you an amazing story about John Wayne, but I didn't dare.* The story is so shocking that I figured Charlie might get mad if I told it. But, like you said last night, neither of us are particularly shockable—you because of your father, who sounds wicked but real cute, and me because of my life here in Hollywood. If you have time, I'd love you to tell me his ten top tips for seduction—you know, the ones you mentioned. I promise I won't tell anyone else.

Anyway, now it is just you and me in a letter, I'll tell you. . . . A few years back, Vice caught John Wayne having sex with a man in a public bathroom in Santa Monica. The dumb cop who arrested him didn't recognize him and didn't believe he was who he said he was, but once they got to the station, they knew immediately and let him go. Hedda and Louella didn't get to hear about it, because, luckily, the studio is good at hushing scandals up for us. I wasn't that surprised about John Wayne, though, because sometimes the most macho men like a little variety and I don't judge them, because I really do think sex is sex and not anything evil. So I'm not a bit shocked and I know you wouldn't be either. But if his fans knew, his career would be over, so please don't breathe a word to another living soul.

I also couldn't stop thinking about what you said at dinner, that everyone thinks Hollywood is a fairy tale, filled with magical beings, but that underneath it all, movie stars are still human. I just wish other people thought like you.

I loved meeting you, Jackie. I just hope you don't think less of me for what Joe did.

---

* The John Wayne story was confirmed to Wendy Leigh (see her 1999 book, *Hollywood Insider* [Honolulu: Baynards Press]) by an LAPD detective who was shown the arrest sheet early in his career.

Love,
Marilyn

P.S. I forgot to write that I think the Senator is very nice and I was glad to meet him as well.

P.P.S. You said in your last letter that you would never tell the Senator that you adore him. I wondered why you wouldn't.

SENATOR AND MRS. JOHN F. KENNEDY

3321 Dent Place

Washington, D.C.

Mrs. Joe DiMaggio

508 North Palm Drive

Beverly Hills, California

August 10, 1954

Dear Marilyn,

Thank you so much for your delightful letter. Now that we have met, I can hear your voice in every line and feel exactly as if you are talking directly to me. Regarding Joe—of course I don't think less of you! None of us is remotely responsible for our husbands' actions.

Your John Wayne story was delicious—I promise never to reveal it to anyone and I think you were right not telling it in front of Charles, or for that matter, Jack. Men are such infants when it comes to their heroes, aren't they!

You were so kind and generous to send me Strawberry Pale. I absolutely adore it. Your thoughtful gift of a lip brush and the accompanying advice is invaluable—thank you. All through dinner, I was mesmerized by the luminosity of your skin and (at the risk of sounding like one of your abortive dates) am longing to know your secret. I once asked another movie star (Zsa Zsa Gabor), whom I met on a plane, for her skin secrets and she instructed me to eat a piece of raw green pepper every single day in order to achieve and maintain beautiful skin. I followed her advice, but noticed no improvement. So, if I might prevail upon you, I should be most grateful for your skin care advice.

I do hope you will like the fictionalized autobiography of Napoleon's first fiancée, Désirée Clary, which I am sending you. It is one of my favorite books (I love that period of history) and I think you might like it as well.

I found our conversation riveting—your life seems so glamorous next to mine. You spend your days on movie sets, mingling with stars like Betty Grable and Cary Grant. I spend mine answering Jack's mail and reading the *Congressional Report*. Yet despite your glittering existence, in person you are so down-to-earth and so far removed from your movie image.

Before you left so suddenly, I wanted to ask you what Betty Grable is really like. My curiosity is grounded in the fact that I believe my father had a brief affair with her.

In the meantime, please forget all about Joe's behavior, because as far as I am concerned, it was not in the least bit reprehensible. In fact, his jealousy was really rather sweet. For my part, I was delighted that Jack was so very thrilled to meet you. After having listened to you at dinner and observed the way in which you constantly underrate yourself, I know you will immediately assume that he, too, merely sees you as a movie star, and not a person. But that is not remotely the truth, because I know Jack genuinely sees the real Marilyn, as I believe I do as well.

You asked why I never tell Jack that I adore him. I don't restrict that maxim to Jack. Before we were married, I employed the identical tactics with all my other beaux as well. You will not be in the least bit surprised, I know, if I tell you that my tactics were dictated by my father's advice on how to attract a man, how to seduce a man, and how to keep a man. Through the years, I have found my father's advice to be infallible—and I know that he would be immensely flattered were

I to share them with you.* Please know, however, that you are the only other woman to whom I would ever dream of entrusting such valuable information, but because we are now firm friends, I do so in the knowledge that you will keep it entirely secret.

1. Be vague and distant from a man—so you play on his imagination.
2. Don't always project the same image with the same man—be a little girl one minute, and a predatory masculine-style seductress the next.
3. Promise a man everything, but give him as little as possible.
4. Be evasive and elusive.
5. Always avoid being predictable.
6. Try and judge a man's mood of the moment, then blend in accordingly.
7. Alternate between being prim and ladylike, and being lascivious and suggestive, between being impish and coy, outgoing and shy.
8. Let a man know that you have many other admirers on tap, all vying for your attention.
9. Be mysterious, yet hint that you have the capacity to be adventurous.
10. Never reveal all your thoughts and feelings to a man.

---

* "As for Jackie: 'She wasn't bothered, not at all,' said Peter Lawford. 'Every man in the room was drooling over Marilyn. Jackie would have thought something was wrong if Jack hadn't stared at her'" (see Bradford).

Jackie wrote in her diary, "If I gave father even a glimmer that none other than MM was riveted by his seduction advice, he'd be on the next plane out to L.A. But I won't. The prospect of him and MM as an item is too harrowing to contemplate. Besides, I like her far too much to subject her to him."

Please, Marilyn, don't think that I follow all the above advice to the last letter at all times (heaven forbid!), but it does tend to color the way in which I treat men—Jack in particular (although, naturally, I will never let him know it, and trust that you will keep my secret, as I do all of yours). That said, I hope my father's maxims, however cynical, will serve to amuse you.

My sister Lee has just arrived for lunch, so I am afraid I must close. Good luck with *The Seven Year Itch*! I am looking forward to seeing it with the greatest anticipation.

Love,
Jackie

Senator and Mrs. John F. Kennedy
3321 Dent Place
Washington, D.C.

September 15, 1954

Dear Jackie,

Thank you for your warm and friendly letter. I started to write you back the day it arrived. But Joe came back in again, saw the name Kennedy, and went crazy. Now, though, I am alone, as he is at Toots Shoor's [sic], and want to write to you at last.

Before I write anything else—and there is a lot—thank you for sharing your father's seduction secrets with me. Looks like I'm going to need them. . . .

What you said about Joe's jealousy was so kind. But he practically punches every man who ever looks at me and he hates all my movie parts and says he is fed up with me playing sluts. I keep trying to explain that playing is all I'm doing and that acting is playing, like baseball. But he can't seem to see it. I keep telling him that it is nice when people fantasise [sic] about me—although sometimes I wish they would real-ise [sic] about me as well. But he is either unwilling or unable to understand.

He says he feels like he is two people and that one of him really wants to be on the set when I am doing a love scene, applauding. The other half wants to kill the man to whom I am making love. This morning, I wasn't doing a love scene with anyone, so I thought it would be fine for Joe to come on the set. I hoped he would be proud of me, but he went beserk [sic]. Joe likes all the crowds to worship him—and they do. But he doesn't want them to even like me. All he wants is for me to hang around at home while he watches TV and drinks beer. He wanted Marilyn Monroe, now he's got her, and all he really wants her to be is a little housewife from Podunk. After all, neither of us, Jackie, are housewives—are we? I remember what you told me about writing in your high school yearbook that your ambition was not to be a housewife but to be Queen of the Circus. I feel the same way because I have far too many fantasies to be a housewife.

Today we filmed a scene outside the Trans-Lux movie theater on Lexington Avenue in which I stand on the subway grate and my skirt blows up in the air, showing my legs. There was almost a riot, but I wasn't scared because the crowd was so warm and friendly. They roared and cheered for two whole hours, and I was real happy and waved and smiled right back at them. A couple of times, I ran back into the theater for a quick cup of coffee because, what with the wind machine and the weather, I was freezing, but I didn't stay inside long because I didn't want to disappoint the crowds. When I went outside again, they roared even louder than before and I loved it. I didn't see anything wrong with what I did, till Joe came along and his face went dark as death. He stormed off to a bar, and now I don't know where he is. So I came back here to write to you. But I am not ashamed of what I did and I think you would approve as well, because it was only acting. Besides, I have never been shy about my body. After all, God gave it to me and I—

October 6. I had to stop writing in the middle of the sentence because Joe burst into the suite and started shaking me so hard that the next morning I had big bruises all over my shoulders. I thought he was going to kill me. I was trembling all over. I wanted to scream, but I lost my voice.

By now you will have heard that we are divorcing. I am not sorry. But I am afraid of being alone again. Before Joe, I always thought of myself as someone whom no one could love. Joe changed all that. Now, I suppose, I am back to square one again. . . .

I am sorry that I have taken so long to answer your questions, but I will now. How strange that you know Zsa Zsa, as I do too, but to be honest, we are not friends. She is married to George Sanders, who made <u>All About Eve</u> with me, during which he took a fatherly interest in me. Zsa Zsu found out and cut me dead, which was very unfair because I had done nothing wrong. George didn't talk to me for the longest time, which made me really mad, because until then, he was so helpful giving me hints on how to play my part. The longer he stayed away from me, the madder and madder I got, till one night when Zsa Zsa was out of town, I slipped on my full-length sable and ran over to his house on South Sherbourne, rang the bell, and when he opened the door, gave him a quick glimpse. Naturally, of course, I wasn't wearing anything underneath. I then ran straight home again. Of course, nothing happened between me and George, but Zsa Zsa still found out and was livid about me and the sable.* Afterwards, I was sorry, because seeing her on the set, always looking elegant, in perfect clothes, with perfect makeup, made me regret that I couldn't get to know her better and learn from her. Did she tell you anything else useful?

---

* Zsa Zsa Gabor's recollections of Marilyn's nocturnal visit to George Sanders differ somewhat from Marilyn's own account. In her book *One Lifetime Is Not Enough* (New York: Delacorte, 1991), she quotes George Sanders as relaying the story to her in the following terms: "Marilyn is so insecure that if a man takes her out to dinner and doesn't go to bed with her afterwards, she thinks there is something wrong with her. You can't imagine what happened the other day! The doorbell rings and there stands Marilyn in a beautiful sable coat. I asked her what she wanted and she opened the coat. Marilyn was stark naked underneath. Who am I not to make love to a woman like that? It was wonderful, but really Marilyn was far too professional. Marilyn knows exactly how to make love to a man. And I didn't pay her afterward either. . . !"

To tell you my skin secrets—they aren't anything special. Every morning and every night, I plunge my face into a basin of the hottest water I can stand and keep it there for as long as I can. Then, at night—if I am alone—I cover my entire face and neck in Vaseline and go to sleep that way. Please be careful not to burn yourself if you try it.

I shall be in New York till the end of October and I really hope you will write to me soon, as I am lonely and love hearing from you. This may sound strange, but it would be safer if you wrote to me under a fake name, because Joe sometimes prowls around the hotel (he wants me back, but I don't think I'll cancel the divorce) and I don't want him seeing any of your letters. He is so jealous that seeing them will remind him of that evening in L.A. and he'll go crazy again. So please write to me here under my favorite alias, Martha—after Martha Washington—I really admire her—Marshall. I'll work it out with the concierge so she gives me the letters without Joe seeing them.

Love,
Marilyn

P.S. Betty Grable is kind, friendly, not the least bit competitive and made your father very happy, I'm sure.

P.P.S. Please forgive me for not mentioning it before—I was so distracted by Joe's terrible tantrums—but I loved <u>Désirée</u>. She had such a fasinating [<u>sic</u>] life, ending up as the Queen of Sweden. I liked the chapters best when she was engaged to Napoleon. It must have been heartbreaking for her to love and be loved by such a powerful man and then to lose him. I thought it was very romantic, and it even took my mind off everything, thank you. Also—and I forgot to tell you this—when I was on the Fox lot doing *No Business Like Show Business*, I actually met *Marlon Brando*, who was playing *Napoleon* in the film.* He was very kind and friendly to me.

---

* Marilyn met Brando when he was shooting *Désirée*, and they continued to meet frequently in 1955, after Marilyn moved to New York; he may well have been instrumental in persuading her of the benefits of working with Lee Strasberg. Rumors made the rounds of an affair between these two stars, based on the many times they were seen out on the town, going to the theater or restaurants. In December 1955, Marilyn was Brando's guest at the premier of *The Rose Tattoo*, after which they went to a celebration dinner at the Sheraton Astor Hotel on Forty-fourth Street (see Victor).

In his biography of Marilyn, Anthony Summers writes that Marilyn told her friend Amy Greene that she secretly referred to Brando as "Carlo," and that he was "sweet, tender."

Ironically, as was often the case between Jackie and Marilyn, both women were to fall under the same man's sexual spell. Brando's undeniably powerful erotic allure appealed to both of them.

Sometime after Bobby's death, Lee and Jackie had dinner with Marlon Brando and his best friend, George Englund, at the Jockey Club in Washington. As Brando confided to a friend, after dinner they danced and "she pressed her thighs against his and did everything she could to arouse him. They talked about going away on a skiing vacation together, just the two of them. Brando could feel Jackie's breath on his ear. He felt Jackie expected him to make a move, try to take her to bed." However, having drunk too much, Brando was fearful that he might be impotent, made his excuses, and left. (See *Just Jackie*, by Edward Klein [New York: Ballantine, 1998].)

Jackie Kennedy
Suite 2222
The Carlyle

Marsha Marshall
The St. Regis

October 11, 1954

Dear "Martha,"

I was deeply saddened to hear of your impending divorce.* I just got into town and almost called you. But I imagine that at a time like this, you would probably rather be left alone. I want, from the bottom of my heart, to express to you how sorry I am that things didn't work out between you and Joe DiMaggio. I know that you loved each other profoundly. It is unfortunate that your work came between you. I often dream of having a career, aside from helping Jack, but I think men generally find it intensely difficult to cope with women who forge separate identities.

In your case, however, that is utterly unfair, because Joe was fully aware that he was marrying Marilyn Monroe. You were Marilyn Monroe when he met you—how could he have expected you to relinquish your identity? But who knows what goes on in the hearts and minds of men?

You must never forget, Marilyn, that you are very special and very

---

* Jackie wrote in the Purple Diary, "MM has given Joe D his marching papers. Wonder how Joe K will feel about her now that she is once more fancy-fee and ripe for the picking. . . . Then again, the poor kid doesn't really need to get in any deeper with him than she already is."

beautiful and that you deserve love and happiness. Do you have a replacement for Joe in mind? Jack and I have been married for over a year now. Sometimes I still feel as if we are gypsies. Jack makes speeches all over the city and is never home for more than two nights at a time. We stay with his family in Hyannis Port a lot, in a little room on the first floor where Jack used to sleep, so it really isn't big enough for more than one person.

I truly wish that we had a home of our own. If we did, it might give our lives some roots, some stability so that Jack would be able to spend more time with me and the children we want to have.

I realize this may not be the appropriate time (and forgive me for asking) but this morning, Jack was admitted to the Hospital for Special Surgery—Cornell Medical Center, here in Manhattan. He is having a very complicated operation—a double spinal fusion. Right now, he is in a lot of pain and feeling very low. It would greatly raise his spirits if you were able to find the time to send him a poster or a photograph of yourself. You could send it here to the Carlyle and I would bring it in to Jack when next I visit. Unfortunately for me, his sisters are staying here, too (we have very little in common), and I would be mortified if they get their hands on it and give it to him themselves. Could you please mark it "Private and Confidential"?

Which reminds me: I just adore your alias. I suppose movie stars invariably require an alias as protection from fans and gossip columnists. At any rate, movie star or not, in case our letters inadvertently fall into the wrong hands, I have made the momentous decision to acquire an alias of my own. You will be amused to learn that I have selected Josephine (after Napoleon's empress)* Kendall. So let us continue our correspondence under our new aliases. Frankly, the prospect of doing

---

* Sarah Bradford tells of Jackie's engraving of Empress Josephine, proudly displayed in her White House bedroom. Norman Mailer interviewed Milton Greene, Marilyn's business partner, and his wife, Amy, for his *Of Women and Their Elegance* (New York: Macmillan, 1980) and they

so inures us against the horrific mishap of either the Hollywood hag columnists or the equally vitriolic East Coast scribes getting their vulgar ink-stained hands on our correspondence. Perish the thought! I always open my own mail, so you could address the envelope to Jackie Kennedy, but then put the letter inside a second envelope, addressed to Josephine Kendall. Also please mark the outer envelope and the inner one "Private and Confidential." I think that phrase describes our correspondence so well, don't you? It is not my normal practice to confide in other women, as the majority are invariably jealous, excessively competitive, and fundamentally untrustworthy. However, due to your open, trusting, unjealous, and friendly nature, I am delighted to be able to drop my guard and do so readily and happily. Apart from which, I am utterly riveted by your tales of your fellow Hollywood luminaries.

Your story about George Sanders and Zsa Zsa Gabor was delicious. As for her tips, in the course of our conversation (we were sitting next to each other on a flight from Paris three years ago when I flew there for the Coronation), she did dispense a selection which she had gleaned from experts at MGM. When I mentioned that my large hands are the bane of my existence, she advised me never to wear pale nail polish, as that would only make my fingers appear longer. According to her, if I wore red or dark red polish, that would serve to truncate my hands. By the same token, she also advised that I create the illusion of long legs by always wearing the same color shoes as my stockings. I am not entirely sure whether these hints will be of any use, but in the light of Miss Gabor's reaction to you in Hollywood, I am amused by the irony of my passing them on to you.

I am unsure as to when Jack and I will return to Washington again. I am so immensely worried about him. The operation he is having on

---

both confirmed that Marilyn was fascinated by Empress Josephine and loved their collection of books on her.

October 21 may be life-threatening. He has always said that he would prefer to be dead than disabled. I hope and pray that it won't come to that. But if you are too busy, please do not, under any circumstances, give my request another thought whatsoever. Just look after yourself and guard against allowing memories of Joe to undermine you.

With my love,
Josephine

The St. Regis

Josephine Kendall
The Carlyle

October 13, 1954

Dear Josephine,

I am so very sorry to hear about Jack's hospitalization and am sending this signed poster by messenger. I hope it isn't too raunchy for the hospital—but it is the only one I have here in New York.

I've had an idea—but please say if you think it wouldn't work. If Jack is in so much pain and so depressed, what if we spring a nice surprise on him? What if I got hold of a nurse's uniform—I could get them to send it out from Hollywood—and sneaked into the hospital dressed that way?* Do you think that might pep Jack up? Or—better still—perhaps I could get you the nurse costume so you could surprise him instead of me. I am sure he would love that even more.

But if you want me to do it, of course I will.

Love,
Martha

---

* After Marilyn wrote to Jackie offering to dress up in a nurse's uniform and surprise Jack, clearly confident that Jackie would agree to her ruse, she called Patty Renoir and begged her to send the nurse's uniform, which she, Marilyn, had worn to audition for *Lady of the Lamp*. "She

P.S. I meant to add that I love the Zsa Zsa nail polish trick because my hands are flat and webed [sic] like duck's [sic] feet, so please don't feel bad about yours.

P.P.S. I also love our correspondence.

---

was talking a blue streak," Patty recalled to her literary agent, Richard Winchester, "all about how now she was going to see 'him,' at last, how she was longing for him, how happy she was. Her voice was high with excitement, like a kid's at Christmas."

The Carlyle

Martha Marshall
The St. Regis

Dear Martha,

Thank you for your extremely kind and considerate note. I am sending this to you via messenger—they are a marvelous addition to our modern age—as well. I think it would be absolutely marvelous if you would dress up as a nurse and surprise Jack.* It would make an enormous difference to him. Of course, you could only stay for a few minutes—so as not to tire him out—but he would just adore it, I know.

The best time of the day is in the morning, as I am usually having my hair done at Helena Rubinstein and the sisters are always sleeping. That way Jack will be on his own and feeling low—so the surprise will be even greater!

You are one of the dearest, kindest people to go to so much trouble for us.

Love,

J

---

* Jackie wrote in the Purple Diary, "Just hope Jack doesn't have a coronary when he sees MM!"

The Carlyle

Martha Marshall
The St. Regis

October 14, 1954

Dear Martha,

You are a miracle worker! When I arrived at the hospital this afternoon, Jack was bright-eyed, bushy-tailed, and a completely new man.*
I wish I knew how you managed it! You did more for Jack than any
doctor could possibly do—and the result is a tribute to the magic of
Marilyn Monroe.

Speaking of which, you never did tell me whether or not you have
a replacement for Joe waiting in the wings???? Someone with your
generous spirit richly deserves love and happiness.

Thank you again for making Jack so happy.

Love,

J

---

* Jackie wrote in the Purple Diary, "This afternoon, when I saw Jack at the hospital, he looked so
young, so fresh, so new. For a second, an unworthy thought regarding MM (and after all, she
nearly did play Florence Nightingale, and we all know how *she* ministered to the sick and needy)
flew through my mind. I ignored it, though. Or rather, as Scarlett would say, 'I won't think of it
now,' or ever. . . ."

508 North Palm Drive
Beverly Hills, California

Josephine Kendall
The Carlyle

October 21, 1954

Dear Josephine,

I wanted to write and say that I hope Jack's operation was a success. He looked so sick that after I left him, I slipped into St. Patrick's, lit a candle for him and prayed that he would get well fast.

Please let me know how he is, and you, too, of course.

Love,
Martha

1095 North Ocean Boulevard

Palm Beach, Florida

Martha Marshall

508 North Palm Drive

Beverly Hills, California

October 28, 1954

Dear Martha,

You are immensely kind to be so concerned about Jack's operation, to have brightened his day and prayed for him. He is making a speedy recovery, so your prayers clearly worked. How I wish I could believe like you do!

You will be vastly amused to learn that before Jack was discharged from the hospital, one of his prospective visitors, his old flame, Grace Kelly (I don't know whether or not you have made her acquaintance), called me.* In the course of our conversation, I told her of your brilliant ruse of dressing up as a nurse and visiting Jack in that guise. She was so beguiled by what you did, and the effect I told her it had on

---

* Jack (perhaps to indicate to Jackie and his other conquests, that they were members of an elite group of women) was open—even boastful—regarding his premarital fling with Grace Kelly. (See *Love, Jack,* by Gunilla von Post [New York: Crown, 1977].)

Heymann cites how Grace dressed in a nurse's uniform and was smuggled into the Hospital for Special Surgery by Jackie.

After Grace Kelly visited Jack in hospital, Jackie recorded in her diary, "Grace was excessively dewy-eyed over Jack and I suspect I made a bad move giving her access to him, even in this condition. For while I may play with the faint possibility that MM might be susceptible to Jack's charms, I don't take my musings at all seriously on that front. However, clearly Grace still carries

him, that she promptly ordered a nurse's uniform for her own visit! Jack, of course, was thrilled.

Now we are in Palm Beach, where he is convalescing. I spend much of my time walking on the beach, and wishing that his recovery will be permanent.

Warm regards and many thanks for your kindness and concern,

J

---

a massive torch for him. But I'll try not to dwell on it, especially now, when Jack is fighting for his life and all I want is for him to get strong and to survive."

Grace continued to excite Jackie's ire, even when Jackie was in the White House and Grace went there on an official visit. As Tish Baldrige recorded, Jack and Grace's romance took place "before either of them was married; that, in my opinion, is why Jackie changed the White House meal in their honor from a four-hour black-tie dinner dance to a small eighty-minute-long seated luncheon—a bit of jealousy, perhaps. Princess Grace, we all noted, stood close to the president and gazed at him with adoring eyes. The photographs of the reunion made us shriek with laughter in the East Wing. She looked like a teenybopper up close to her favorite rock star."

MARILYN MONROE
Cedars of Lebanon
Beverly Hills, California

Josephine Kendall
1095 North Ocean Boulevard
Palm Beach, Florida

November 8, 1954

Dear Josephine,

It is past midnight, I can't sleep, and my thoughts are jangling around in my head like an out-of-tune tamborine [sic]. I am still on heavy-duty painkillers, ones the hospital gave me, and some I bought along myself.

I have been very sick with endometriosis. They operated on me two days ago. Now I am terrified that I won't ever be able to have a child. I want a child more than anything else in the world, at least, sometimes I think I do. Other times, I am afraid the child will turn out to be another Norma Jeane, unloved and unhappy like I was. Sometimes, I don't know what will make me happy. When I first started making movies, I used to go up by the Hollywood sign, look down and think, "Someday I am going to own this town." Tons of other girls, I know, say the same thing. Except, for me, it came true, which is part of the problem. The dream was far better than the reality.

Just now when I looked out the hospital window, there were no stars in the sky—but I know they will be shining up there another night and that gives me hope. I've got your last letters with me in the hospital; I just read them again, and they are so warm and friendly. In one, you asked me if I

79

found a replacement for Joe. I didn't answer that question then, but you are so kind and caring to worry about me, so tonight I will, although I shouldn't. Years ago, I slept with a few men whom I didn't love. I would be telling a lie if I said I didn't, and although I did love Joe, no one has ever touched my heart the way one very special man has. I can't tell you where and when I met him—it doesn't matter and it was a long time ago, and I can't even tell you his real name either, because I made a sacred promise that I would never tell another living soul. I call him Mr. G, but he can't be a replacement for Joe, you see, because—please don't be shocked—he is married. He is tall, dark, and handsome, has brown eyes and reminds me of Clark Gable so much. But no matter how much I love him, and I do, we have no future together, only the present. He lives in Paris and comes to America a lot (to see me), but his wife (she is very small and blonde and French) is sick, and no matter how much he loves me, he can't divorce her. I mustn't say any more and I probably shouldn't even have said this much, except you were kind and asked.

I never knew Jack dated Grace. If I were you and married to him, I would kill myself before I let her within a million miles of his hospital room, but then you aren't me. You have nothing to worry about because you are married to him and she isn't and never will be, and no Hollywood blonde will ever get him away from you, I know that.

You said you didn't believe in religion but I thought you were Catholic, was I wrong? An orderley [sic] has just walked in—I'll give him this to mail right away and will stop writing because I am sure you have better things to read than me.

Love,
Marilyn

Jackie wrote in her diary, "Marilyn has made the sweetest confession—albeit when under the influence of. . . . . She is engaged in an illicit liaison with a mysterious tall dark stranger whom she has dubbed 'Mr. G.' She is obviously not talking about old Joe K, and he is clearly out of the picture, and has been for some time. So who could her mysterious illicit beau be? Could it be Sam Goldwyn? Nubar Gulbenkian? Paul Getty? Gary Cooper? She is achingly earnest about it, as in 'I made a blood oath never to reveal a word about him, not even under torture' sort of thing. She has such a vivid, Hollywood-style imagination. Still, I suppose I shouldn't take all this lightly, because, in reality, there is a wife and God knows how many children. None of whom stand a soupçon of a chance should Miss Marilyn gaze mistily and bustily in their daddy's direction. . . . Little does Mrs. G, whoever she may be, know how insecure and fragile Marilyn really is."

8336 DeLongpre Avenue
Hollywood, California

Josephine Kendall
1095 North Ocean Boulevard
Palm Beach, Florida

November 9, 1954

Dear Josephine,

I am praying that you are out of town and haven't read my last letter, or that it didn't get to you yet.* But when it does, please don't ever read it. I just wasn't myself when I wrote it—my brain had gone because of the painkillers—so I don't really know what I wrote and didn't mean any of it anyway.

Last night is fuzzy, but I remember writing for hours to you, and then begging the orderly [sic] to mail it at once. I wish to God he hadn't. But he was trying to please me and didn't know.

---

* The following morning, when she awoke from her drug-induced sleep and remembered what she had written to Jackie, Marilyn made a hysterical call to Patty Renoir, who recalled "I could hardly understand a single word. She was crying and crying. 'I've ruined everything, everything. Now she'll know. And he'll kill me. He'll never see me again, and she'll never forgive me. I wish I were dead. I should be dead. Deserve it, want it, need it. Should be punished. Will be. I fuck up everything good I ever have,' and on and on. I talked to her for about an hour, talked her down so she stopped crying and went calm again. Next time we talked, didn't say a word to her about what she said before. Nor did she. Might as well have never happened. Then that's how things always were with her."

Marilyn by then must have known that her letter had crossed with Jackie and that she had no choice but to brazen out the consequences of her confession.

Anyway, please, please, please don't read it. Just tear it up and, when I am not so sick, I'll write a real letter to you instead.

Love,
Martha

3321 Dent Place
Washington, D.C

Martha Marshall
8336 DeLongpre Avenue
Hollywood, California

November 12, 1954

Dear Martha,

Your letter so alarmed me that I am writing back instantly. You sound so sad and depressed, so I sincerely hope that this scarf will cheer you up a little and that you will soon be on the road to recovery.

First of all, I am absolutely convinced that you should never give up on becoming a mother. You would love, cherish, and nurture a child so deeply and make a perfect mother, so don't lose heart.

As for my religion—I was, indeed, raised a Catholic. However, because of my parents' divorce, I have always felt somewhat of an outsider in the society in which I live and my religion only intensified that feeling. Consequently, perhaps to my detriment, I allowed my Catholicism to lapse. Nonetheless, I believe in the precepts of the religion concerning divorce, particularly after my own experience in the aftermath of my parents'.

Your Mr. G sounds divine and I am flattered that you decided to confide in me. However, I am fearful of the consequence to your career in the eventuality that the affair ever becomes public knowledge. Although I suppose the studio would protect you from the resultant scandal. That concern aside, please don't think that I am in the least bit shocked about your new romance with a married man.

How could I be, given the way in which my father cheated on my mother during their honeymoon, and later told me all about it, and his subsequent illicit affairs as well? My primary concern, Marilyn, is not about the morality of the situation—the heart, as we both know, beats to its own moral code—but that you may get hurt. Mr. G, I assume, is probably much older than you and, if he is anything like most men, can take good care of himself. Of course, I feel sorry for his wife, but French women are bred to endure their husbands' infidelities, and who knows whether or not she has driven him to cheat. My mother certainly bore some responsibility for my father's infidelity, so no doubt Mr. G's wife does as well.

But please take care of yourself, dear Marilyn, in negotiating this perilous situation. You may be worldly on the surface, but knowing you as I do, I am profoundly aware that you can also be somewhat naïve. So I hope you will shield your heart as best you can. That said, please do not, under any circumstances, jump to the erroneous conclusion that I am judging you in any way whatsoever. Nothing is further from the truth, for I am sure that if I had never met Jack, I, too, might well have fallen prey to the blandishments of an older, experienced, married man of some charm and sophistication. Consequently, I am certainly not judging you, nor would I ever, as I am much too fond of you. Please take great care, cherish your times with Mr. G, but do guard against giving away your entire heart to him.*

---

* Jackie's ability to guard her heart and restrain her emotions was masterly. Maria Mencher has made available to the editor her tapes of off-the-record interviews that she used for background on her groundbreaking 1977 biography of Jackie titled *Jackie Unmasked* (Düsseldorf: Muller Books, 1977). "During one of her trips to London to stay with Lee (shortly before Jackie married Ari) Jackie summoned one of her beaux, a lovestruck Philadelphia oil and steel millionaire named Gray Partland. He reserved a suite for them at the Ritz, and Jackie checked in at lunchtime. Partland arrived at the hotel at three, jet-lagged but wild for Jackie and desperate to see her. He strode into the suite, in a high state of passion, ready for Jackie to fling herself into his arms. But when he reached out for her, Jackie took a step back and said, 'Wait. Not yet.' Then, cool as a cucumber, she sat down at the dressing table and proceeded, extremely slowly, to apply

Warm regards,
Josephine

---

her makeup. Partland watched, dumbstruck, unable to move, unable to touch her, as his desire mounted. Finally, after she had checked her makeup, Jackie got up and walked away from Partland, toward a closet. Then she took out a large picture hat, walked back to the mirror, where she spent an inordinately long time arranging the hat to her satisfaction. By now, Partland—this six-foot-three Philadelphia oil and steel tycoon with money to burn and overwhelming charisma—had turned to Jell-O. Jackie smiled a slow smile, gave him an extremely direct look, beckoned, and said, 'Now.' Partland was hers forever."

8336 DeLongpre Avenue
Hollywood, California

Josephine Kendall
1095 North Ocean Boulevard
Palm Beach, Florida

November 18, 1954

Dear Josephine,

Thank you for the beautiful gift and your kind and friendly letter. Reading it, I realize that you must have got my other letter before you knew not to open it. I am so embarrassed and hope you will forget whatever—and I still can't remember what—stupid things I wrote in it.

The scarf you sent me is beautiful. It makes me feel so glad to know that someone—no—not someone—you—so far away still cares about me, even though I don't deserve it. I never owned a Hermès scarf before. Doesn't "Brides de Gala" sound romantic? I loved it so much that I called Paris, found out Hermès made one with Napoleon on it—why not Josephine? So unfair . . . So here it is and I hope you like it.

By the way, did you see Eisenhower's historic first televised cabinet meeting last month? I think it is wonderful that television cameras can now bring us so close to the President. I never dreamed of seeing the President in action like that. I don't like being on television myself—the lighting is difficult to control and the makeup is different—but I think it is wonderful that the people can see what the politicians are doing, don't you? I've been a registered Democrat for as far back as I can remember and I want to know as much about our politicians and their ideals as possible.

I forgot, because of the hospital, to give you the big news that, just before I got sick, we finished shooting <u>Seven Year Itch</u>, and Charlie Feldman gave a dinner in my honor at Romanoff's.* I borrowed a bright red chiffon ball gown from wardrobe and I was glad I did, because guess who I danced with? Clark Gable! The orchestra played "Bye-Bye Baby," Clark held me a little close, and I felt like Cinderella dancing with Prince Charming. During the dance, I was so shy that I just kept on smiling, but when it ended, I told Clark how much I admired him and that I longed one day to do a picture with him, and guess what, he said he had seen <u>Gentlemen Prefer Blondes</u>, thought I had "magic"—I remember you once said that about me as well—and that he wanted to work with me as well! So you will get to meet him after all—I'll make sure of it!

Thinking back to that wonderful evening makes me so happy, which I need to be now, what with Thanksgiving round the corner and not having anyone I love here with me. Today I heard a song which really made me cry, "I'm Dreaming of a White Christmas." It was almost as if I wrote it myself, except for the line "just like the one I used to know"—because I have never known that kind of Christmas, but it sounds wonderful, and maybe one day I will.

Your advise [sic] about Mr. G was very kind and, I am sure, right. I know I'm wrong seeing him. But I just can't help myself. If you knew him, I'm sure you'd understand. At least, I hope you would.

---

* The party, thrown in Marilyn's honor by Charles Feldman, was a dinner for eighty guests. The guests included Darryl F. Zanuck, Samuel Goldwyn and Jack Warner, Humphrey Bogart, Gable, Claudette Colbert, Gary Cooper, Susan Hayward, and Loretta Young and Billy Wilder. On each round table, the centerpiece was a cardboard cut-out of Marilyn in the skirt-blowing scene from *The Seven Year Itch*.

Please write me soon and forget about that stupid last letter.

Love,
Martha

P.S. Sometimes I just don't know what's real and what isn't. Please forgive me.

1095 North Ocean Boulevard

Palm Beach, Florida

Martha Marshall

8336 DeLongpre Avenue

Hollywood, California

January 8, 1955

Dear Martha,

Your letter was so interesting and descriptive—thank you. I adore
my beautiful new Napoleon scarf and think of you every time I wear
it. You were extremely kind and generous to have sent it.

You will have realized from my last letter that your second letter,
imploring me not to read the first, arrived too late. Consequently, I
had, indeed, already read the first letter. But you must not reproach
yourself for anything you wrote in it. It was sincere, heartwarming,
and your secret is utterly safe with me—as I know all mine are with
you—so please don't feel anxious.

You may think me presumptuous, but despite your reassuring
words regarding Mr. G, I am still a trifle concerned that your new
romance may, in the long run, have a negative impact on you. It would
set my mind at rest, I think, if I knew more about him, his marital situation, and his intentions toward you. What is his profession? Does
Mrs. G know of your relationship? Does he have any intention of
leaving her and, now that you are free, marrying you? Are you prepared for the fact that, given that she is French, and probably Catholic,
her religion will preclude divorce? I hope you will not consider these

questions intrusive, Marilyn, but you know that I have your best interests at heart.

On a lighter note, I was ecstatic to learn about your dance with Clark Gable and I am now uncontrollably impatient for you to begin filming with him forthwith! But even I, stuck here on the East Coast, know that things materialize relatively slowly in Hollywood and will thus endeavor to control my impatience!

As for the benefits of televising our political proceedings—I am not convinced. Ambassador Kennedy's creed, as he will have told you, is "It doesn't matter who you are, it only matters who people think you are!" In the same vein, I fear that if the people one day get too close to the politicians who represent them, the entire process will be forever tarnished. I imagine that television will only ultimately benefit those politicians who are able to combine the showmanship of P. T. Barnun with the thespian ability of John Barrymore.

Yesterday I read in the *Palm Beach Daily News* that you are now a corporation (along with Milton Greene). Congratulations! It all sounds wonderful and now that you are moving to the East Coast, I hope you will be happier.

I am afraid I have to close this letter now, because Eunice, Jack's sister (his favorite, although I can't imagine why), has just materialized. If she chanced to learn the identity of my secret correspondent, her cackle would echo all the way to L.A. By the way, I am unable to conceive why most people are so enthralled by Jack having so many siblings. Now that I've been part of the family for a while, I've come to the inescapable conclusion that large families are not so great at all. Jack is forever in his late brother Joe's shadow, Eunice is in her late sister Kathleen's, and all the other kids veer between being far too close to one another and being so virulently competitive that every single one of them would rather die than lose a cretinous game of touch football to the other.

I do my utmost to avoid them whenever I can, and so divide my time between reading Proust, walking on the beach, and shopping on Worth Avenue. Yesterday, when I came back from Saks with a new turquoise Balenciaga ball gown, Eunice had the gall to demand the price! Of course, I did not respond, but borrowing a gown from the studio and not having to answer to anyone seems to me to be a much more desirable way of life. In the meantime, I try to brighten Jack's days by playing checkers, categories, and twenty questions and the new game, Scrabble, with him—all of which he relishes, just as long as he can win . . .

Please write when you are settled and let me know your new address.

Love,
Josephine

Jackie wrote in her diary, "Marilyn obviously has no scruples whatsoever about hurting Mrs. G and any children the couple may have. But perhaps I shouldn't be surprised. I guess part of M's charm lies in her fundamental amorality. Rather like Jack, I suppose."

The Gladstone Hotel
East 52nd Street
New York, New York

Josephine Kendall
3321 Dent Place
Washington, D.C.

February 24, 1955

Dear Josephine,

I am sorry I haven't written for so long, but moving back East has been so crazy, in a nice way, that I haven't had a moment. I am taking acting lessons with Constance Collier and am reading Ulysses and George Sand's letters. I want more than anything else, more even than being rich, famous, or loved, to learn. Also, I want to do something right in my art when so much is going wrong in my life—all except for Mr. G. The good news is that being here hasn't meant being apart from Mr. G for too long. He has managed to come out here—from Paris—and we have had lovely times together.

I want to answer all your questions as well as I can. Mr. G is president of an insurance company. I don't think Mrs. G knows about me yet. I sure hope not. I never ask him about her, because when I am with him I want to pretend that he is all mine. But I get mad when he tells me that he doesn't have sex with her. All married men say that, you see, and I find it really insulting. I would rather he and Mrs. G were having sex all the time, but that he still wanted me. I've said that to him, but he just changes the subject.

You asked if he was planning to divorce Mrs. G. Well, ever since I married Joe, Mr. G always says how great it is that we are both married to other people. He calls it "the seesaw effect," which he says means that we are equal because, being both married, we each would suffer if we were found out.

So when Joe and I split up, at first I didn't tell Mr. G. We met for dinner in a suite at the Algonquin and I didn't say a word about Joe. I was wearing leopard skin stiletto boots. Mr. G said he loved them, so I kept them on all evening, all through everything. Then, just as he was leaving, I told him about Joe. After, I turned away, because I started crying and didn't want him to see. If he had, I would have expected him to hug me and kiss me, but he isn't really that sort. After I told him about Joe, he went very quiet, then he said, "You are a very strong lady, Marilyn." I said I didn't feel very strong and he said, "You and I would get the last piece of bread in the concentration camp." I didn't like that, so I said, "But I'd share it with everyone else." He didn't say anything, then he left. I cried all night, thinking he would never call me again, but he did, the very next morning, just to check that I was OK. He called lots of times after that, too, and we still see each other, but I would never think of asking him to leave Mrs. G. I am just happy that now I've come East, I can see so much more of him—because New York is far more convenient for him than Los Angeles, being closer to Paris, I mean.

Had to stop because I got a call from Milton. I've been spending a lot of time with him and his wife, Amy—who is lovely—at their home in Connecticut, where they live in a beautiful old house—the kind you probably grew up in. The living room was once a stable, with vaulted ceilings and a big old fireplace. I've never sat in front of a fireplace before, because we don't have them in California, but now I love to gaze into the flames for hours and just dream.

On March 30, one of the dreams I used to dream as a child will come true and I'll be thinking of you wanting to be Queen of the Circus because I shall actually be in the circus, riding a pink elephant, for a benefit.* It means a lot to me, because I never went to the circus as a kid and now I am actually going to be in one! Mike Todd is running it. I quite like him, he's very handsome, strong, and determined. But he isn't Mr. G. No one is.

But going back to Amy Greene. At first, I think she was afraid I'd make a play for Milton, which I never would. Also, she didn't really seem to trust my mind or my word much. Anyway, after the press party announcing the formation of my corporation, I wanted to take everyone to the Copa, where Frank Sinatra was singing, but Amy said the show was sold out for months and we wouldn't get a table. I explained that I thought I could get one, but I could tell that she didn't believe me. I got mad and said, "Watch this, Amy," picked up my ermine wrap, and told everyone to follow me to the Copa. Although they probably secretly agreed with Amy, out of politeness—and I guess because sometimes it helps that I am Marilyn Monroe—they all followed me. At the Copa, the doorman took one look at me, got us inside, and the maître d' put down a table and chairs just for us. Then—and this was the best—Frank, who was right in the middle of singing "Always," stopped dead, stared right at me, and winked. Amy almost fainted dead away. Then she whispered to me, "I stand corrected." Since then, she believes in me and we are friends—but of course I would never dream of confiding in her as I do in you.

---

* On March 30, 1955, a benefit was given at Madison Square Garden for the Arthritis and Rheumatism Foundation. Milton Berle was the ringmaster. When Marilyn first met him—mindful of Berle's reputation, still unchallenged even today, as being the best-endowed man in Hollywood—she greeted him with the words "Mr. Berle, I'm finding it really difficult to keep my eyes on your face. . . ." He returned the compliment by announcing Marilyn as "the only girl who makes Jane Russell look like a boy!" Marilyn made a breathtaking entrance on a pink elephant named Karnaudi and the 18,000-strong crowd went wild.

I hope Palm Beach is fun for you. I'd love to go there and perhaps we will be there together one day. That would be nice.

Love,
Martha

Jackie wrote in the Purple Diary, "So Marilyn's Mr. G has a propensity for leopard skin stiletto boots. . . . He obviously possesses the soul of a Pigalle pimp coupled with the aesthetic sensibilities of Hugh Hefner. Still—if that's what makes MM happy . . . On the other hand, he (and don't they all—the ones who attract us) clearly has a well-developed vein of ruthlessness—witness his concentration camp remark. And applying it to Marilyn as well . . . interesting . . ."

3321 Dent Place
Washington, D.C.

Martha Marshall
Gladstone Hotel
East 52nd Street
New York

April 10, 1955

Dear Martha,

Thank you for your enchantingly evocative letter. It seems such a long time since I last wrote to you, but life has been extremely hectic, so I hope you will forgive my lapse. I quite agree with you that meeting in Palm Beach would be wonderful when things have calmed down a little.

How marvelous that you are now taking acting lessons (although I cannot imagine why you would need them, as you are already so accomplished), that you are reading vociferously, and that you had such a glittering evening at the Copa. By now, you are probably accustomed to my undying curiosity regarding the Hollywood gods and goddesses who inhabit your dazzling universe, thus I am certain you will not be in the least bit surprised when I reveal my abiding fascination with Frank Sinatra and my desire to discover more about him.* I

---

* Jackie wrote in her Purple Diary, "Now and again, can't help myself from fantasizing a little about Mr. Sinatra. Nothing explicit, just defused images, but all extremely pleasing. Tend to drift into that state during those evenings when Jack is at the Mayflower, doesn't call me and when I call him, his voice is strained and his mind elsewhere. As for his body, who knows. . . ."

should love to learn any details/anecdotes/gossip you have time to share with me.

Jack and I have just returned from what will be our new home, a white brick Georgian mansion, on six acres of woodland overlooking the Potomac, complete with stables, where I house my horses, and an orchard. The serenity of the house, the river flowing nearby, and the tall trees surrounding the house transports me back to Merrywood, the home in which I spent much of my childhood and sometimes still yearn for. But at last Jack and I have a home of our own! Perhaps we can finally be a family.

Marilyn, I hope what I am about to tell you will not upset you (and I firmly believe that it is only a matter of time before you find the man of your dreams—who is available—and will then follow suit) but I wanted to write and share the news with you that I am pregnant. I know that you will wish me well and understand when I tell you that I am simultaneously thrilled and scared, excited and nervous. I wonder what the next nine months will bring.

I only wish Jack could spend more time with me here. But he often has to stay over in Washington (at the Mayflower Hotel, where he has a permanent suite) because he works so hard. The Ambassador is playing an increasingly large part in our lives. He is determined that Jack one day attain high political office. Naturally, I feel exactly the same. As for Jack, he lives and breathes politics all day long. Joe says he intends to sell Jack like cornflakes—I am not at all sure that I appreciate the analogy. All in all, I am not altogether convinced that being married to a very busy politician is the easiest way of life, but I intend to make the best of it. The pictures of you on the pink elephant were glorious, by the way.

Love,

J

P.S. Are you dating anyone else, or are you true to Mr. G?

Martha Marshall
Suite 2728
The Waldorf-Astoria Hotel

Josephine Kendall
3321 Dent Place
Washington, D.C.

April 19, 1955

Dear Josephine,

Thank you for your letter. I am very glad about your news. Congratulations to you and Jack. I am sure he will make the best father in the world and you, of course, the best mother. Sometimes I sit in the park and watch the children play. I can't remember ever playing in the park as a child, but I suppose I did and wish that I was expecting Mr. G's child. But that will never be, for, tragically, he is unable to father children—due to a childhood attack of measles, I think. It is very sad for him, because every man wants to be a father and he will never be one, ever.

You asked if I was true to him. The answer is yes—but I don't think he would care if I wasn't. He always says, "The day you get married again, Marilyn, I'll be standing in the wings applauding." I never like it when he says that, because, to me, it means that he doesn't care much. Once, I asked him why he would applaud. He said, "Not because I don't want you." Then he clammed up. I was afraid to ask any more. I don't really know what to believe, except that I don't think I'll be seeing too much of him anymore.

I am afraid I am feeling very blue right now. Yesterday, Einstein died and although I never met him, I always hoped I would. In any case, he was a wonderful man who did a great deal of good in the world, so I am sad.

I have recently moved into the Waldorf Towers—27th floor. You spent your honeymoon here, didn't you? Perhaps one day I'll do the same. I hope things go well for you and the baby.

I've started seeing Margaret Herz Hohenberg, a psychoanalist [sic] five times a week, which may seem a lot. Lee Strasberg suggested I try psychoanalisis [sic] so as to help my acting by exploring my inner self. Most of all, I want to be wonderful, an artist and true. Sometimes, though, I don't know what to say to Margaret. Other times, I can't stop talking and afterwards I feel great. But that feeling doesn't last for long. I suppose the only things that endure in life are the important ones— like babies and, sometimes, love.

You asked about Frank and I will tell you as much as I can.* Frank and I are good friends now, but once upon a time, as they say in fairy tales, we were lovers. Frank can be like chili peppers one minute—so mad that he flares up and burns you real deep—and the next like velvet—so gentle that you want to nestle right into him and feel safe forever. He is kind and generous—he gave me pearls—he gives all his women pearls. At first, when you sleep with him, he is real restless and dreams the same dream over and over each night. He told me so, but I didn't dare ask what the dream was,

---

* In 1958, Marilyn's maid Lena Pepitone observed that Marilyn loved to listen to Sinatra's "All of Me" as well as "Every Day I Have the Blues" and "The Man I Love."

Pepitone and Marilyn had a detailed conversation about Sinatra, which Pepitone records in her book, *Marilyn Monroe Confidential* (New York: Simon and Schuster, 1979):

"One night, she told me, she got so drunk that she totally forgot Frank's strict orders. She absentmindedly wandered downstairs—with nothing on—to look for Frank. She said that she was lonely and just wanted to talk to him. After walking through one empty room after another, she finally cracked open the door to the smoky room where the card game was in session. Frank

only each night in his sleep he'd say the same thing over and over, "*They're chasing me, they're chasing me!*"* Underneath, he is caring and tender, I like him very much, but I don't love him.

Martha

---

noticed her before anyone else had a chance to. 'He hit the roof. Frankie slammed his drink down so hard he broke the glass,' Marilyn said. Frank jumped up and pushed Marilyn out of view before the others could figure out exactly what was happening. 'He yanked me aside and ordered me to get my "fat ass" back upstairs. How dare I embarrass him in front of his friends? He looked like he was going to kill me on the spot. I ran back to the bedroom and cried for hours. Here was Frankie being so nice to me, and I let him down.'

" 'No one in the whole world's sweeter than Frankie. When he came back later and kissed me on the cheek, that made me feel like a million.' Marilyn beamed. 'From then on, I always dressed up for him. Whether or not anyone was coming over.' "

* Sinatra giving all his woman pearls and talking in his sleep from Wendy Leigh interview, "Hollywood Insider," with Tiffany Bolling, who had an affair with him during the making of *Tony Roma*.

Chesham Place
Belgravia
London

Martha Marshall
The Waldorf-Astoria
301 Park Avenue
New York, New York

July 15, 1955

Dear Martha,

I am sorry I have been so long in writing, but I lost my baby in May and, since then, have been traveling. But now that I am in London at last (I am on my own and staying with my sister, Lee, and her family) I can relax and finally write to you. But I promise not to allow so much time to elapse between letters again.

I was spellbound by your Sinatra revelations. He sounds intensely complicated and endlessly intriguing. What a pity you can't bring yourself to love him. But then none of us can love—or stop loving—at will, can we?

Mother mailed Lee a copy of *Life* and I read in it that not only was June 1 your birthday, but that *Seven Year Itch* opened that day as well and was a stupendous success, so I hope you are feeling happier than when you last wrote to me and that this birthday heralds a new beginning for you. *The Seven Year Itch* sounds wonderful, although I suppose it may evoke painful memories for you. Isn't it sad that just when we think we have the man of our dreams, everything dissolves and reality sets in? I have come to the conclusion that it is a mistake to expect too much of life, or of men.

Between us, and in confidence, I have not been altogether happy. Lee and I are going on to the South of France and I may even stay there with her for a while, for some fun and a few giggles. But although she is my sister and I love her, I seem unable to confide in her, as I am in you. Something you wrote to me recently has stuck in my mind. You quoted Mr. G as alluding to "the seesaw effect" between the two of you, and in a strange way, a parallel dynamic exists between both of us as well. Apart from the fact that we both feel a mutual sense of respect and friendship, we both know we will always be discreet about each other's confidences, because we each have as much to lose as the other.

On that note, I must ask you a question and should appreciate it if you would reply as honestly and sincerely as you always do. In the past six months, I have been besieged by rumors of Jack's infidelities and I find myself compelled to ask you if these have reached Hollywood— and if you have heard them.*

Given my father's history, the concept of an unfaithful husband is hardly foreign to me, and I could probably cope with the reality. It is just these deafening rumors which I find difficult to bear.

If, indeed, you have heard any, please be assured that none of them bear the slightest resemblance to the truth. For if Jack were as rampant an adulterer as the rumormongers allege, he would be either eternally exhausted or just plain dead.

---

* "Probably made a dreadful mistake," Jackie wrote in her diary, "but was feeling somewhat low at the time. I lost my sangfroid sufficiently to write and ask Marilyn if she had heard any of the Jack-as-Casanova rumors swirling around. I can't think why I broached the subject to her and now feel foolish for having done so. After all, even if she'd heard anything, she wouldn't tell me, would she? Not with her eager, puppy dog persona. Then again, to be fair to her, would I tell her if I chanced to learn that her beloved Mr. G happened to have another mistress? Probably not."

In any event, I suppose things can only get better. At least I hope so. For both of us.

Love,

J

The Waldorf-Astoria Hotel

Josephine Kendall
Chesham Place
Belgravia
London

July 28, 1955

Dear Josephine,

I was sad to get your letter and I am dreadfully sorry about the baby, and that you are feeling blue. I feel so bad for you hearing all those dreadful things about Jack. Is it Grace? I saw her at the <u>Seven Year Itch</u> premiere and don't think she is nearly as pretty as you, or even me. Or is there another woman? I really hope not. I don't want to believe Jack would ever be unfaithful to you. I am sure it is all lies and that you are the one and only woman whom Jack truly loves. I've got to stop now to go to therapy but will write more when I get back.

Later—You may not be in the mood to answer this next bit, but if you do, I would be very grateful. A friend of Aristotle Onassis, the Greek tycoon, has suggested I should marry Prince Rainea [<u>sic</u>] of Monaco.* I keep joking that Rainea [<u>sic</u>] ought to be called Prince Reindeer. I really do like the idea of becoming Princess Marilyn of Monaco. But although the

---

* Onassis's friend was George Schlee, who exhorted Gardner Cowles to approach Marilyn on Rainier's behalf, proposing that she marry the prince. (See Robert Lacey, *Grace* [New York: Putnam's Sons, 1994].)

title sounds grand, I haven't even met the Prince yet and have no idea as to whether or not I could ever love him. But it would serve Mr. G right if I did marry him, and I think I might. Have you met Rainea [sic]? What do you think of him? Does Jack know him, too? Maybe you could ask him if I should marry Rainea [sic] or not. Thank you.

Please write and let me know what you think—and what Jack does as well.

Love,
Martha

P.S. Yesterday, I met Garbo, just for a minute.

Chesham Place
Belgravia
London

Martha Marshall
The Waldorf-Astoria
New York, New York

August 10, 1955

Dear Martha,

I was so touched by your kindness and concern on my behalf regarding all those ridiculous rumors regarding Jack's alleged floozies. Thank heavens (because she would, indeed, be strong competition) Grace's name has not been evoked in that connection. On reflection, I now feel that I reacted a trifle prematurely to mere gossip, which, as you so rightly say, is probably patently untrue.

I should love to hear about Garbo—how very thrilling that you met her! Lee and I are about to leave for the Eden Roc, and you can write to me there.

How riveting about Rainier! Monte Carlo is divinely elegant; the Palace, a dream; Rainier travels most of the time. In fact, if Rainier asked me, I should not think twice. When I asked Jack how he viewed a possible marriage between you and Rainier, he merely shrugged. However, don't take his reaction as meaning indifference to you or your question—it is just a symptom of the current state of our relationship.* What does Mr. G think about you marrying Rainier?

Good luck.

Love,
Josephine

---

* During her trip to Europe in the summer of 1955, Jackie was so upset about Jack's indiscriminate womanizing that she told friends she was leaving him. "Jackie left Jack Kennedy at that time," said Peter Ward, an English friend who joined them in Antibes. "They were split. She said, 'I'm never going back,' in my presence several times" (see Bradford). However, within days the Kennedys and Lee and her husband were dining together in Monaco.

Rumors of a divorce brewing in the Kennedy household made it into print. First Drew Pearson reported the rumors in his syndicated column. *Time* printed a story that Joe had met with Jackie and offered her $1 million not to divorce Jack.

When she read the story in *Time,* Jackie supposedly phoned Joe and called him a "cheapskate. Only one million? Why not ten million?" Joe, convinced that a divorce would shatter Jack's chances of ever occupying the White House, did indeed step in to broker a peace between his son and daughter-in-law. He flew to New York from Hyannis and pleaded with Jackie not to divorce Jack.

"Jackie was forthcoming on the matter with Gore Vidal. 'Yes,' Vidal said, 'Joe did offer Jackie the money to stay with Jack and she took it. Happily'" (see Bradford).

In an exquisite irony, Marilyn, notorious for her rendition of "Diamonds Are a Girl's Best Friend," was ultimately far less materialistic than Jackie. For while Jackie's incipient materialism is a matter of record, Marilyn rarely wore jewelry, nor did she gravitate toward rich men.

The Waldorf-Astoria Hotel

Josephine Kendall
Chesham Place
Belgravia
London

August 17, 1955

Dear Josephine,

*Thank you for your letter about Rainea [sic]. Mr. G does know that I'm thinking about marrying Rainea [sic] and he isn't the least bit pleased.** *He said that if I did marry Rainea [sic], it would become impossible for us to carry on meeting because if I become Princess Marilyn of Monaco, we would be watched more than ever. I was glad he felt that way. He also said that Monaco is too close to Paris, so it would be dangerous for me to live there in case his wife found out about us.*

I am really embarrassed about Garbo, but as you asked, I will tell you.† *I was in Berydorf's, trying on some silk lingerie just flown in from Paris. I stuck my head round the door, wanting Elise, who looks after me, to check the fit of my bra, and came face-to-face with Garbo. My mouth flew open—*

---

* According to Lem Billings, Jack's lifelong friend, who was staying in Palm Beach when Jackie told Jack that Marilyn was contemplating getting involved with Ranier, Jack showed no reaction (see *Forever Jack* by Charles Cabot-Winthrop III [Washington, D.C.: Hookstead House Books, 1965]). But as soon as Jackie had left for her habitual beach walk, he called his old flame, Grace Kelly (who happened to be in the South of France, filming), and told her Marilyn was going to pursue Rainier. According to Grace's masseur, Reginald Carrera, "The moment Grace heard Marilyn was in the running for Rainier, although she hadn't been at all crazy about him she contacted him at once.

109

I've always admired her, especially as Maria Valeska [sic] in that movie with Charles Boyer—and I stepped back into the room. "Marilyn!" she said, walked into the room after me, and closed the door. I froze solid. She put one finger on her lips. I know you will want to know this—her nails were bitten, she didn't have polish on, and her lipstick was whitish brown. She gazed at me for a moment, then whispered, "Shhh." I was still speechless, then she leaned forward, cupped my face in her hands, and kissed me. I didn't mean to open my mouth, but, out of habit, did. She smelled of cheap soap, so I pulled away. Thank goodness, at that moment Elise knocked on the door and I was saved.

I must stop now or I'll be late for analisis [sic] and you still have to pay if you are, but will write when I have made my last and final decision about Rainea [sic]. A lot depends on Mr. G and how he treats me over the next few weeks—so wish me luck!

Love,
Martha

————

They met, he proposed, and Grace, knowing that she didn't have a hope of getting anywhere with Jack again, accepted." (See *Grace, My Princess* by Reginald Carrera [New York: Premier Books, 1983].)

† Marilyn most likely relayed this story to Jackie in the hope that she would repeat it to Jack, whose lesbian fantasies were rampant, and in order to titillate him. In her memoirs, *One Lifetime Is Not Enough*, Zsa Zsa Gabor recalls a similar encounter with Garbo. "Greta asked me if she could drive me home. I said yes, but I was afraid of her. We got to my hotel (I was living in the Savoy Plaza) and for a moment I felt like inviting Greta in. Then she said, 'Darling, would you like to come to my apartment?' I was paralyzed. Then she kissed me straight on the mouth. And I couldn't help kissing her back because she was so overwhelmingly strong and so beautiful."

Marilyn was quite relaxed about arousing lesbian emotions in other women. She was blasé about the fact that her drama coach, Natasha Lytess, clearly had sexual designs on her. "She was in love with me and she wanted me to love her," Marilyn said.

Marilyn told Lena Pepitone, "I let Natasha, but that was wrong. She wasn't like a guy. You know, just have a good time and that's that. She got really jealous about the men I saw, everything. She thought that she was my husband. She was a great teacher, but part of it ruined things for us. I got scared of her, had to get away."

Hotel du Cap

Antibes

France

Martha Marshall

The Waldorf-Astoria

New York, New York

August 28, 1955

Dear Martha,

Thank you for your entertaining letter and vivid description of Garbo. I was mesmerized and, henceforth, will always view her through jaundiced eyes. Cheap soap, indeed! How disillusioning!

You and I live in such an incredibly small world! In an amazing coincidence, this evening I met Aristotle Onassis. Jack and I were invited to a party for Winston Churchill, held on a floating palace, the most beautiful yacht of which I could ever conceive. A crew of 60, a masseuse, two chefs (one French and one Greek). Belonging to none other than Aristotle Onassis himself! He isn't movie-star handsome like Jack, but the more you talk to him, the handsomer he becomes. In a way, he reminds me of my grandfather Bouvier. He spins such fantastic tales about his early days when he worked as a telephonist for 25 cents an hour. He was utterly charming, a diamond in the rough, but with a way of talking to you that completely envelops you in his warmth and interest. Would I still find him attractive had he fallen off the back of a truck and not been one of the world's wealthiest men? To be absolutely truthful, I probably would not. In any event, although he is conventionally ugly, he had a tremendous impact on

111

me. For once, Jack (did I tell you he is now here with me?) actually noticed. Afterwards, we had an enormous fight. Mostly, I suspect, because Jack was dressed in a white dinner jacket and I cracked that Churchill must have thought he was a waiter . . .

After the fight subsided, Jack sulked for ages. Ultimately, because I was bored with his silence, I said, "Jack, I wasn't laughing at you, but at Churchill, being eighty and probably gaga!" Consequently, he was mollified, while I, for my part, felt a strong surge of guilt, knowing as I do that since April, after he resigned from the British premiership, Churchill has been deeply depressed. It is so sad, isn't it, when great men go into decline.

I get the sense that you decided not to marry Rainier. But I think you might like Onassis better. If you want (and your Mr. G doesn't mind), I can arrange an introduction.*

Love,
Josephine

P.S. Since last night, Jack seems inexplicably reformed. Perhaps we are now destined to live happily ever after at last.

---

*Jackie wrote in her diary, "The idea of MM and Onassis is divine. He radiates a rough-hewn masculinity, is strong, masterful, experienced with women, yet kind, not to mention stratospherically rich. Perfect for M, if only for a brief interlude. Mrs. G should really thank me. . . ."

Here, Jackie was unconsciously picking up on the fact that she and Marilyn shared similar sexual and emotional desires. To the seasoned observer of both women, it is possible to picture Marilyn happily married to Maurice Tempelsman (Jackie's last love) and Jackie finding marital happiness with Arthur Miller.

2 Sutton Place
New York, New York

Josephine Kendall
1095 North Ocean Boulevard
Palm Beach, Florida

October 31, 1955

Dear Josephine,

Your letter must have traveled by pigeon, as it took months to get to me, but maybe it's my fault because I've left the Waldorf, as my lease expired. Thank you for being so sweet and telling me all about Onassis, but they sent me his picture and I said no. I didn't like his lips. More important, I don't want to marry anyone while Mr. G is being so attentive to me.* If that changes, I will consider Mr. Onassis more seriously as a prospect.

But a man with too much money makes me nervous. All men try to buy you in one way or another, the process is always the same, and it is only the price that is higher or lower. Sometimes it is things, other times it is words, and I don't trust any of it. I care about what men do, not what they say, and about their minds.

---

* For the first time in his life, when Jack was confronted with the possibility of losing Marilyn to Rainier, he was compelled to face the fact that Marilyn—out of all the legions of women in his thrall—had infiltrated his carefully constructed facade. Consequently, at this time, he directed all his emotions, charm, and tenderness toward her.

How exciting for you to meet Churchill—I would love to meet him one day, as he is one of my heroes—along with Mr. G.

Love,
Martha

1095 North Ocean Boulevard
Palm Beach, Florida

Martha Marshall
2 Sutton Place
New York, New York

December 20, 1955

Dear Martha,

I have been meaning to write to you for the longest time, but today heard something that made it imperative for me to pick up my pen at last.

Rainier has finally chosen his bride—and she is none other than Grace! Jack was a trifle miffed when he heard the news and, under his breath, just loud enough for me to hear, muttered, "She would have married me if I had asked her."* I had great difficulty in stifling a smile!

I am afraid I am dashing this letter off in great haste, as I gave Jack a faithful promise that I would sail with him to Hobe Sound this

---

* "Jack was a consummate actor—the best," wrote Charles Cabot-Winthrop III, who was present when Jack and Jackie read in the newspaper that Grace was engaged. "Of course, he already knew about the engagement from Grace herself. But he threw Jackie the bone of pretending to be jealous. Clever, that. Making Jackie think she had scored points, when all along it was Jack who was doing the scoring. Typical of him. In control, always. Except, perhaps, when it came to Marilyn. Because, really, for Jack, no matter how many he had (and he had plenty), deep down where he really lived, it was always Marilyn, and he knew it." (See *Forever Jack* by Charles Cabot-Winthrop III [Washington, D.C.: Hookstead House Books, 1965].)

afternoon, just the two of us, for once, without the horrendous sisters. All too inviting an opportunity to miss!

I hope you will have a happy and prosperous New Year and that all your dreams will come true in 1956.

Warmest regards,
Josephine

2 Sutton Place
New York, New York

Josephine Kendall
Hickory Hill
McLean, Virginia

March 15, 1956

Dear Josephine,

It's three in the morning, I can't sleep, and I want you to be the first to know the reason why. Tonight I went to the opening of <u>My Fair Lady</u>, the Lerner and Low [sic] musical, and finally made up my mind to marry him at last.

Not Mr. G, because I wouldn't have him anymore, even if he crawled over broken glass, naked. When he thought I was going to marry Rainea [<u>sic</u>], for a few weeks, he was everything I have ever wanted—except not married, but that is too much to ask, I know. He treated me as if—to quote <u>Romeo and Juliet</u>, the play I am studying with Lee Strasberg—I was "spangled with stars." But then, as soon as he knew that Rainea [<u>sic</u>] was definately [<u>sic</u>] marrying Grace and not me, he was back to his old ways again. No more compliments, no more red roses, no more midnight calls. Just the same old G. And I couldn't bear it.

My new analyst, Dr. Brandt, says I definately [<u>sic</u>] shouldn't blame myself because G is a classic narcessist [<u>sic</u>], a loner whose defenses I temporarily penetrated but who, when he was sure of me again, reverted back to his old pattern. G's armor, he said, was once more firmly in place, and I

117

didn't have a hope in hell—my language, not his—of penetrating it again, unless I found another love with whom to threaten him. But that isn't why I picked Arthur. I picked Arthur because I want to spend the rest of my life with him. Arthur, as in Arthur Miller. Writing his name sends shivers up and down my spine. . . .

We met many years ago—he spent the entire evening just stroking my toes—I was too young, too dumb, and too much in love with Mr. G to really appreciate him. Now I realize what a wonderful, brilliant, and insightful man he is. My very own Professor Higgins.

He is so different from Joe. I once gave Joe a gold medallion engraved with that saying from the _Little Prince_— "True love is visible not to the eyes, but to the heart, for eyes may be deceived." Joe just looked at it as if it were written in Korean—which he doesn't even speak. I tried to explain the _Little Prince_ to him, tried to teach him, but he didn't want to learn. Not that, not anything. But now the tables are turned. Now Arthur teaches me instead. But I am in love with ALL of him, not just his mind. And loving him has made me feel so special, knowing that someone as brilliant as him loves me back.

Nothing will be announced in the press for quite a while, so please keep my secret secret, like we always do. But do tell Jack, if you like, and wish him luck in his run against Stevenson. Lots of it, and yourself, too.

Love,
M

P.S. Please forgive me for forgetting the most important thing—Grace marrying Rainea [sic]. I am so glad, and I'll bet you that from now on, Jack will be faithful to you again forever.

Hickory Hill
McLean, Virginia

Martha Marshall
Old Tophet Road
Roxbury, Connecticut

March 20, 1956

Dearest Martha,

I know from the press that you are in Phoenix filming *Bus Stop* (and really admired those pictures of you in the rodeo), but assume this will ultimately reach you.

First of all, I want you to know that I am utterly delighted that you have chosen Arthur Miller as your husband. I've admired his work for as long as I can remember, know that he is an erudite and charming man, and am thrilled that you finally have found the mentor and the husband whom you so richly deserve.

In many ways, Martha, strange as this may sound, I almost envy you the wonderful opportunities which you now have at your disposal for learning from an older, wiser man who can guide and teach you.

For while I adore Jack, as far as our relationship is concerned, I am the teacher, but merely in sartorial terms—as before we met, his style of dress was generally crumpled and boyish, as opposed to suave and sophisticated. There is little reciprocity. All in all, had life turned out differently, it is highly likely that (much as I love Jack) I would have opted to marry a Professor Higgins of my own. . . .

On reflection, though, Martha, please don't pay too much attention to my meanderings. They are, in part, prompted by the fact that I am pregnant again but, instead of resting, am on the campaign trail with Jack. He craves victory so strongly that I feel I have very little choice but to support him, albeit that our private life is virtually nonexistent. The house is always full of his political associates or his family—which, to all intents and purposes, practically amounts to the same thing. Sometimes, I feel as if I am running a small hotel.

Through it all, I am still haunted by the fear of Jack's infidelity. You were kind to reassure me that now that Grace is married, he will once more be faithful to me, but frankly, I don't see the connection, as I don't believe Grace is still one of his paramours.

Whatever the case, all my focus must now be on the baby.

In the meantime, please know that I am thinking of you and wishing you and Arthur much happiness in your new life together.

With my warmest regards,

J

P.S. What does Mr. G say about your marriage?

Jackie wrote in her diary, "Mailed a congratulatory letter to MM but, on reflection, think my pregnancy must have temporarily unhinged my mind. Arthur Miller, indeed! Well, yes, he is an intellect, and a great playwright, but he is hardly an Adonis, nor a charmer of Jack's caliber. . . . Still, I wish her well, and hope that she will, at last, find peace."

꧁

Senator and Mrs. John F. Kennedy
1095 North Ocean Boulevard
Palm Beach, Florida

Mr. and Mrs. Arthur Miller
Old Tophet Road
Roxbury, Connecticut

July 5, 1956

Dear Mr. and Mrs. Miller,

Please accept this gift as a small token of our esteem, which brings with it our congratulations on your marriage and our best wishes for your future happiness.

With warm regards,
Senator Kennedy and Jacqueline Kennedy

MR. AND MRS. ARTHUR MILLER
Parkside House
Englefield Green
Egham
Surrey
England

Senator and Mrs. John F. Kennedy
Hickory Hill
McLean, Virginia

August 6, 1956

Dear Senator and Mrs. Kennedy,

Arthur and I were thrilled with the beautiful silver Cartier picture frame. We would love it if you would send us a photograph of yourselves—as neither of us can think of anyone else's picture we would rather have in such a beautiful frame.

Love,
Marilyn and Arthur

Parkside House
Englefield Green
Egham
Surrey
England

Josephine Kendall
Hickory Hill
McLean, Virginia

August 11, 1956

Dear J,

Your picture frame was lovely, thank you. I only wish I could write you the kind of glowing, happy letter a new bride is supposed to write, but I am glad that I have a true friend with whom I can be myself and be honest.

I think I may have made a terrible mistake in marrying Arthur. I already felt that way the day before our marriage, but it was too late. So, here I am in England with Arthur, making Prince and the Showgirl, with Sir Olivier—or is it against him? Sir Olivier, I mean. Or perhaps I mean Arthur, I don't know anymore—at times, they feel like one person, both of whom despise me.

Before I forget, you asked what Mr. G thinks of my marriage. Well, at first he said all the friendly and encouraging things, and wished me luck. But now that he knows how wrong everything is, he is right here for me. Not here, exactly, but not too far, and maybe . . . if I am lucky, this weekend . . . but I had better not jinx it by writing any more. Not that I don't trust you, just that things have been so tough, and I am so desperate to see him.

123

Part of it is Sir Olivier. Maybe if I wasn't married to Arthur, and we could have taken things somewhere personal—I know he doesn't love Vivien Leigh anymore, I can tell and it's really sad—things might have worked out better between us. After all, I was so thrilled to be working with the greatest actor alive, and I really did believe that he wanted to work with me as well.

Instead, he says all the right things in his snooty British voice—"How simply ravishing, my angel, how divine," all that kind of stuff—when all the time he looks at me as if I were a pile of bad fish and he is about to throw up all over me.

For a while, I tried being Marilyn and funny. You know, when he first said "fuck" in front of me, I played Her, opened my eyes real wide, and said, "Gee, do they have that in England too?" Trouble is, Sir Olivier thought I was for real and didn't laugh.

I hate acting with him—acting at him is what it feels like. Meanwhile, Arthur seems to be more on Sir Olivier's side than on mine. Neither he nor O is anything like I thought he would be—wise and strong, like Mr. D'Arcy [sic] or Max de Winter. Just patronizing and old, and derizzive [sic]. All of which makes me want to be bad. Just to test them. Or are they testing me? I am not sure. Only that I don't like it.

Isn't life disillusioning?

Good luck with the campaign, and tell Jack good luck from me as well.

Love,
Marilyn

1095 North Ocean Boulevard
Palm Beach, Florida

Martha Marshall
Parkside House
Englefield Green
Egham
Surrey
England

August 19, 1956

Dear Martha,

Yes, you are right, life is disillusioning. I am eight months pregnant, yet Jack is off on a Mediterranean cruise with his cronies. I try and console myself with all those clichés about boys being boys and so forth, but sometimes it is difficult.

A couple of days ago, I was by his side at the Democratic Convention, supporting him, shaking countless hands, and smiling a myriad of bright smiles, despite the great heat and my considerable discomfort, both with the climate and the activity. When Stevenson won, naturally, I was on hand to console Jack as well. Yet now he has left for France, and I am here, in the sweltering Palm Beach heat, waiting.

But I don't want to bore you with my complaints and did want to say that I so admired your photograph on the cover of *Time* and that, as always, you looked lovely. At the same time, it struck me forcibly that it is probably far better for a woman to be a person in her own right, with her own career (despite such vicissitudes as Olivier), rather than merely being the frame to some man's picture.

So Jack is off on his cruise and his own adventures. Leaving me to wait here until the baby is due. Before I end, I must say how sad I found it to learn from you that Olivier is no longer in love with Vivien Leigh. Has her beauty faded, or do you sense other reasons why he should fall out of love with her after such a grand passion? When you have time, do write and tell me all about her.

Love,

J

On August 17, the same day as Jack lost his bid to become vice president, Marilyn chanced upon Arthur's notebook, in which he had confided his deep disillusionment with her. Devastated, and already yearning for Jack, she sent him a distraught message, suggesting they meet in Paris, if only for one night. Unable to resist Marilyn's charms, as well as the urgency of her plea, on August 25, Jack slipped away from his cruise and (after Marilyn flew to Paris incognito, under the alias of Zelda Green) spent one night with her at the Ritz. (See *My Summer with Marilyn* [Honolulu: Baynards Press, 1965], the memoirs of Delia Hamilton, Marilyn's personal assistant during *The Prince and the Showgirl*.) In the meantime, on August 23, unbeknownst to Jack, who couldn't be reached for a week, Jackie gave birth to a stillborn child.

Parkside House
Englefield Green
Egham
Surrey
England

Josephine Kendall
1095 North Ocean Boulevard
Palm Beach, Florida

August 31, 1956

Dear Josephine,

I am so extremely sorry about your stillborn baby. I ran into Peter at the studio and he told me. I couldn't stop crying when I thought of it struggling to live, then failing and dying. I feel terrible. I hope Jack does, too. He should have been by your side, instead of in Europe having fun. Whoever was with him—his friends or whoever—must feel terrible. I know God probably will punish them in the end.

But I wouldn't blame you one bit if you decided to end the marriage. I definately [sic] have deep doubts about mine, deeper every day. Arthur treats me as if I were even less than Eliza Doolittle was before she met Higgins. I am pregnant again—I wish it was Mr. G's, but he can relax, because it can't be (in Paris I took care of him) . . . and I don't think the baby will make things better between Arthur and me. All he really loves is writing. And maybe money.

You asked me about Vivien Leigh. In a way, I wish I had never met her, because she isn't Lady Hamilton or Scarlett at all. Maybe that sounds silly coming from me, being an actress and knowing that it is all fake, but I do feel that way. I so wanted her to be wonderful, and she isn't. She's beautiful and scared, fragile and frosty. She drinks a lot—and why not, being married to Sir Olivier—is overshadowed by him, and is almost like a shadow herself.

More than anything else, she makes me terrified of growing old in this business. When we arrived here, the producer, Terrenz [sic] Rattigun [sic] gave a party in my honor. Everyone was there, Tyrone Power (very dark and gorgeous, a bit like Gable, and if I didn't have Arthur, and didn't love Mr. G . . .), Margot Fonteyn, Sir John Geelgood [sic], Peggy Ashcroft, and Sybil Thorndike. The garden was decorated with Chinese lanterns, they served lobster, and it was lovely, except at the last minute, Vivien didn't show up. Later, I found out that it was because her dress didn't fit. Then on another day, she refused to pose with me for a picture. Very politely, but firmly, and I guess it was because I'm younger. I feel so sorry for her, but I can't help wondering how I'll feel when I'm her age, and I'm not nearly as beautiful as she is.

Arthur is at the door, I have to go. I am so sorry about the baby.

Love,
Martha

P.S. I don't know why Sir Olivier has fallen out of love with Vivien. I don't think he has anyone else. And even if he did, he might still love her a little.

1095 North Ocean Boulevard
Palm Beach, Florida

Martha Marshall
Roxbury, Connecticut

November 21, 1956

Dear Martha,

I am extremely sorry that I haven't communicated with you recently, but life stood still for me when my baby was born dead. This may sound a trifle strange, but although my baby never saw the light of day, to me she—and it was a girl—was already a person.

All during the nine months when I was carrying her, I was constructing a dream future for her. I imagined her to grow up being a combination of Jack, my father, and me. I pictured her first smile, her first word, and all the years to come.

When the doctor told me she was dead, all feeling drained out of me. Worst of all, Jack was not there to share my anguish.

If I have been too emotional in my sentiments, please understand. In fact, I should appreciate if, in your next letter, to which I am naturally looking forward to, you do not allude to my darkest hour. I know I must go on.

I've been thinking of you so much recently, particularly as Lee and I are about to go on a trip to Paris and your Mr. G lives there. Wouldn't it be strange if we met him, without knowing it? Or Mrs. G, for that matter. Does Mr. G talk about her, or give you any clue as to her appearance or anything else about her?

Forgive me for rambling, though—I was a bit tired yesterday what with preparing for the trip and Thanksgiving. My main reason for writing (and I have been intending to for ages, but things have been heating up in terms of Jack's political career) is to say that I hope you and Arthur have managed to work things out and that you are happier.

If we don't write before the end of the year, please believe me when I say that I will be wishing you a happy 1957 and that I have a strong sense that next year will be wonderful for you.

Warm regards,
J

P.S. I apologize for being somewhat cryptic as regards Jack's career—but you will read about it soon enough, so . . . Spurred on by his father and the rest of the family, as well as by his own abiding ambitions, he is definitely going to make a run for the Presidency. Am still mulling over the consequences, but shall, of course, support him all the way.

444 East 57th Street
New York, New York

Josephine Kendall
3307 N Street
Washington, D.C.

March 17, 1957

Dear Josephine,

I am sorry not to have written before, but I've been really doing all I can to make things work with Arthur—and I think we are starting to be happy at last.

Men are so difficult to figure, aren't they? But, of course, you know that, and I remember you saying so, in different words, when we met all that time ago in L.A. Most of everything that went wrong between Arthur and me was really my fault. I really thought that because Arthur is so much older, and so brilliant, I could depend on him for everything, that he would take care of me just like my father would have done, had I had one. But it turned out that he needs taking care of just as much as—and maybe more than—I do. So that is what I am doing, and I like it.

You asked about Mr. G and Mrs. G—which was so kind of you—but really, now that I am trying to make things work with Arthur, Mr. G isn't on my mind much anymore. Still, to answer your questions. Mrs. G is small and doll-like and blonde (Mr. G said), with violet eyes. He once said we have similar voices, but I think he was just kidding around, and I didn't appreciate it, because I do know that my voice is unique.

By the way, what do you think about Elizabeth Taylor marrying Mike Todd? I liked him a lot when I met him—remember, the pink elephant—and, had I not fallen for Arthur or loved Mr. G, might have gone for him myself. He certainly knows how to put on a show—15,000 flowers at the wedding, oceans of champagne, and mountains of caviar, they said in the papers. Elizabeth is very lucky.

So, by the way, is Brigitte Bardot. I don't know if you've seen <u>And God Created Woman</u>, but I heard from Dee Dee Crawford—who did her makeup for the London premiere, where we met when I was over there—that Roger Vadim guides her career every step of the way. I wish Arthur was like that. I guess, though, I'll just have to guide my own career, like I always have. Except when Mr. G gives me advice.

Speaking, I mean, writing, about careers—I'm working real hard at the Actors Studio. The other day, had to sing "I'll Get By As Long as I Have You" to the class, and suddenly burst into tears. For a moment, I didn't know why, but then realized it was because of Mr. G and that I don't have him. But I do love him a lot.

I hope you don't think I am crazy feeling that way, and that you will never ever show any of my letters to Jack. I am sure you won't.

Take care of yourself.

Love,
M

———————

When Jackie received Marilyn's letter, she wrote in her diary, "Strange letter from MM, veering between love and disdain for Arthur Miller, and harking back to 'Mr. G' far too often to render her avowed love for Arthur the least bit convincing. Then a bizarre plea that I not show the letter to Jack. In any event, he is far too busy and self-absorbed right now (and probably always) to pay attention to anyone or anything except politics. His true mistress . . . "

1095 North Ocean Boulevard
Palm Beach, Florida

Martha Marshall
444 East 57th Street
New York, New York

March 28, 1957

Dearest Martha,

Just a brief note to assure you that I would never dream of showing any of your letters to Jack or, indeed, discussing the contents with him or anyone else. As far as I am concerned, our correspondence is private and confidential, and you have my word.

In haste, and with great affection,

Yours,
Josephine

Jacqueline Kennedy
3307 N Street
Washington, D.C.

August 4, 1957

Dear Jackie,

Arthur and I want to send you our deepest sympathies on the death of your dear father, Jack Bouvier. He sounded like a wonderful man and I am only sorry that we never had the opportunity of meeting him. I am sure he was extremely proud of you and loved you very much.

In sympathy,
Marilyn and Arthur

P.S. If there is anything I can do, please let me know and I will do it.

P.P.S. Have just lost my baby. Am getting accustomed, though, to the idea I shall never be a mother. Perhaps it is for the best—the baby could have turned out just like me.

1095 North Ocean Boulevard
Palm Beach, Florida

Mr. and Mrs. Arthur Miller
Stoney Hill Farm
Amagansett, New York

August 10, 1957

Dear Martha,

How like you to think of me amid your own sorrow! I understand only too well what you must have gone through, and you have my sympathy. I was sad, too, to read your emotions regarding your own fitness for motherhood. With your kind heart and loving nature, I think you would make a wonderful mother, and I am sure, when the time is right, you will have the opportunity you so richly deserve.

Since the death of my father, for which I suppose I should have been prepared but which, strange as it may sound, took me entirely by surprise, I have been reflecting on my life and remembering my childhood.

I find that my father's death has affected me in the same manner as an earthquake. For despite his unconventional behavior vis à vis women, my father was the best person in my life, the strongest influence I have ever known, and I don't think anyone will ever love me that way again, or I them. He was the wisest, kindest, most intelligent man I ever knew and no one, not even Jack, will ever live up to him. Except, of course, in one particular area, in which we both know Jack outstrips my father, and every other man: his sexual insatiability and virtually unlimited capacity for infidelity.

But enough of that—I despise self-pity and, close as we are, Martha, do not wish to inflict it on you. I must admit, though, that this has been the most difficult time of my life. Ironically, it began the day before my birthday, when my father checked into Lenox Hill for a series of routine tests.

Initially, they revealed nothing. I, of course, had flown up to see him but, thinking that he was in the clear, returned to Hammersmith Farm to celebrate my birthday with my mother, who (even at a time in which my father's health appeared to be in jeopardy) still found herself unable to jettison her deep and abiding bitterness regarding him. An example to me, if ever I saw one . . .

In any event, I relaxed into my habitual blithe mode of existence at Hammersmith (reverting, I suppose, to my youth in that serene and peaceful environment which is so familiar and so dear to me) when, on August 3, I received word that my father had lapsed into a coma.

Although Jack and I rushed there, posthaste, we arrived at the hospital too late and I never saw my father alive again. Consequently, I had no opportunity to say good-bye to him. In retrospect, however, I think it was worse for Lee, who only arrived from Italy in time for the funeral.

I never saw her cry, of course, nor she me—as both of us were drilled, from an early age, not to display our emotions. Instead, I cried in private, then resolved to create a funeral worthy of my father's memory, one that reflected his intense love for life.

It was held at St. Patrick's, and his coffin, according to my instructions, was garlanded with daisies and cornflowers, all reminiscent of the flora at Lasata, the Long Island home where we shared so many idyllic and happy days together.

Lest I bore you with my somewhat maudlin sentiments, I shall now attempt to amuse you with the following. No fewer than eight of my father's paramours were present at his funeral, all perfectly coiffed—as he would have wished it—all weeping profusely, all convinced that they were the alpha and omega of his desires. I must, at this point, confess that one of them—Mimi Formosa—the Texan oil field billionairess who was one of my father's many last loves—actually made me laugh when she had the effrontery to whisper to me, "Honey, tell your kids that their granddaddy was the very best in bed. I should know. After Black Jack, no other man will do. . . ." A fitting epitaph, don't you think???

I do have some other news, Martha, news which I feel somewhat tentative in imparting to you but, aware as I am of your good heart and the kind impulses which you have always manifested toward me, feel that, in the interests of being honest, I must share. I am, once more, pregnant. Whether or not I carry the child to term is, of course, with my track record, another subject. However, I can only pray that God, having taken from me the person whom I loved most in the world, will now be compassionate and give to me another human being to love.

I apologize for my meanderings, but know that you will understand.

With my love,
Josephine

MR. AND MRS. ARTHUR MILLER
444 East 57th Street
New York, New York

Senator and Mrs. John F. Kennedy
3307 N Street
Washington, D.C.

November 28, 1957

Dear Jackie and Jack,

Arthur and I are thrilled to learn about the birth of Caroline. We wish you all a great deal of happiness.

Love,
Marilyn and Arthur

SENATOR AND MRS. JOHN F. KENNEDY
3307 N Street
Washington, D.C.

Mr. and Mrs. Arthur Miller
444 East 57th Street
New York, New York

January 2, 1958

Dear Marilyn and Arthur,

Jack and I just adore the beautiful christening robe which you sent us upon the birth of our daughter, Caroline. The lace and the work is exquisite and we shall always treasure it.

We both enjoyed *Bus Stop* immensely and look forward to your next movie with great anticipation.

Warm regards,
Jackie and Jack

3307 N Street
Washington, D.C.

Martha Marshall
444 East 57th Street
New York, New York

March 26, 1958

Dear Martha,

The moment I heard about Mike Todd's tragic death in a plane crash (what fate that Elizabeth was sick and couldn't travel with him at the last moment) I wanted to express my condolence. I know how much you admired him.

I don't know how Elizabeth will go on without the love and support of such a man. I feel deeply sorry for her, don't you?

Thinking of you during this sad time.

Love, as ever,
Josephine

The Beverly Hills Hotel

Josephine Kendall
3307 N Street
Washington, D.C.

August 3, 1958

Dear Josephine,

I feel really guilty telling you this, but I probably don't have as much sympathy for Elizabeth as I should have. * It's just that she has always been so lucky, you know, born rich, always loved, praised for her acting, and having such great men in her life.

But I shouldn't complain — and have been feeling a bit brighter, though a little scared, because I am starting a new film tomorrow, Some Like It Hot, with Billy Wilder, who did so well for me with The Seven Year Itch. So maybe this time I'll be lucky as well. . . .

---

* Throughout her career, Marilyn always felt inferior to Elizabeth Taylor, standing in awe of Taylor's English background, her voice, her refined manner, and consequently was extremely jealous of her.

In later years, when Marilyn heard that Taylor was getting a million dollars to make *Cleopatra,* she was outraged. What bothered her most was that Taylor's huge fee was coming from Marilyn's own studio, Twentieth Century–Fox. Marilyn received only a hundred thousand dollars a picture. According to Lena Pepitone, "It seemed like a fortune to me, but to Marilyn, it now seemed like nothing. She was insulted. Was she only one-tenth as valuable as Elizabeth Taylor?"

Hope you are having a happy summer.

Lots of love,
Martha

Jackie's letter in response to this one from Marilyn is unaccountably missing from the correspondence.

444 East 57th Street
New York, New York

Josephine Kendall
3307 N Street
Washington, D.C.

December 16, 1958

Dear Josephine,

I know I haven't written for the longest time, but I have been dividing my time between the movie—<u>Hot</u>—and working at being Arthur's wife—the more difficult of the two jobs. . . . I've even been trying to cook—although he can't stomach the pasta dishes I learned from Joe's mother—and encouraging him while he writes a brilliant—I think—new script for me called <u>The Misfits</u>. I hate the title, but Arthur says I am projecting. Only I think he is.

The <u>Time</u> spread on you and Jack was lovely, you seem so happy together—I mean, you look it and being a father has obviously changed Jack a great deal. I am glad. Congratulations on Caroline. She looks just like Jack and is beautiful like you.

I also saw you and your mother-in-law, Rose Kennedy, on a TV show. She must be really interesting—she'd have to be very tough, to survive him—Joe Kennedy, I mean. And all those children. What is she really like?

Speaking about what people are like, I've always wanted to ask you if you knew anything about the Duchess of Windsor and what tricks she used to make the Duke give up all of England just for her. I'd love to know—specially as I can't even get Mr. G to answer my messages, never mind give up a country for me—only, of course, he doesn't have a country to give up, just an insurance company. At least Arthur is a writer.

Lots of love,
M

Martha Marshall
444 East 57th Street
New York, New York

January 18, 1959

Dear Martha,

I was delighted to hear from you. Thank you for asking about Caroline. She is a good baby, but I am determined not to sink into motherhood and stagnate. For no matter how much she touches my heart, I know that the role of mother is one which often diminishes a woman—something which, dear Martha, you must always bear in mind when you have regrets that you do not, at the moment, have a child—in terms of her feminine allure.

In that spirit, rather than enthusing interminably—as so many women are prone to do—about the baby, I shall answer the questions in your last letter as honestly as possible and shall, in the bargain, enjoy doing so—thus reminding myself of the larger, more glittering world beyond my current new role.

First, the Duchess of Windsor. To be perfectly frank, I know more about the lady than one might wish—all of it deliciously titillating. The source is one Bridget Maria Collins—a former maid of my mother's whose identity I do not find it necessary to conceal from you. First, because we trust one another. Second, because she was found to have stolen a garnet and pearl broach from my mother and summarily dismissed from service.

That said, I believe that her story about the Duchess can be believed implicitly—as others have whispered similar stories to me as well. In any event, Bridget M—who, I almost forgot to mention, before becoming employed by my mother worked for many years for the Duchess—claims that the Duke's entire demeanor when in private with her speaks of his regret at having relinquished his throne for her.

So that while he does not, in the course of their many and virulent arguments, reproach her with the recrimination "To think what I gave up for you," he continually exhibits an attitude toward her which speaks volumes.

During the day, that is. In daylight hours, he requires her to curtsey to him, treats her dismissively, and regularly criticizes the (I think) somewhat contrived appearance she strains to create. One epithet BM heard him hurl at her was "Wallis, you can buy a million couture gowns and have a thousand face-lifts, but as far as I am concerned, all you will ever emanate is the allure of a rotting chicken wing."

Yet at night, things change dramatically. Bridget M heard the Duke repeatedly address the Duchess as "Nanny," and the villa often echoed with his pitiful wails as she chastised him. All in all, a classic example of the well-known English vice and perhaps an answer to your question regarding the tricks by which the Duchess succeeded in enslaving the Duke. All of which reminds me of one of my father's time-honored maxims: "Once you have a man's perversions, you have that man." In any event, I thought you might find the story diverting. Tragic, yet fascinating, don't you think??

Which brings me to my mother-in-law, the celestial Rose Kennedy. One day, in the far distant future, I imagine I could well be in her place, and a mother-in-law. That awareness should, I know, cause me to temper my remarks. However, two months here in Palm Beach, in close and constant proximity to her, has not enhanced our relationship remotely.

You may know from my father-in-law that Mrs. Kennedy, while

matriarchal on the surface and fearsomely well organized—each child's illnesses, problems, and preferences are catalogued on an index card—a feat, given the number of children involved—and though she has borne tragedy (the loss of two of her children to death and one to illness) bravely, in reality, is far from saintly.

Her coldness to Jack, her rejection of him as a child, her constant forays to Paris to view the collections (trips which I, of course, understand and cannot, in truth, afford to condemn) left him feeling lonely and unloved. The result, I firmly believe, was to entrench within him a steely resolve never to put his heart or his trust into the hands of one woman alone. Hence the infidelity. For which, perhaps, I blame my mother-in-law. Easier, of course, than constantly blaming Jack, and, perhaps, a contrivance on my part.

That said, my mother-in-law and I do, even now, engage in a subterranean battle of wills. Jack and I have our own suite of rooms in the compound, and during the time in which we are absent, my mother-in-law is prone to moving the furniture around to her satisfaction. Whereupon I, on arriving, move it back. Only to find it in Mrs. Kennedy's preferred position on my return. All of which is only the tip of the iceberg.

I have to confess, though, that I am being a trifle unfair. Without wishing to reproach you in any way (for I know he is an attractive and beguiling man), the fact of Joe Sr.'s philandering does try her [Rose Kennedy] sorely.* So perhaps she should be forgiven for her petty manipulations.

---

*Dr. Joseph Brandt's widow, Ida Brandt, has graciously granted the editor access to tapes of Marilyn's therapy sessions, recorded with her consent by Brandt and hitherto not made public. When Marilyn received Jackie's letter, she was elated. Two hours later, she kept her appointment with Dr. Brandt, whose transcripts from the taped session include the following dialogue, starting with Marilyn's comments: "See, Joseph, I've really got her now. If he saw this, he'd kill her. Or, better still, leave her." "So, Marilyn, what are you going to do with the letter?" "What do you

I hear Jack's voice and must seal this letter and mail it quickly. For no matter how much his mother has hurt him, he would protect her—and her image—to the death and would not look kindly on my words.

With my love,

J

---

think I should do, Joseph?" "You know better than that, Marilyn . . . don't throw the question back at me." (Long silence on the tape.) "Well, I guess I'll look like a bitch if I show it to him. And then I'll have to explain." (Change in voice.) "But I want to do the right thing by her. I've hurt her enough so far, even though she doesn't know it, and she's been good and kind to me, so I won't show it to him." (Further silence.) "And I do owe her because now that I know about Jack and his mother, when I do see him, I'll give him what he needs. And then we'll see. . . ." Then, in a different voice, she went on: "She still thinks Joe Kennedy is having an affair with me. I'd really like to set her straight, but then I think it isn't a bad idea she thinks I am, because maybe if she does, Jack might as well, which ought to get him hot, because he always wants to beat his father at everything. Also, maybe it stops her guessing about Jack and me and I'm glad. I'd die if she knew. I'd feel bad, real bad, if she did—and Jack would kill me."

The day after mailing this letter to Marilyn, Jackie wrote in her diary, "I am absolutely appalled at my own indiscretion regarding Rose. But my depression at the alien status accorded to me in this rough-and-tumble household, coupled with my loneliness, cause me to write an extremely graphic letter to MM about my mother-in-law. My frankness was, I know, also partly prompted by my guilt at having a child and MM being barren. I wanted to amuse and divert her, and in the throes of such 'noble' emotions, went overboard. I feel mortified, am inclined to ask her to return the letter to me, but know full well that doing so would only alert her to the value of my indiscretions. Then again, perhaps my fears are groundless. Her own letters, all of which I have retained, contain a great deal of information which I am sure she would not wish made public. Nonetheless, when the moment is right, much as I am entertained by our correspondence, and genuinely do care for her, and am intrigued by her adventures and her universe, I shall attempt to draw her out on what I understand, via Jack (although how he knows this, I can't imagine), to be her lurid past as a call girl. A letter on that subject will, I know, be my safeguard against any revelations she might, in future, consider making regarding my own indiscretions."

444 East 57th Street
New York, New York

Josephine Kendall
3307 N Street
Washington, D.C.

March 10, 1959

Dear Josephine,

I know you are busy with the campaign—I read about it all the time in the newspapers, and am rooting for Jack and for you—but thought I would write to you and let you know that I've been thinking of you a great deal

I'm writing to you on the plane to L.A. from Chicago, where I've been promoting Some Like It Hot.* Before I tell you all about it, I wanted to thank you for your kind and interesting letter. I loved it all, particularly all the bits about the Duchess and about RK. I wanted also to tell you that I promise never to show that letter—or any other that you have written me— to anyone else in the world. I thought I would say that in case you were worried, which you shouldn't be.

Chicago was thrilling, but exhausting. After I left—on the plane—I read that Jack was also here, seeing Mayor Daley. I expect you were with

---

*On March 18 Marilyn was in Chicago, promoting *Some Like It Hot*, and Jack was also in the city, meeting with Mayor Richard Daley. She and Jack spent one night together in his suite at the Ambassador.

149

him, too, although they didn't mention you in the newspaper. I am very sorry to have missed seeing you both.

I wonder how the campaign is going for you. Do you think Jack has a chance of making it right to the White House? Is it exciting for you? And are people thrilled at meeting Jack on the campaign trail? I am sure they are, and you, too, of course.

Love to Caroline and Jack and to you,
Martha

3307 N Street
Washington, D.C.

Martha Marshall
444 East 57th Street
New York, New York

May 20, 1959

Dear Martha,

Forgive me for not writing to you sooner, but all this campaigning has exhausted me. The extremely belated answer to all your questions is yes to everything. Sometimes I look at Jack and he seems truly blessed, golden, like Gatsby, with a pure spirit and an honesty which should prevail. At other times, I could just throttle him, but that's another story altogether. . . .

This is just a short note to add my thanks to Jack's for your most generous campaign contribution.* You are such a good friend to us both.

I do think it is sad, though, that you didn't get to say hi to Jack during your mutual stay in Chicago. That way he could have thanked you personally for your generosity.

In any event, I am writing this on board the *Caroline,* Jack's campaign plane, a present from Joe K. It's a DC-3, with a dining area, a sleeping area, and a galley, where I invariably end up making Boston clam chowder for Jack, as he loves it so. The plane is now Jack's campaign center and he spends far more time here than at home. When-

---

* Marilyn donated $25,000 to Jack's campaign (see Heymann).

ever I can, I fly with him, but usually spend most of my time doing needlepoint or reading—most recently, *Lolita* (which I didn't like) and *Bonjour Tristesse*, which I did.

I am starting to get accustomed to the hectic pace of the campaign. In the end, I hope it will all be worth it. I can't believe how many hands I have to shake. Many of the women are even shyer than I am. And I tend to spend most of my time wondering how Caroline is getting on without me.

We are about to land in Des Moines—but before we do, I wanted to say that I adored *Some Like It Hot* and laughed until I cried.

Love,
J

444 East 57th Street
New York, New York

Josephine Kendall
3307 N Street
Washington, D.C.

June 15, 1959

Dear Josephine,

Just a quick note to say that I am also real sorry I didn't see Jack in Chicago. I have to confess the reason why I didn't see him is because I was with Mr. G. I didn't want to tell you before, because of Arthur, but I guess it doesn't matter, and I know you won't judge me for having been unfaithful to Arthur, because we both know that the marriage is on the rocks. So G and I met in Chicago, but I couldn't see Jack as well, because, crazy though this may sound, G is so possessive that he goes ape at the thought of me spending even a second with another man—even one as happily married as Jack, and as serious a politician with so much integrity. So I couldn't see Jack when we were both in Chicago at the same time, and hope you understand and that he will too, although you don't have to tell him, because I am sure he was far too busy to think of me.

Hope the campaign is going well.

Love,
M

3307 N Street
Washington, D.C.

Martha Marshall
44 East 57th Street
New York, New York

October 20, 1959

Dear Martha,

I've been wanting to write to you for ages, but thought of you a great deal when I was in Louisiana campaigning for Jack. I tried something new, my idea, which was speaking French to the people there, and they all (100,000 of them) seemed to really appreciate my doing it but then, all of a sudden, went wild and surged forward toward me. I was petrified. Then I remembered the film I saw of you in Korea, how joyful you seemed, how elated by the crowd, how unintimidated, and (for that moment) imagined I was you, and thus sailed through the entire experience. Consequently, from now on I shall always remember your example and have it in my mind whenever I am confronted by a large crowd, and hope to act accordingly. All in all, I owe you a big thank-you for having thus inspired me.

I also wanted to say that although I never met him (did you?), I was sorry that Errol Flynn died. He always reminded me so much of my father. Do tell me if you know anything interesting about him—it would be exhilarating to be distracted from politics and transported into your glittering world, if only for a moment.

In haste,
Warm regards,
J

444 East 57th Street
New York, New York

Josephine Kendall
3307 N Street
Washington, D.C.

November 12, 1959

Dear Josephine,

Thank you for your letter—I am glad I helped, even though I didn't know I did. I wonder if you've been hypnotized by the quiz scandal like I have and the rest of the country as well.[*] I just can't believe that all those quiz questions were fixed and the contestants lied all the way through. In a way, though, it has started me thinking about all the things we—I mean me—do or say that aren't right or true.

It also made me think of a question which Freud used to ask his patients: "Imagine you are starving. You discover that if you press a red button, a ninety-year-old Mandarin in China will instantly drop dead. As a result of pressing the button, you will get one million dollars. Would you press it?"[†] I don't think I would. At least, I hope not. Would you?

---

[*] On October 19, 1959, congressional hearings commenced regarding the fixing of big-money quiz shows, including *Twenty-One,* on which distinguished Columbia University professor Charles Van Doren won $129,000 in prize money.

[†] See Dr. Erika Padan Freeman, *Insights: Conversations with Theodor Reik* (Englewood Cliffs, N.J.: Prentice Hall, 1971). Freud termed this particular story "Tuer son Mandarin."

You asked about Errol Flynn. Well, I do have a great story to tell you about him but I am not sure whether or not I should, because it is very dirty. To tell you the truth, I am a little nervous about telling you, as there is no easy way to tell it without using four-letter words. Now that you are a mother, and Jack is running for President, I think that would be wrong. But if you would like me to tell you it—and can forgive my bad language—of course I will. Please write when you have time, and I'll tell you it if you really would like me to.

Arthur just walked in looking glum, so must stop.

Love,
M.

3307 N Street

Washington, D.C.

Martha Marshall

444 East 57th Street

New York, New York

December 5, 1959

Dear Martha,

Your letter gave me food for thought and I'm grateful. Much as I despise myself for admitting this, honesty forces me to confess that (as I have never in my life known either hunger or cold, and the prospect petrifies me) I should, indeed, press the button.

However, not that I wish to indulge in one-upmanship or assuage my considerable guilt at my own venality, I have to ask you to reevaluate your answer were I to rephrase Freud's question as follows: imagine that if you pressed the button, Mr. G would be yours for keeps (as the teenagers call it). Would you press it? I'd be extremely interested to learn your answer, if you feel like considering the question further.

On another front, your reticence regarding Errol Flynn was commendable, yet tantalized me almost beyond endurance. Please don't feel that because I have become a mother, I either am less of a woman or have become fragile and unable to countenance the saltier side of life. My father, as you know, was utterly blunt regarding the subject of sex, as I myself have always been.

So, dear Martha, please don't hesitate to express yourself as freely as possible (four-letter words included) regarding Errol or anything else.

We know each other far too well by now to play games or prevaricate in any way.

With great anticipation,
Yours,
Josephine

Josephine Kendall
3307 N Street
Washington, D.C.

January 30, 1960

Dear Josephine,

I really wanted to reply to your letter honestly, so here goes. I have to be honest and admit that of course you are right. If I could have Mr. G, I would press the button, I would in a heartbeat. Afterwards, though, I'd feel sorry for the old Mandarin and his family and would try and make it up to them, but, yes, I would still press the button.

As for Errol Flynn. Well, to be truthful, about a hundred years ago, when I had just become a model, I went to a party, and there was Errol, in all his glory. All of a sudden, he took out his—forgive me, but I don't really know another word—prick and played "You Are My Sunshine" with it on the piano.* He looked so pleased with himself—it was big and beautiful— the prick, I mean, not the tune—but I felt like saying, "Don't think you are so great because you've got a big prick. I mean, it isn't like winning the Nobel Prize because you are a genius. You didn't do anything to deserve it,

---

* See Truman Capote's essay "A Beautiful Child" in *Marilyn Monroe* (Munich: Schirmer/Mosel, 2001).

you were just born with it." But I was young and shy and I didn't say anything. So that's my Errol story.

Have to go now, as I've got a costume fitting.

Love to you and Jack,
M

3307 N Street
Washington, D.C.

Martha Marshall
The Beverly Hills Hotel
Beverly Hills, California

February 28, 1960

Dearest Martha,

I am writing to you in an extremely distraught state of mind, but know that you, above all women, will understand my emotions. I have discovered that Jack has acquired a permanent mistress, one Judith Campbell, and that he is enthralled by her. They met in Las Vegas only lately. But the affair is ongoing and, as far as I am concerned, a great threat.

If you chance to question the manner in which I obtained this disturbing information, the answer is simple. Taking a leaf out of *Désirée,* the book which you and I both love, I have recently followed in Napoleon's footsteps (vis à vis Fouché, his most trusted spy) and engaged a private detective to keep watch on Jack. If you judge me to be excessively devious and underhanded, and I hope you won't, please imagine how you might have reacted were you to be in my position, loving Jack as I do and aware that a serious rival (she is said to be tall, dark, beautiful, and well versed in the art of lovemaking) looms large on his sexual horizon.

Forgive the somewhat distraught nature of this letter, but I know you will understand. There is, on reflection, very little you can say to my news, but I look forward to hearing from you when you have time.

Love,
Josephine

Seymour Hersh's interviews with Judy Campbell (see *The Dark Side of Camelot*) provide an insight into Jack's wooing techniques and ability to sustain an illicit extramarital relationship:

"'He was very interested in the fact that I was from a large family and that I was Catholic,' Exner told me. 'We talked about everything—the same things that you'd talk about to anyone that you find attractive. He was an amazing man. When you talked to him, you felt you were the only person on the planet, much less just in the room. He never forgot anything you said—good or bad. He didn't just pretend to be listening to you—he listened to you. He absorbed everything.'"

As time went on, according to Campbell, "Jack always wanted to know where I was at all times. He wanted to know who I was seeing, who I was having dinner with. He loved gossip, just thrived on gossip. I used to tell him, 'Go out and buy a movie magazine.'"

Although her relationship with Jack was to last for several years, when Jack became sexually complacent, Judy, unlike Marilyn, became jaded with him in that arena: "Slowly I began to feel that he expected me to come into bed and just perform. . . . I understood about the position he had to assume in lovemaking when his back was troubling him, but slowly he began excluding all other positions, until finally our lovemaking was reduced to this one position."

1095 North Ocean Boulevard
Palm Beach, Florida

Martha Marshall
The Beverly Hills Hotel
Beverly Hills, California

April 12, 1960

Dearest Martha,

I am thinking out loud, Martha, as I often do when writing to you. Since I dispatched my desperate missive to you, I have reevaluated the situation regarding JC. I believe now that Jack has won the New Hampshire primary, his bid for the Presidency will engender a sense of caution within him and cause him to curtail his propensity for adultery.

But I am not altogether sure. His sexual allure (glittering as it is and, as far as I am concerned, unmatched by any other man) will surely be even more enhanced by the patina which power will inevitably bestow on him. Where that will leave me, I am not altogether sure.

In a way, his passion for politics threatens me more than his affair with JC. I feel so very excluded from all the hoopla and the festivities. To give you an example, on the night on which Jack won the primary, the family threw a victory party during which they gathered round the TV to watch and applaud his speech, which he had recorded earlier in the day. Throughout the entire evening, Jack and the rest of the clan (the gaggle, as I sometimes think of them, as in geese) completely ignored me. I spent most of the evening sitting on the stairs, reading, and (when the time to depart for the airport drew nigh) escaped into

The Beverly Hills Hotel

Josephine Kendall
3307 N Street
Washington, D.C.

April 5, 1960

Dear Josephine,

Your letter shocked me so much. How could Jack be such a louse? Specially now that he's running for President as well. I almost hope he doesn't make it. But I hate the thought of you suffering so much, and hate Judy even more. If I were you, I would divorce him this minute. I'm thinking of divorcing Arthur myself.

In a way, your letter came at just the right time. Although I've seen G—he doesn't deserve the title Mr., because he isn't a gentleman—now and again during my marriage to Arthur, I always felt that seeing G didn't count as infidelity because, in a strange way, I was married to him before I ever met Arthur. Or at least till now I thought I was.

Now, though, I mean to go ahead and start seeing someone else. Someone about whom I think I could get really serious. I expect you will have guessed by now who I mean. Everyone knows we are working together. And I know you will always keep my secrets.

He looks a bit like Joe, but is far brighter and more sensitive. In some ways, he reminds me of G because he can be sweet and sensitive and sexy. But unlike G—who is spoiled and pampered, had everything he ever needed but is still cold and selfish—he came up the hard way, like I did.

The good news is that we have a great deal in common. The b[...] that he is married. But she—his wife—is more like his mother. [...] should feel bad about borrowing him from her for a while—or long[...] she is much luckier than I am, and has a lot more to be glad ab[...] maybe she won't care too much.

I know I sound like I'm speaking in riddles, so I'll be up front, be[...] I always am with you. She is Simone Signoret—and she really is l[...] because she's just been awarded the Best Actress Academy Award for[...] performance in <u>Room at the Top</u>. Of course, she <u>was</u> good, but then so u[...] the part. I'll never get a part like that. Or if I did, they would never gi[...] me the Oscar, or any other awards either. She is so lucky, she probably wil[...] be so busy celebrating that she won't even notice about Yves and me. So[...] now you know who he is. Yves Montand.

Until I got your letter, I wasn't going to do a thing about him, but now[...] everything you told me about Jack made me realize that I am crazy to be[...] true to Arthur, or even G. So watch this space!!!

Arthur is calling me, so I had better stop in case he reads what I said about Yves. But he probably wouldn't even care. Nor would G.

I'll be keeping a good thought for you, Josephine, and feel so bad for you.

Love,
M

After Marilyn wrote to Jackie, she called Dr. Brandt, begging for an emergency appointment. According to his transcript of the session: "'The bastard's having an affair. Probably a real tacky one. But I fixed him. I wrote and told her that I was planning to fuck Yves, and I'll bet that she will tell him. Even if she doesn't, I'll still fuck Yves. I really will, and I'll like it as well.'"

the car, where I waited for Jack to join me. He did, giving me nary a thought. Such is the fate of the political wife and I guess I had better become accustomed to it. For Jack, I know will, for as long as he lives, no matter how high he climbs or low he falls, remain beguiled by (to mix metaphors) the thrill of the crowd and the lure of the greasepaint.

On that subject, I want to congratulate you for having won the Golden Globe for *Some Like It Hot*. You certainly deserve it. I so admire your acting abilities. I have to confess (and I believe this is my first confession in this arena) that I have always nurtured a secret desire to become an actress. Naturally, I shall now never be able to live out my desire. Except, of course, if I become First Lady, a thought which fills me with a combination of dread and excitement. However, to continue my train of thought, if I do, I know I shall require every iota of acting talent I possess to play the part to the satisfaction of Jack— and history.

You may think I am being presumptuous assuming I have acting talent.* My only basis for thinking I might is my childhood, during which I was continually compelled to keep up a front, to hide my grief at my parents' divorce and my knowledge of my father's rampant infidelity, about which, thanks to his somewhat inappropriate honesty, I knew every detail (who, what, when, where, and even in what position . . .). Against all odds, I was compelled to hide the truth from my mother, my school friends, and, of course, Lee. In short, I was compelled to become an actress—in life, if not in art.

So that from the age of around seven, I had to pretend constantly

---

*On Jackie's acting ambitions, see Gore Vidal interview in Bradford: "One afternoon, Vidal took Jackie, whom he described as being 'fascinated by Hollywood and movie stars,' to a rehearsal of his television drama *Honor*. Vidal remembers that they were drinking coffee and watching the rehearsal when suddenly Jackie blurted, 'I'd love to act.' When Vidal asked if Jack's political stardom wasn't more interesting, she replied, 'For Jack it is. Not for me. I never see him.' When Jackie pushed the acting issue, Vidal told her he was sure a studio would cast her for the novelty alone."

that things were not as they were. When I wasn't pretending, I escaped into a dream world in which I pictured myself as Queen of the Circus, Madame de Staël, or Josephine and above the fray and the pain of my parents' splintering marriage.

But I digress. Back to JC. After a great deal of anguish, I have concluded that my best course is to ignore the entire affair. To sweep it under the carpet, as it were. After all, by now I should know the pattern of Jack's dalliances. They begin with high intensity, and burn out quickly. Besides, now that he has scented victory, my sense is that all his energies will be focused on the Presidency, and not on JC.

To answer the rest of your letter. I trust that your romance with YM is progressing happily and that the errant Mr. G has been eclipsed in your affections. However, perhaps "errant" is an understatement. You called him "selfish, spoiled, and cold"—which, now that I think of it, sounds exactly like Jack. That, as far as I am concerned, is a further justification for your having transferred your affections from Mr. G to Mr. M.

By the way, does Simone know, do you think? I saw Yves recently on the newsreels and think he is very handsome and erotically appealing. Do write back and tell me all about your romance.

In great anticipation,
Josephine

The Beverly Hills Hotel

Josephine Kendall
3307 N Street
Washington, D.C.

July 2, 1960

Dear Josephine,

Thank you so much for writing to me. I am feeling very low these days.
I hated making the movie *Let's Make Love*, think the script was awful,
despise Cukor, and feel like I've failed at life.

My romance with Yves, which you asked about, is over and I feel like a
fool. It started out great, of course, as romances always do. At first, he was
so sweet and shy. So—because I knew how much he wanted me—I did the
same thing as I once did with George Sanders all those years ago, put on
my fur—a white mink this time, not a sable—and knocked on the door of
his bungalow here at the Beverly Hills Hotel. Simone, of course, was out of
town, promoting her movie.

The moment I closed the bungalow door, I slid straight out of the coat.
All my life, I've loved being naked. I even have dreams in which I am naked
in public. I started having them when I was ten years old and I'll never forget the first one. I was lying naked on a big table in front of all the girls and
all the teachers in the orphanage and they were all examining my naked
body. I felt proud and less lonely. Since dreaming that dream, I've had no
shame or sense of sin about being naked.

So it all started then with Yves and me, and for a time it was bliss. I felt bad about Simone, of course, but not about Arthur. He has aliunnated [sic] me on every level. The last straw was his actions after the Screen Actors Guild went on strike. I had always admired and respected him for his communist beliefs and support for the workers. Imagine my shock when, in the dead of the night, he broke the strike by working on the script.* Looking back, though, I don't know if Yves is any better. I like to think he is, but it's difficult, as now that filming has ended, he has ended everything with me as well. Same old same old. "On location it doesn't count. . . ." And I hate that. I still miss Mr. G so much.

On another front, as you would say, I guess because I donated money to his campaign, I have been invited to hear Jack speak at the Convention here in L.A. Will you be there, too? I sure hope so. If you are not going to be, though, I am not sure whether to accept, as I am still mad at Jack because of Judy Campbell and how badly he made you feel. Please let me know whether you think I should go or not, and I shall do whatever you think.

Love,
M

---

*Miller, according to Yves Montand's memoirs, *You See, I Haven't Forgotten* (New York: Knopf, 1992), "came running back from Ireland to rewrite some scenes, pocketed a check (from Fox) and complained about prostituting his art."

In her memoirs, *Nostalgia Isn't What It Used to Be* (New York: HarperCollins, 1978), Simone Signoret recalled the letter that Yves wrote Marilyn and her reaction: "Don't leave me to work for hours on end on a scene you've decided not to do the next day. I'm not the enemy. I'm your pal. And capricious little girls never amused me. Best, Yves."

According to Simone, on receiving Yves's note, Marilyn went to his room and burst into tears, weeping, "I'm bad, I'm bad, I'm bad. I won't do it again. I promise."

3307 N Street
Washington, D.C.

Martha Marshall
The Beverly Hills Hotel
Beverly Hills, California

July 10, 1960

Dear Martha,

Sadly, because I am pregnant again, I shall not be accompanying Jack to the convention in Los Angeles. But please don't hesitate to go. I have long forgotten about JC and I know Jack would love to see you. Moreover, your support, which I know will garner a great deal of publicity, will only add to his luster.

I look forward to reading about the convention, and your visit there, in the papers.

Warmest regards, as ever,
Josephine

Jackie wrote in her diary, "I couldn't have stopped her going, even if I had tried. So (on the basis, better the devil you know) I encouraged her. After all, I have no proof and I really am not sure. Just that now and again, I wonder. In any event, if I am right, the continuing presence of Mr. G in her life clearly precludes her having any other deep involvements. So on that count, at least, I shall relax, enjoy the summer, and wait for November and the new baby."

Marilyn did, indeed, attend the Democratic Convention on July 12 (see Summers) and then spent the night with Jack afterwards and the next few days as well.

Room 614
The Maples Hotel
30 North Virginia
Reno, Nevada

Josephine Kendall
3307 N Street
Washington, D.C.

July 29, 1960

Dear Josephine,

I am sorry I didn't write after the convention when—for just a few minutes—I saw Jack. He probably complained to you afterwards that I was cold and distant. If he did, he was right. I meant to be—because of JC, of course. I don't know how you live with it.

My big news, though, is that I am out here in Nevada working with Clark Gable—am enclosing a signed picture for you. He is everything we both always thought. We've already done one sex scene together, but in his case, I would rather call it a love scene. I was so thrilled when the moment came in the script when he kissed me. Luckily for me, we had to do the scene over several times. When the sheet dropped and he put his hand on my breast, I got goose bumps all over. Whenever he was near me, I wanted him to kiss me and kiss me and kiss me. We did a lot of kissing, touching, and feeling. I never tried harder to seduce a man, but Clark is happily married— his wife is pregnant—and I knew I didn't have a chance. But, oh, I wanted to, I really did. Because if I had, I know I would have been happy forever.

172

When I am with Clark, I feel as if he doesn't just know Marilyn, he knows Norma Jeanne as well—and also the third woman who is in me and who ultimately controls everything I do and everything I am. She kind of hovers above me, rarely says much, but decides which me I should be each day. She doesn't have a name—except that I think of her as "the puppet mistress."

Clark knows all of me, though, all three of me. He knows all the pain, and all the desperate things in me. In the movie, when he put his arms around me and said he loved me, I knew it was true. Or was it? Sometimes, like I told you once, I don't know the difference between what is true and what isn't. Like with Mr. G. I love him, but I know that he will go away soon (because he is being promoted and transferred to Africa—I think the place is called Mogambo) and will not have too much time for me anymore.

I am sorry if I sound confused. I guess I am. The movie isn't anything like I hoped and I haven't been well and have been taking things to get better. I'll write when I am.

Hope you are well and happy.

Love,
M

In his autobiography, *Monty and Me* (Chicago: Hart & Richardson, 1963), Montgomery Clift's double, Ben Gordon, remembers Marilyn writing a letter, which he mailed for her, and says, "She was drugged out and disheveled. I felt sorry for the recipient of the letter, because, given M's condition, it could hardly have been coherent."

3307 N Street
Washington, D.C.

Martha Marshall
882 North Doheny Drive
Beverly Hills, California

November 20, 1960

Dearest Martha,

Thank you for your congratulatory telegram. I can't believe it yet either. Jack is President of the United States of America and I am First Lady—which, in my view, sounds akin to being a racehorse or a brand of hair spray. Nonetheless, I guess I have to become accustomed to both the title and the office, and quickly.

However, as you know from my previous communications, I am terrified about my new role and what the future may bring.

I did, however, want to say that I am deeply saddened regarding the death of your great friend, and my hero, Mr. Gable. How fortunate, though, that you were able to have the opportunity of working with him at last. I am also grateful for my signed photograph of him, which, much to Jack's amusement, now has pride of place in my boudoir. I owe you a great deal for having secured it for me.

I have not, of course, referred yet to the subject of your divorce from Arthur. Partially, I suppose, because I have always intuited that in your heart, from the first moment you made the fateful decision to maintain your relationship with Mr. G (is he still on the scene?), you had also resolved to divorce Arthur.

I know, too, that your decision is the right one. Marriage is difficult enough without being bound to a partner whom, no matter how high his status, one no longer respects.

Forgive me if this and my subsequent communications in the near future are somewhat truncated. I appear now to be living in the eye of a storm and my time is no longer my own.

On another front entirely, have you seen *Butterfield 8*? Jack and I went to see it when it opened a few days ago. I know your feelings regarding Miss Taylor, and thought of you when I saw the movie. Yet despite my loyalty to you, I found myself admiring her portrayal. Long after we came home, the following question lingered in my mind and (in the same vein as your Freud question, which, you will gather, made a strong impression on me) I asked myself if whether or not, under the right circumstances, I should be able to sell myself to the highest bidder. Or, to set an example in terms of bluntness, could I ever be a call girl and have sex for money? I must confess that, after having mulled the matter over at great length, I concluded given the right circumstance and, of course, the right man (or men), I could imagine myself succumbing to that particular temptation.

In all honesty (and our mutual honesty is one of the factors which render our correspondence so refreshing and important to me), how do you feel? The debate is, I think, an interesting one—and one about which I know you will be truthful.

Do write as soon as you have time. Please know, as well, Martha, that you remain in my thoughts and that, as always, I wish you well.

Warmest regards,
Josephine

After mailing this letter, Jackie wrote in her diary, "I feel a bit Lucretia Borgia in having done this, but I set the trap for MM at last, because I think the time is right. I seized the moment (or rather, the movie, *Butterfield 8*, which Jack and I saw right after it opened) and, in so many words, asked MM the question whether or not she has ever been a call girl. My guess is that she will reply, and in detail. I do feel a trifle guilty, though, for having thus entrapped her, but feel that given Jack and my respective positions, I feel justified, if only as a safeguard."

882 North Doheny Drive
Beverly Hills, California

Josephine Kendall
3307 N Street
Washington, D.C.

December 15, 1960

Dear Josephine,

I wanted to write and congratulate you on the birth of John. I am so glad for you—and for Jack. Strange that you gave him the same name as Kay Gable gave Clark's baby as well. I feel so bad about Gable, and it was all my fault. I kept him waiting for me—kept him waiting for hours and hours on the set. After he died, I asked Dr. Brandt if I had left Gable waiting because he reminded me of my father, and I wanted to punish my father, so I got even with him for all those years he kept me waiting. Dr. Brandt said that my explanation was interesting, but not necessarily valid.

Before I forget, you asked me about Butterfield 8*. At first, I wasn't going to tell you—and I am trusting you with my life and my career by telling you this—because although I did survive the calendar scandal, through following the advice of a good and dear friend, I don't know whether I would survive if the following story was made public. But then, I know you would never do anything to hurt me, or I you.*

Please forgive my language, but it is the only way in which I can tell what happened, and I know you once said it was OK for me to use that type of language and that you wouldn't mind.

It was a long time ago, before I was a star, or even an actress. I can't remember the date and I don't remember the hotel—just that it was in Vegas. I was broke then. Broker than you can imagine. Lived on air, really, and hope, and dreams. A Cuban girl called Treasure Malone told me about Vegas, said that I could clean up in just a week, with no hassle, no one would know. So I made up a name—Sheba Langtry—bought a long black wig, changed my makeup, and pretended I wasn't me. Although, in my heart, I knew I was.

At the Flamingo—I guess I've remembered the name now—I did what Treasure said and introduced myself to the bell captain. Otto, his name was, and he came from Bulgaria or Bavaria or some place starting with B and ending in A. Treasure told me about the split. 60% to me and 40% to Otto. All I had to do was check into a motel and just wait for the call to come in from Otto, telling me the time and the room number. I liked it that way, because it meant I didn't have to deal with any bitchy girls. Otto and I got kinda friendly and he told me a bit about how the whole thing worked.

The men would call him up, you see, and say they needed a pillow. In my case, Otto said—because he was hoping, I think . . . he tried real hard and used to say, "Sheba is young, beautiful, busty, brunette, and aims to please, you'll love her." So, because of Otto—and I guess I was nice to him, for a few minutes, in a way—I got lots of calls. The men paid me cash up front—or threw a chip my way. I didn't like that much, because it made me feel cheap—although I don't really understand how a girl can be called cheap if she works out of an expensive hotel and makes as much as I did.

You learn a lot, you know, Jackie, being that kind of a girl, if only for a week, and I don't regret it, because it helped me with my acting. Not that I acted in bed. Far from it. I was probably more real with those men than I have ever been with any other man, except perhaps Mr. G—a lot of good it did me. . . . You see, because of being Marilyn, most men these days are scared of me and treat me like a princess or a fragile piece of china. I want that out of bed, and the respect, too, and the kindness. But not in bed. In bed I want them to be themselves.

They all wanted the same things from me—and all of them, the clever ones, picked up on what I wanted as well. You would never think it, at least I didn't, but even if they are paying, men really want to please you. So the men I had in Vegas pleased me by being a bit rough with me and not phony. If they had pretended to love me or given me compliments or kissed me, I would have felt dirty. This way, when it was over, I always felt clean.

I am embarrassed to tell you this, but the ones who made me feel the cleanest were the ones who slapped my ass. Not real hard, but as if I was a bad girl. That felt right, because I knew that what I was doing was wrong and that I needed to be punished, and I was. So when they slapped me— and most of them said things like "bad bad bad little girl" in time with the slaps—it felt like I deserved it and I felt good afterwards. Like I got justice or something. Funny, though, the men felt real bad afterwards—one kept his wedding ring on when he spanked me, and the next day I looked as if a tiger had scratched over every inch of my ass—and then they tipped me extra. I used to take it, but I'd always tell them not to feel bad, that they didn't hurt me— I even told the tiger man that, because he felt so guilty, like a kid who'd been caught with his hand in the cookie jar—and that I liked it. Which I guess I did. In a way, though, I felt sorry for some of the men because they were real cute, and it seemed sad that their wives didn't care about them and that they were far from home and needed that little bit of affection.

When I left Vegas—a week later, and it really was only a week—I did make enough dough to eat for a while—even some to send my mother and some to save.

So it all worked out in the end: no one got hurt and I got some money and survived. I don't regret it, not one bit, although I don't want anyone to know. Not now. Also—and this is real important, if there is only one thing in my life I am proud of, it is that I have never been a kept woman. Never, and I never will be.

Wishing you and Jack and John and Caroline and everyone a Merry Christmas and 1961.

Love,
M

———————

According to Dr. Brandt's transcript of Marilyn's session held the next day, she began: "I know I should have asked you first before I did it, Joseph, but the letter came and I just went with it— the way you just go with a scene when you act, playing the moment like Mr. Strasberg always taught me. When she asked about whether I have ever been a call girl, I spun her a story that I was. I did it hoping she would tell Jack. He loves call girls, and he isn't shy about letting me know it. 'The greatest women in the world,' he calls them. 'No frills. They just give you what you want and leave. Please you without asking for anything back. Every man's dream.' Well, I always thought I was like that anyway, or at least I try to be, but perhaps I haven't done it right, at least as far as Jack is concerned, so I thought I would try this—so he would see it in me, you know, and give up Judy Campbell. So I told Jackie, hoping she would tell him. Let's see who comes crawling now . . . Even if he is President . . ."

Did Marilyn make up the Vegas call girl story or not? We may never know. Moreover, when she was approached by Billy Wilder to play the streetwalker with the heart of gold in *Irma La Douce*, Marilyn instantly turned him down, citing her unwillingness to play that type of a role.

As for Marilyn's sexuality, Peter Lawford, who knew her well, alluded to her "masochism" (see Heymann), as did her psychoanalyst Dr. Ralph Greenson. As to her sexual submissiveness, according to her friend Harry Rosenfeld, "Marilyn told me she hardly ever had an orgasm. She tried above all to please the opposite sex."

3307 N Street
Washington, D.C.

882 North Doheny Drive
Beverly Hills, California

December 20, 1960

Dearest Martha,

I felt compelled to write at once to tell you that I was stunned and impressed that you were so open and honest in your last letter to me. Please know that I respect and admire you for your capacity to trust and be so frank.

On some level, too, I think I envy you. For although I would die were a man to even contemplate raising a hand to me, there is, indeed, something fundamentally honest (or is it primeval?) about a man paying, and paying well, for sex. Looking back on my father's life, I think he might have led a less tangled romantic existence had he restricted his extramarital straying to liaisons with women who catered to his needs without expectations of any emotional involvement. Then again, I guess my father's ego craved the knowledge that, to the end of his life, he was capable of winning the chase and seducing any (and every) woman who aroused his lust. So that if he paid for it, I think he might have missed the triumph of conquest.

In a way, perhaps, a woman who charges for sex (and I know we are discussing the highest class of woman—latter-day Madame de Pompadours—not streetwalkers) is the ultimate conqueror, for she knows her price, takes it, and then moves on. Something one can hardly do vis à vis a marriage, no matter how unsatisfactory that marriage may be.

Forgive me for ending abruptly, but Maud Shaw, John and Caroline's nanny, has just arrived and needs briefing.

Wishing you happy holidays, dear Martha, and a wonderful 1961.

Love,
Josephine

Jackie wrote in her diary, "I know I planned this after I'd been indiscreet about Rose and wanted to inveigle Marilyn into being indiscreet as well, but now that it is done and she has fallen into the trap, I feel deeply guilty and wish so much that I hadn't set it. Of course, Jack must never set eyes on her letter (or any others she has sent me), for I know it would arouse him beyond belief. To that end, I shall sequester it in the safety-deposit box at once and never use it against her."

Columbia-Presbyterian Medical Center
Room 719
622 West 168th Street
New York

Jacqueline Kennedy
The White House

February 12, 1961

Dear Jackie,

You are in the White House and I am in the Nuthouse. . . . I just hope you don't think badly of me. I wanted you to know that I haven't really lost my mind, or whatever they call it. I'm not here because I am crazy—like my mother. I was always haunted by the fear that I was like her and that I was doomed to end up in a place like this, and that because I was her daughter, I was exactly like her. I felt so scared, till I started analysis and Dr. Brandt said to me, "Purple shouldn't feel scared because it has blue in it." Which explained everything.

So I am not here because I'm crazy. I'm here because of Mr. G, only he doesn't know it—and also because <u>The Misfits</u> *turned out to be just that— a misfit for my career and I feel like a failure, a bad actress and useless.*

But back to Mr. G. It isn't really his fault, but recently I have been feeling so lost and lonely, what with him being so occupied—in Africa— and not able to see me much anymore. One night, when I'd had too much champagne and the bad reviews were pouring in, I was all alone in the apartment, thinking of G and wishing I were with him, close to him, even

183

married to him. For a moment, I thought back to my marriage to Arthur and, in particular, the wedding. The Jewish wedding ceremony, you know, includes the groom breaking a glass. So—although I wasn't a groom, and there wasn't a wedding—I started smashing glasses, as if there was—a wedding and it was me and Mr. G getting married. When I'd finished—I must have smashed at least thirty Baccarat crystal glasses—I was covered in blood and there was glass everywhere. I forgot to say as well that I was playing Frank all through it. Just one song, "All the Way," and I kept playing it over and over and over.

Anyway, when they found me, they called my analyst and I ended up at Payne Whitney. First thing they did was wash away all the blood. They thought I was trying to slash my wrists—but that wasn't true. If I wanted to slash them, they would have been slashed, but I didn't. I just wanted to feel married to G, if only for one night. It oughtn't have been too much to ask—but it obviously was. Funny thing, though, when I was all cleaned up, I had just one deep cut—on my wedding ring finger. I hope I'll have the scar for the rest of my life and if I do, I'll be glad. At least that way I'll feel married to G.

As soon as I was cleaned up and was put in a kind of cell, the door opened and a man who looked like W. C. Fields—you know, a big red nose and a fat face—came in and introduced himself as Dr. Woolfmann. The first thing he did was ask me how old he was. "Around 47," I said, trying to be polite. He shook his head and said, "No, Marilyn, I am 102." I didn't know what the hell he was playing at, so I didn't say a thing. He didn't say anything either for a while—you know, the silence trick that interrogators in movies play—then asked me if I knew what was wrong with me. I decided that as he was really stupid, I would give him a really stupid answer and said, "No, that's your job." He was standing real close to me and I felt like he was about to touch me. "So what are you going to do with me now," I asked. He gave me a long slow look. "What am I going to do with you, Marilyn? I am still thinking about it." Then he paused, the way men do when they have just said something like "I don't want you to get hurt"—then, after the pause, tell you they don't want to see you anymore—although I doubt that has ever happened to you.

In the end, when the pause was over—and it was a long one—he said, "I think I'll put you in a locked ward in manacles." I knew he wanted to scare me, but I didn't want to give him that satisfaction, so I said I had to go to the bathroom. Once I'd got away from him, I got someone to call Joe. He came and rescued me and now I am in a better place.

But it still isn't great here. All night long, there is screaming from everywhere. The worst thing about it is that one of the screamers is a man from Tunisia or Algeria or somewhere ending in A who keeps screaming things in a deep voice in some kind of an Arabic language. So you get to hear the noise, the yelling, but don't know what he is saying. Then there is an old lady called Betsy who has got yellow gray hair and who has this fear that the floor is crawling with maggots, so she carries sheets of newspaper—the Van Nuys Sentinel—around with her every day, and puts them on the floor in front of her before she takes each step. Then there is a girl here called Gail Volman, very tiny, with long blonde curly hair and pretty. This morning, she showed me her arms and they were all scarred up. I didn't know what to say, but she did and said, "Because of a lover." I nodded sympathetically. "It's always the man, isn't it?" I said. Gail looked surprised. "No, it was the woman," she said. Then she told me all about having met this cabaret singer who enslaved her and then kicked her out. No different, really, than any man might treat you, I suppose, and I felt sad for her.

LATER Just had a real bad experience. I've been trying to make some calls, but each time I do, there is a woman called Linda Duggan-Chapman in the call box. She is an ox of a woman, one of the hefty ones, with greasy black hair, wears glasses, and has a voice like one of those plum-in-the-mouth British actresses. Sort of like Sir Olivier, only female. I hung around for the longest time, waiting for her to finish her calls, but she never did, and I couldn't help hearing her tell the operator, "I want to make a collect call to Lima, Peru, to my cousin, Dido Percival," and, "I want to make a collect call to Delhi, India, to my uncle Nigel Northwick." She never got through, ever, or else they didn't accept her calls, but I still had to wait while she made them. Now and again, she caught my eye, so I smiled at her because I don't bear anyone in here any bad will. After all, they are poor, suffering human beings who deserve respect and probably don't belong here in the first place.

So I felt warm toward Linda and, when she finally did come out of the call box, gave her a friendly smile and said hi. She took a step toward me, as if she was going to hit me, and said, "Don't you hi me, bitch. I know just how ugly I am. I've got an ugly pig mind, an ugly pig face, ugly pig feet, and an ugly pig body." "You're not ugly," I said quickly, even though she was—but I was trying to make her feel better. "Just fuck off, you Jew whore," she said. I didn't say anything back, although what I did want to say was "I might be Jewish—[I am through conversion]—but you'll never make any money as a whore," only I didn't. I went back into my room, but I can't stop thinking about Linda.

LATER STILL I just couldn't keep quiet, so I went over to Linda and asked if I could talk to her. She seemed in a better state and said yes. So I sat down next to her, took her hand, looked deep into her eyes, and said this to her: "Linda, I want you to know that I understand how you feel and how you hate everybody. I do too, sometimes, as well. But you shouldn't say anything bad about Jews. My three-year-old little brother was thrown into the oven alive and burned to death, and if you say anything bad about Jews, you are acting like the Nazis who did that to him." She didn't say a word, so I just came back here. They've just brought dinner. Dinner? A piece of green-looking fish and some potatoes that taste like sugarless cotton candy.

THE NEXT AFTERNOON When I woke up this morning, there was someone banging on my door. Linda. I let her in, and before I could stop her, she threw her arms around my neck. "Marilyn," she said, "I couldn't sleep all night. I am so sorry I called you a whore, and I'm sorry about your little brother. Please forgive me." I said I did, she went off to breakfast, and I thought that was the end of it, but it wasn't. She came over to me again and said, "Marilyn, I want you to know that I am getting to love you." I said, "Thank you." Then she came closer. "I have to make a call, and I need some cigarettes, but they won't give me any money. . . ." I went into my room and got her some. Next thing I knew, about two hours later, she came over to me again, grabbed me by the arm, and said, "I've got to have your number, please, please, please." I asked her why. "Shhh," she said. "When I get out of here, I've got nowhere to stay . . . please, Marilyn, please."

I felt dreadful for her, but I knew I couldn't give her my number. So I just mumbled something and slunk back in here. But I know it is just a matter of time before she comes after me again.

THE NEXT DAY They had to smuggle me out the back way because of Linda, and now I am back home. But I can't stop thinking about her and all the other sad and lonely, frightened people back there.

I have to end now—appointment with my analyst. I wanted also to say that I understand if, now that you are First Lady, you—and Jack as well—want to forget all about me. I don't expect to ever hear from you

187

again, although I would love to, and to hear what life is like for you inside the White House. If you don't have time to write, or don't want to, of course I will understand.

But if you ever can, please think good thoughts for me.

Love,
Martha

Martha Marshall
882 North Doheny Drive
Beverly Hills, California

February 18, 1961

Dearest Martha,

Your letter touched my heart immeasurably. How could you possibly think that I would not have the time or interest to reply to your patently sincere and highly detailed letter! I am immensely flattered that you feel able to write to me in such honest and direct terms and hope very much that your horrendous ordeal has come to an end and that you are now safely home again. As for that psychiatrist, your instincts, Marilyn, are so acute that I have no doubt whatsoever that his intentions were less than honorable. Thank God you had enough strength and self-preservation to remove yourself from his evil reach. Your description of the other patients was most moving and I only wish something could be done to alleviate their suffering. Your own actions in that direction are praiseworthy and I deeply admire your sensitivity and commitment.

Of course I should be delighted to tell you all about my strange, bewildering new life inside the White House. Before I start, though, please know that if ever you come to Washington, both Jack and I should be delighted if you would plan to come here and amuse both of us in this dreary Maison Blanche.

In any event, thank heavens all the furor is over. Since the campaign, I've felt so mercilessly exposed. Now I can think of nothing I'd rather do than write to you.

I'm writing this late at night in the Queen's Bedroom (my new bedroom), where I sleep each night in Andrew Jackson's bed. One of my first actions, you will be pleased to learn, has been to purchase for my bedroom wall an early-nineteenth-century engraving of the Empress Josephine.

But lest you imagine the Empress Josephine's boudoir, think again! The White House is a million miles removed from Malmaison in style or grandeur. I am absolutely horrified by what I have found here and desperately want to renovate it, starting with the Oval Office. I adore the view from there of the Washington Monument and the Jefferson Memorial, but I hate all that morose blue. And as for the East Room, it reminds me of a roller skating rink with those awful orange walls. In most of the other rooms, the carpets—including the spectacular Aubusson rugs which I adore and are priceless—are covered in spots. The draperies are tattered and torn. The fireplaces don't even function.

To give you a flavor of the shabbiness of the entire White House (and I am now quoting from my detailed plan of action), there are 412 doorknobs (should be polished twice daily), 147 windows (should be cleaned biweekly), half an acre of marble corridors (must be polished twice daily), half an acre of carpet (must be vacuumed thrice daily). The linens are yellowed and need replacing, and the china (all 10,000 pieces) is chipped and cracked.

Most of the furnishings look like something left over from a yard sale: jumbled, dusty, with very few pieces that are of historical importance. Before Jack and I moved in, I toured the place with Mamie. Her decorating taste, you will probably surmise, was, to put it kindly, deficient. Her bedroom wall was decorated in a horrendous combination of vomit green and rose pink, and on either side of the door leading from the Oval Office sitting room into the main upstairs hall, two portholes had been built expressly for the Eisenhowers. When I chanced to inquire as to their purpose, an usher opened them, revealing a television sequestered in each porthole. Apparently, Mamie and Ike favored TV dinners, of which they partook in front of the televisions, with Mamie watching soaps on one and Ike, Westerns on the other.

Somewhat dispirited, I explored the house, and was elated to discover in the basement an 1817 Pier table. Some cretin had sprayed it with gold radiator paint but I think it can be rescued. There is also a wonderful Hepplewhite mirror I love that belonged to George Washington. If I could find more pieces like that, perhaps the White House could be made livable after all.

Really, the whole place desperately needs renovating so that it reflects the glory of the nation. The White House should be the grandest residence in the land. Thomas Jefferson would have understood (he ordered silks and furnishings from France when he lived here), but I doubt that Jack will. He is so uninterested in decor that he probably thinks chintz is a small animal. . . .

Of course, I wouldn't touch some things—like Lincoln's Bedroom, which, to me, is inviolable. Sitting on Lincoln's rosewood carved bed earlier this evening, I felt that he was watching me. I wonder what my life would have been like had I been married to him. Probably not much better . . . If I could have picked any American President as a husband, Jefferson would have been my choice. If only for his taste . . .

Back to my plans: I intend, first and foremost, to dispense with as much stuffy protocol as possible. I shall abolish that dreadful custom of serving guests seven-course dinners. Imagine living in Grant's day and having to plow one's way through twenty-nine! All the women must have looked like giant pandas. . . . I also intend to dispense with that stupid custom of men and women being segregated after dinner, too; women assembled in the Red Room for coffee, and men in the Green Room for brandy and cigars—dreadfully mannered and affected.

Living in the White House would probably have been greatly facilitated for me had I been born in Poughkeepsie, for then I might not have had small, instead of great, expectations. I wouldn't have been so disappointed in my surroundings, and instead of noticing the dirt, dust, and dreariness, I would have been dazzled by the White House. Instead (and I know this may sound spoiled, but given your honesty, I do not intend to prevaricate with you), I dread the prospect of spending four years living in this soul-destroying mausoleum. I feel as if I have been sentenced to prison.

Since we moved here, I have been confronted by a series of less than pleasant surprises. On our first night here, I returned to my room alone (I don't want to speculate where Jack was, or with whom . . .), only to realize that I was famished because I hadn't eaten all evening for fear of spilling something on my white Givenchy.

Consequently, I dialed the kitchen, and the following dialogue (which I hope will amuse you) ensued.

"This is Mrs. Kennedy," I said. "I should be extremely grateful if someone could bring up some Scottish smoked salmon, toast points (brown bread, please), and a bottle of Dom Pérignon."

There was a silence while a female on the other end of the line digested the information.

"Of course, Mrs. Kennedy. Is this on your account?"

To cut an extremely disconcerting story short, it transpires that unless they are entertaining in an official capacity, the First Family actually has to PAY for every single solitary one of their White House meals! Horrifying! I thought it would be Beluga all the way. . . . I suppose it is my fault; I was so caught up in the whirlwind of the campaign (which can age you thirty years in just one day—my mouth paralytic from all that smiling, my hand practically crippled from all that shaking) that I didn't consider all the ramifications of living here.

It has also become clear to me that one of the major obstacles confronting me is the ever-present, forever-intrusive media. The reporters appear set on stalking Caroline, and are determined to turn her into a ghastly Shirley Temple figure. I shall fight tooth and nail to prevent this from happening. Fortunately, I have managed to create a little playroom for her and a few friends in the third-floor solarium. It consists of a sandbox, rabbit hutches, fish, guinea pigs, and plants.

Since we moved here, I have managed to cajole Jack into establishing a regimen in which at 1:30, each and every day, he has a swim, and afterwards we take a nap together. No matter what I am doing, however important, I join him. We close the bedroom door, no calls are put through, and, for once, I have Jack to myself.

However, as you know from my previous letters, that is somewhat of an illusion. Apart from the usual situations which we both know simmer beneath the surface of our otherwise pristine marriage, even when Jack and I are together in a group of people, we differ dramatically in our way of relating to them. Jack generally talks to everyone with great animation, asking penetrating questions, sparkling, focusing. Whereas I become shy, distant, restrained, find myself unable to laugh or drink or relax, and fail completely to be myself.

Someone is at the door—one of the hazards of living in the White House—one is never allowed to be alone for long.

My caller turned out to be a page with an invitation from Lady Bird to take tea with her next Thursday. I am less than eager. For although she has been incredibly kind and welcoming, I have scant respect for her subservient attitude to her husband. If Lyndon so decreed, she would waltz down Pennsylvania Avenue naked.

I am constantly beset by cabinet wives, and have very little patience for the breed. As you know (and we share this), I have a great disdain for hordes of women en masse. From our first evening here, I have endeavored to retain the intimate quality of our social life. Our first guests, on the Sunday after the Inauguration, in fact, were Mr. and Mrs. Leonard Bernstein and Mr. and Mrs. Franklin Roosevelt, Joe Alsop, and Bill Walton. The eight of us dined in the Oval Office sitting room on ten pounds of fresh caviar (a gift from a Palm Beach supporter) served out of an enormous yellow metal bucket, plus Dom Pérignon. The atmosphere was congenial, friendly, and almost resembled our pre–White House evenings.

One drawback, however, when entertaining more than eight is that we are compelled to utilize the Family Dining Room, which, apart from being gloomy (with burgundy carpets, curtains, and walls), is also extremely cold. The White House central heating system is archaic and the fireplaces haven't been used since the year dot. I also want to initiate the custom of placing ashtrays in each room, as well as fresh flowers (white tulips and yellow carnations in the Blue Room, yellow tulips and red carnations in the Red Room) and a bar in the State Dining Room, enabling our guests to drink alcohol, which was banned under Mamie.

I have just re-read this letter and am compelled to laugh at my own bravura style and confidence. Underneath, I am dreadfully insecure, petrified of the scrutiny under which Jack and I will henceforth live, and of the impact it will have on our children. Nonetheless, I will try. Jack expects no less of me.

Forgive me for ending now, but tomorrow I shall be welcoming Lee and her husband to the White House, and must prepare for their visit. I hope it will not be long, dear Marilyn, before you, too, grace us with your presence.

Naturally, I am assuming that you are well on your way to recovery—for you are a strong lady with a profound intelligence and a deep capacity for spiritual regeneration. All my thoughts and good wishes are with you. Please know that my current circumstances render me as open to you and to our correspondence as ever and that I welcome your letters and your friendship with continuing eagerness and warmth.

Fondest regards,
Josephine

Extensive accounts of Jackie's life in the White House can be gleaned from all related books in the bibliography. Sarah Bradford casts further light on Jackie's first days there: " 'I felt like a moth banging on a windowpane when I first moved into this place,' Jackie said, 'it was terrible. . . . They were painting the second story and they moved us way down to the other end. The smell of paint was overpowering and we tried to open the windows in the rooms and we couldn't. They hadn't been opened for years and years. Later, when we tried the fireplaces, they smoked because they hadn't been used. Sometimes I wondered, "How are we going to live as a family in this enormous place." ' "

882 North Doheny Drive
Beverly Hills, California

Josephine Kendall
The White House

March 5, 1961

Dear Josephine,

I loved your letter, and felt as if I had actually been inside the White House with you. It seemed so real. I also meant to say that I am really glad that Jack and you take a daily "nap." In the past, you've always been so open and honest about sex, but when I read your letter, I suddenly realized that, with all the things you've told me about Jack, you never told me whether or not you still . . . you know . . . It feels a little funny asking the First Lady that kind of question, but I have known you long enough, so I guess I can—still have sex together? Or does "nap" mean "sleep"? I hope it doesn't, I hope it means sex, because I would much rather Jack was happy with you than fooling around with JC or any other woman either.

Warm regards,
M

Martha Marshall
882 North Doheny Drive
Beverly Hills, California

March 18, 1961

Dear Martha,

Your last letter was so cute—and so refreshing, amid the sea of idi
otic communications from cretinous women. Imagine, we get liter-
ally thousands a week, and I have to deal with them all—answering
such profound questions as what brand of shampoo I use and how
many curlers I wear in bed and whether or not Jack objects to my
doing so. Worse still are the women who persist in sending me their
photos, along with the sentiment "Everyone, just everyone says I look
exactly like you." They are even presumptuous enough (or perhaps a
better term might be "insecure") to ask for my advice regarding the
toilet training of their children. Tedious beyond belief, I am sure you
agree.

However, to answer your perfectly sane and understandable question. Nine times out of ten, Jack really does take a nap. The tenth
time, he requires certain sexual services to which I am quite unequal.
Forgive me for being reticent, but I do have a horror of talking about
that particular phenomenon, and always have.

However, please don't feel that my current and relatively new status
is holding me back or preventing me from communicating with you
as before. Quite the reverse. Being your pen pal has been and contin-

ues to be an enriching experience, one which I should not wish my role to curtail.

Apart from the fact that I am in the habit of looking forward to your letters, you are one of the few women in the world—perhaps the only one, apart from the Queen of England, with whom I have very little empathy—with whom I can feel secure in the knowledge that your own glittering career and stratospheric fame ensures that you will never feel any jealousy or sense of competition with me. Which is more than I can say for some of my immediate family, or Jack's, or my friends and acquaintances.

No, Marilyn, only you and I know what it feels like living our lives in the white heat of limelight, forever on display, forever having to present ourselves in the most glowing of aspects. For example, next week I am compelled to attend a White House lunch for a gaggle of female journalists—all of them dubbed illustrious, and each and every one of them baying for my blood.

You, in contrast, have had years of experience with the terrors of being at the mercy of their spite and the sharpness of their malicious yet powerful pens. Contemplating the prospect of being in their company is, for me, akin to having all my wisdom teeth out on the same day (something I did at the age of 14), only this time without anesthetic.* At least that would be a one-time experience. This, however, will, I fear, be a regular occurrence, and these harridans an integral part of my life. Your help and advice would be most welcome.

On another front, I see that your erstwhile "rival," Elizabeth Taylor, is currently splashed all over the rags as a consequence of her adulterous romance with the extremely fetchingly masculine Richard

---

*See Yusha Auchincloss in Bradford on Jackie's having all her wisdom teeth out on the same day.

Burton. If you have any gossip, I should welcome it as a delightful diversion from the drudgery of politics and life inside my Washington fish bowl.

Love,
Josephine

Josephine Kendall
The White House

March 26, 1961

Dear Josephine,

I am so flattered that you have asked for my advice, and will do my best to give it to you. First of all, be prepared that when the press conference is over, your ears will be ringing—because being with all those female journalists, with their high-pitched voices all chattering at once, is like being stuck in a cage with a thousand squealing starlings. As for the flashbulbs, all popping at you from every direction, sometimes you feel like you are going blind.

The important thing is to talk to yourself beforehand and say this: "Even though most of them are vile and ugly and, no matter what I say, are going to write mean and unkind things about me, in the end, so long as they spell my name right, I'll get the best of them." Sometimes, before I see them, I picture myself as a queen in a parade, and them as little dogs, all yapping at my ankles. Because, in the end, no matter what they write about me, they are writing about me. I'm not writing about them. They aren't important enough and the more they write about me, the more famous and important I'll become.

You have to prepare yourself, though, Jackie, that when one of those unfair articles about you hits the press, everyone you know will call up, saying how sorry they are, but no one will ever call you if and when fair and

200

kind articles are published about you. For years, I kept saying to myself, "How strange. Everyone always gets to see the bad stories, but they never get to see the good ones." I felt that way for ages, until a good friend (Mr. G, actually) said to me, "Sometimes you really are a dumb blonde, Marilyn. Don't you realize that everyone sees every single article about you but only ever bothers to call about the bad ones? Human nature." I always wonder why the expression "human nature" is applied only to the dreadful side of people, don't you?

In the end, you just have to assume that everyone has read the good articles as well as the bad, but mention only the bad ones because they are jealous. When I get mad or upset about their jealousy, I give myself a good shaking—not really, of course, but in my mind—and say, "If you don't want them to be jealous, Marilyn, give up being a star and move to Podunk and be a housewife instead." Then I end up feeling OK.

Of course, you are in a different position, Jackie, because you didn't choose the spotlight. But there must be some good things about being married to the President and you must be proud—specially when he does the right thing like he did this week, in creating the Peace Corps. If I had a child, I would want him or her to join it. I think it is wonderful and you can tell Jack I said so, if you want.

Another thing to remember, before I forget, when you talk to the press, is that no matter what you say, their minds are already made up and they will probably write what they want about you anyway. If I can, and if the studio lets me, I try not to talk to them at all. Or I request male journalists, who are always much nicer than female ones. In fact, I have a little group of male journalists whom I trust and who are generally nice to me. You might want to pick a group of your own who are nice and trustworthy as well. I think that would help. And if you do have to see the hags, just be polite and say as little as possible.

To answer your question about Elizabeth. I think she is really lucky to have Richard Burton, because he really is supposed to be the ultimate stud who really knows how to make a woman happy in bed.* Only the first time, he didn't make love to Elizabeth in bed at all. Francesca Le Frenais, one of the makeup artists at Fox who is working on <u>Cleopatra</u> with Elizabeth and Richard, called Patty, my beautician, and told her that Burton first made love to Liz on the backseat of George Cukor's Cadillac on the back lot. Apparently Elizabeth screamed so loud that Burton had to honk the horn to stop everyone from hearing. I feel sorry for Sybil, though, because Elizabeth and Richard are so unkind to her that they even French kiss right in front of her. I would never do that to Mrs. G. First of all, because I don't know her. Second, because I wouldn't. Thank you again for asking for my advice. I hope it helps.

Love,
Martha

---

*"In bed you must love a woman as if you were blind and your hands were reading Braille. You must learn her body as you think a great musician would orchestrate a Divine theme. You must use everything you possess—your hands, your fingers, your speech—seductively, poetically, sometimes brutally, but always with a demoniacal passion."
  —Richard Burton to Wendy Leigh in *What Makes a Man G.I.B.* (New York: NAL, 1979)

Martha Marshall
882 North Doheny Drive
Beverly Hills, California

April 11, 1961

Dear Martha,

Thank you for your stellar advice. Thanks to you, the press lunch wasn't such agony after all. You were right, of course, about the ringing in my ears afterwards. Fortunately, no one can ever accuse either of us of creating such a cacophony . . . as we both have soft and gentle voices.

On the subject of soft and gentle, I also feel sorry for Sybil. Not really for Eddie, though, because I think he took advantage of Elizabeth's loneliness after she lost Mike Todd. On the other hand, I can understand her turning to Eddie after she lost Mike. It seems natural to me that after you lose the love of your life, you turn to the man closest to him for love and support.

In any event, I am watching events unfold on the *Cleopatra* set with extreme interest, and am thankful that they are deflecting attention somewhat from me and Jack and our closely chronicled lives here in the White House.

Forgive me for making this a short letter, but duty calls. . . .

Warmest wishes,

J

The Waldorf-Astoria Hotel

Josephine Kendall
The White House

July 26, 1961

Dear Josephine,

I am thinking of you so much as I know it is your birthday on the 28th. I wanted to write to you before, when you came back from Paris. The photographs of you were beautiful and I'll bet that JC (does he still see her?) was pea green with envy when she saw them. She could never compete with you—and nor can anyone else either.

Am feeling a bit blue today, what with the news of Hemingway's death. Although I didn't like his books and hate the way he hunted and loved bullfighting so much—I always feel so sorry for the poor bull, after all, he hasn't done anything to deserve being taunted that way—I think it is still sad when someone kills himself.

I once read somewhere that the world is divided between people who— were they given a choice—would either commit murder or suicide. I, for one, would never commit suicide—at least, not on purpose—because I have put everything I am into creating Marilyn and if I killed her, I would be killing her, all my efforts, and Norma Jeane as well. Far too many people, don't you think? Also, I am an actress and I'd never intentionally mark or harm myself. I'm that vain. . . .

But I definitely could commit murder. At the moment, Mr. G is acting cold and distant, even though I need him more than ever. I'm writing this letter at Kenneth's, by the way, my hairdresser at the Waldorf, but will have to slip out the back way, as there are 200 fans waiting for me outside. At least, everyone says I should. Slip out, I mean. But I probably won't. After all, they are people, too, and if I can make them happy by smiling at them for a second or two, or signing an autograph, at least I will have done something good today.

On a different subject, as you would say, I nearly laughed out loud when I saw your pictures with Sukarno and the ones with Khrushchev as well. It's strange, really, that although I often get things wrong about what people say and what they mean, I have a real talent for reading pictures and I could see from the pictures that both of them went wild for you. I know all of America is—but I could tell from their eyes that they both practically fell in love with you. Which tickled me because both of them were real adoring to me when they met me as well. Funny, isn't it, how we seem to attract the same men, even though we look so different?

Mr. Kenneth has just started taking out my curlers, so I guess I'd better end. Think of me sometimes, Josephine, and give Jack my love as well. Is he still seeing JC? I hope not.

Lots of love to you,
Martha

1095 North Ocean Boulevard
Palm Beach, Florida

Martha Marshall
882 North Doheny Drive
Beverly Hills, California

August 31, 1961

Dearest Martha,

I was so delighted to hear from you. The image of you sequestered inside the Waldorf, besieged by 200 fans, is one that is not unfamiliar to me, and I must commend you for the grace and generosity with which you handle your fame. I am not finding it so easy, perhaps because as you once so rightly observed, I didn't ask for it. Which doesn't make me a better person, by the way, just more unprepared.

At the moment, both Jack and I are pretty shaken by the developments in Berlin—the wall being erected and all that entails. However, I could also shake Jack as well. You asked about JC and I'm afraid my answer is this—he is seeing more and more of her. I don't understand the nature of her hold over him, just that his lust for her appears to be unbridled. According to my spies, that is. Sometimes I wish I had never engaged them. I wonder if Napoleon ever felt that way about his. . . .

As for murder or suicide—my answer is exactly the same as yours. If I had a choice, it would be murder, and right now it would be Jack who'd be my victim. Perhaps we could get a package deal. . . . I shouldn't joke about such things, though, but when I write to you, I seem able to relax.

Jack has just walked in. I told him I was writing to you and he seemed most tickled, to use one of your phrases. He said to tell you that he hopes you will be able to make it to the fund-raising dinner being held in L.A. in November.

If I know you are going to be there, I'll try and make it as well. I should so enjoy seeing you again—off screen, I mean.

Love, as ever,
Josephine

882 North Doheny Drive
Beverly Hills, California

Josephine Kendall
The White House

November 26, 1961

Dear Josephine,

I was so sad that you didn't come to the fund-raising dinner. Jack will have told you that I went. I went because I support the President and believe in everything he is doing politically, but I hate that Jack sees JC and is so disloyal to you. But he is my President and I must be loyal to him because of that. I hope you understand.

Love,
Martha

After Marilyn attended the fund-raiser, she slipped away to a bungalow at the Beverly Hills Hotel and, as arranged, waited there for Jack. Afterwards, she confided to Dr. Brandt, "He was tired and, when I looked at him, seemed suddenly older. I could tell he needed to relax, so I gave him a massage. Then, instead of doing what we always do, right away, we had some Dom Pérignon. To make him laugh, I started making toasts to tons of people, Nureyev, Khruschev, Nabokov, like a rhyme. Then I toasted 'sweet Adeline' and, before I could stop myself, toasted 'baby Caroline.' Jack sat up sharp and I knew I'd made a mistake. I said I was sorry but that I often thought of her and, every time I saw her picture, was glad for him that he had her. He smiled at me then, that smile which sweeps right through me every time he smiles it. The kind of smile which you know comes from his heart, his soul, his mind, his spirit—all directed at you— hot and warm and friendly—like an invitation and a blessing, all at once. 'Yes,' he said, 'I love her so much.' Then he patted the bed and I knew he wanted me to sit next to him. I put my arms around him, and for once, he didn't shrink away. He looked straight at me—with those blue eyes that see right into you—and said, 'I love her, I love John, and my marriage is for life, but still . . . Marilyn . . . ' I knew what was supposed to come next, but I was still thinking of Caroline. 'Tell me about her,' I said. He thought for a second. I knew he didn't really want to, because it was me he would be telling, but then—because he loves her so much, because he is so proud of her—he did tell me about her. How smart she is, how sweet she is, how adorable. Then he looked guilty. 'Right now, I should really be back at the White House, with her, like I always try to be every night before she goes to sleep.' I asked him if he read Caroline bedtime stories—the way I always dreamed my father would read them to me—and he looked shocked. 'I don't read to Caroline,' he said, all proud. 'I make stories up for her specially.' 'Tell me one,' I said, and he did, all about a bear called Gramble—pink, with blue eyes, who has all sorts of adventures. I loved it when Jack told me all about Gramble. If I could live my life again, Dr. Joseph, I'd want to come back as Caroline Kennedy."

MARILYN MONROE
882 North Doheny Drive
Beverly Hills, California

President and Mrs. John F. Kennedy
The White House

December 2, 1961

Dear Jackie and Jack,

This teddy bear is a Christmas present for Caroline. I think he looks like Gramble Bear, don't you? Happy Christmas, Caroline. And happy Caroline's Christmas to John and both of you, too.

Love,
Marilyn

Marilyn Monroe
882 North Doheny Drive
Beverly Hills, California

December 8, 1961

Dear Marilyn,

This is not an official answer to your last letter nor a formal thank-you for your Christmas gift to Caroline. That will be dispatched at a later date. It is just that I am intensely curious regarding exactly how and where you learned of "Gramble Bear."

He is a character whom Jack invented specifically for Caroline. He tells her Gramble Bear bedtime stories most every night. However, as both of us care so deeply about preserving the privacy of our children, we have not relayed that fact to the press or to anyone else, for that matter.

All in all, I cannot imagine how you learned of Gramble and should be grateful if you would assuage my curiosity.

Regards,
Jackie*

---

*Jackie has jettisoned her alias here and that of Marilyn, as Marilyn's gift and letter to Jackie (and Jack) were sent to her in her official capacity as First Lady.

WESTERN UNION TELEGRAM

☫

MARILYN MONROE
882 North Doheny Drive
Beverly Hills, California

Jacqueline Kennedy
The White House

December 15, 1961

Dear Jackie,

I'm devastated that I upset you. I wouldn't have dreamed of doing that for all the world. I guess I should have explained that when I met Jack at the fund-raising dinner—somehow—and I can't remember how—we started talking about Caroline and him being a father. Anyway, I asked Jack—and I don't know why—what Caroline's favorite bedtime story was. So, of course, he told me about Gramble Bear. I hope that answers your question and that you aren't mad at me anymore.

Please write or cable and tell me that we are still friends and that you still care about me. Please don't give up on me. I need your letters and your friendship desperately.

Love,
Marilyn

Marilyn Monroe
882 North Doheny Drive
Beverly Hills, California

December 16, 1961

Dearest Marilyn,

Please forgive me for my rudeness. I don't know what I was thinking when I last wrote to you. Perhaps it is the pressure of life in the
White House and the continuing specter of JC that gave rise to my
sudden flash of paranoia.

Of course I understand, and it is quite understandable that you, and
only you, would have such a cute and personal conversation with Jack
at the fund-raiser. After all, you have known each other for so many
years, if only mostly by proxy via me, and it is only natural that you
would express a motherly interest in Caroline. Thank you for doing
so, for lightening Jack's burden, if only momentarily, and for being
such a good and true friend.

I hope that you will have an extremely happy festive season and a
wonderful 1962.

Warmly,
Jackie

After writing this letter, Jackie wrote in her diary, "It still seems too intimate, too unlike Jack, too
like pillow talk—the kind of kitsch in which MM would most likely indulge were she having a

dalliance with him. Dalliance? The wrong word, perhaps. It must be something more. They do, after all, possess a similarity in that they are both charismatic, kaleidoscopic, deeply self-absorbed, radiate sex, are disarming, ruthless, and, as Mr. G (or was it Jack?) once said, would get the last piece of bread in the concentration camp. If I am right—and Jack is Mr. G—because, re-reading my last sentence, I guess that deep down I have always intuited that he might be—then I must be Mrs. G, and Marilyn, my Judas. Maybe yes. Maybe no. If no, I am a fool to think it. If yes—I must, at all costs, retain my sangfroid and bide my time."

THE WHITE HOUSE

Marilyn Monroe
882 North Doheny Drive
Beverly Hills, California

December 22, 1961

Dear Marilyn,

Jack and I were touched to receive your kind and concerned letter regarding the stroke which his father, Joe Kennedy, recently suffered. Your sympathy is most welcome and we are grateful.

With warm regards,
Jack and Jackie

Jackie Kennedy
The White House

May 5, 1962

Dear Jackie,

Although I haven't heard from you for the longest time, I am writing to you now because your letters mean so much to me and you are still my closest friend in the world. After the misunderstanding over Gramble Bear, I want to do the right thing and not have anything like that ever come between us again.

Peter has asked me to sing a song to the President at his birthday party on May 19 and I am not sure what to sing, what to wear, or about anything. I am very aware of the honor I shall be getting—singing to the President—and I want to be wonderful, to please Jack and, of course, you.

I so much want to sing a serious song, but I am not an opera singer. Peter says I should sing "I Can't Give You Anything but Love, Baby," but I think that is disrespektful [sic], both to the President and to you. Also, the whole world will be watching me, as the party will be televised, and I want to do the right thing.

My first idea was to rewrite the words of Judy Garland's song "Dear Mr. Gable" and change them to "Dear Mr. President." I got as far as "Dear Mr. President, I am writing this to you, and I hope that you will

216

read it so you'll know. *My heart beats like a hammer and I stutter and I stammer every time I see you on the picture show*"—but I couldn't find the right words to replace "picture show," so I stopped.

My next idea was to sing "Mr. Wonderful," but then I thought it sounded personal, which, of course, my song is not—and I don't want anyone else to think it is either, especially you.

I feel privileged that I, a poor orphan, an ex-factory worker with a crazy mother, will be up there singing to the President of the United States in front of the entire world. Every girl in the universe will be wishing that she was me, and I want to do her, and Jack, and you, justice. I shall be singing to the President on behalf of the people and, if it's the last thing I ever do in my life, I want to do it right.

Please write back as soon as you have a moment, as I really don't know how to handle anything.

Love,
M

P.S. I don't even know what to wear.

Marilyn Monroe
12305 Fifth Helena Drive
Brentwood, California

May 12, 1962

Dear M,

Thank you for your letter regarding your participation in Jack's official birthday celebrations. Before I respond to your flattering request for advice, I wanted to tell you (for you have probably read about it in the newspaper) that Arthur was one of our guests at the dinner we held last night in honor of André Malraux. I was extremely impressed by Arthur, he is everything you said he was when you first wrote to me—an erudite, charming man. He was particularly attentive to me, and I found our exchange hugely stimulating.

I have given your concerns regarding Jack's birthday celebrations a great deal of thought and feel most strongly that they are absolutely unfounded. America loves Marilyn Monroe, and Marilyn Monroe is who you must be. At the risk of alienating you (I hope momentarily), I shall quote Olivier: "Act sexy, Marilyn, act sexy." Your public will expect it of you, and Jack will, no doubt, find it eminently endearing.

So my advice, in essence, is to throw your inhibitions to the wind, enjoy yourself, and BE yourself. Have you thought of contacting Marlene Dietrich's designer, Jean-Louis, to create a gown for you? Jack always says that her dresses give the impression she is wearing little else than flesh plus diamonds, and (remembering "Diamonds Are a Girl's

Best Friend" and "Falling in Love Again," the song played by the music box you sent Jack and me as a wedding present) I think that kind of gown would be most appropriate for you.

As for the song, I think you should consider singing "Happy Birthday," but making the song entirely your own—through your inimical delivery. Taking a leaf from your "Dear Mr. Gable," idea, you could address the song to "Dear Mr. President." I think Jack would like that.

I can't wait for May 19 to see the effect your performance will have on him. Not to mention Miss Judy Campbell, who (as you so rightly observed) will probably be "pea green with envy." Which reminds me, do you think Mr. G will resent your serenading Jack so publicly? I suspect not, as I am sure you have told him that your friendship with Jack is above reproach, and how close you and I are, as well. That way, I am sure he will understand that you would never betray our friendship.

Please know, Marilyn, that I shall be applauding more loudly than anyone, and can't wait to witness your show-stopping performance.

Love,

J

Jackie wrote in the Purple Diary, "I can no longer hide from the truth. And while I still care about her, there is no choice. I shall do what has to be done. Will I ever forgive her? Probably not. Although, in the end, it is probably just a case of the scorpion and the frog, as in the Aesop fable. It's just her nature. Just as it is his. Of course, I forgive him less. After all, he owes me. Not that he will ever admit it. Or act accordingly. Sometimes, at times like this in particular, I don't know how to go on or how to bear it anymore."

MARILYN MONROE
12305 Fifth Helena Drive
Brentwood, California

Jackie Kennedy
The White House

May 14, 1962

Dear J,

Thank you so much for your lovely letter and great advice. Knowing that you will be watching and applauding will make it so much easier for me to sing to the President in front of so many millions of people. I was so nervous, but now that you have told me how to handle everything and are rooting for me, I think I will be fine. More than fine, I hope. I want to be wonderful.

I've already arranged a fitting with Jean-Louis, telling him I want flesh with diamonds. Thank you for a wonderful idea. Like I said before, I really want JC to be pea green with envy. Mr. G, though, won't mind, because by now he knows how much I love him and that I would never ever be interested in any other man.

I want to be wonderful for all the people, for the President, and for you. Now that you've told me to "act sexy" — and I don't mind you quoting Sir Olivier, because I know you mean the best for me — I will feel right being that way in front of the President of the United States. And if anyone asks me why I was so sexy, I can say, "Because the First Lady told me to be!"

Thank you again for being so very kind to me and helping me to do the right thing for the President and for the country.

See you on May 19!

Love,
M

Marilyn Monroe
Madison Square Garden

Jackie Kennedy
The White House

May 19, 1962

Dear Jackie,

I've just got off the stage and I can't believe you weren't in the audience, with Jack.

I did everything you said, was everything you said, but you weren't there to see me. Peter said you were away riding, but I don't believe him.* I don't know what to believe. Now he is banging on the door, ready to take me to the party, but I don't want to go. I just want to know the truth.

M

---

* Jackie was, indeed, spending the day of the birthday party riding. She and Caroline attended the Loudon County Horse Show in Glen Ora, Virginia.

Marilyn sang "Happy Birthday" before 17,000 Democrats and a huge assortment of stars who had gathered to fund JFK's upcoming presidential campaign. Marilyn also paid the $1,000 admission price. The evening's entertainment included Ella Fitzgerald, Peggy Lee, Henry Fonda, Maria Callas, Harry Belafonte, and Jack Benny.

Marilyn was sheathed in a sheer flesh-colored gown shimmering with hand-sewn rhinestones, designed by Jean-Louis. Marilyn worked very closely with the designer, whose brief was to "make this a dress that only Marilyn Monroe would dare to wear." The $12,000 dress did precisely that. When the spotlights hit Marilyn, the silk became almost transparent and she looked as though she were glistening and nude.

Marilyn sang the first verse of "Happy Birthday" and then waved her arms to encourage the audience to sing along for a reprise as a six-foot cake with forty-five oversize candles was carried onstage by two chefs.

MARILYN MONROE
12305 Fifth Helena Drive
Brentwood, California

Jackie Kennedy
The White House

May 20, 1962

Dear Jackie,

The President hated every single second of my performance, I just know it. In public, he thanked me for singing in "such a sweet and wholesome way," but I know I wasn't sweet or wholesome. You told me not to be. The President was just acting. He was acting at the party afterwards, when he thanked me, acting, acting, acting. Acting all the time, nothing but acting. Acting and lies. Lies and acting. Only I'm the actress and he's the President. A cat may look at a king and an actress can sing to a President. Especially if the President's wife says so.

The President was acting onstage, acting at the party, acting all the time. He didn't think I was wonderful. He said I was sweet and wholesome, but I wasn't. He said that to make a fool out of me. He didn't think I was sweet and wholesome, he thought I was a tramp, a nothing. Perhaps I was. Perhaps I am.

Dorothy Kilgallen wrote that "it seemed like Marilyn Monroe was making love to the President in direct view of 40 million Americans." That isn't true. Marilyn Monroe doesn't need to make love to the President in direct view of 40 million Americans, or any other way, for that matter. I wasn't making love to him. I was doing what you told me to. I was singing the way you said, the way you wanted. I was singing to him for the people.

I called Jack this morning to explain that none of it was my idea, none of it was me, but he wouldn't take my call. I just don't understand.

m

Marilyn Monroe
12305 Fifth Helena Drive
Brentwood, California

May 23, 1962

Dear Marilyn,

I am sorry you were so traumatized by Jack's reaction to your appearance at his birthday party. I think he was just unprepared for the sexually charged nature of your performance, but afterwards probably realized that your performance was motivated by your open-hearted desire to please him and that you did it out of love and that your intentions were both honorable and patriotic.

It goes without saying that I am sorry that I unwittingly led you astray. My advice to you was based on what I believed to be my knowledge of Jack, his tastes, and what I thought would entertain him on his birthday. I now realize my mistake and hope you will accept my profound apologies.

You and I share so many very happy years of corresponding together and life is far too short—as they rightly say. So let's just put the birthday party behind us and continue our warm and happy friendship.

Love, as ever,
Jackie

MARILYN MONROE
12305 Fifth Helena Drive
Brentwood, California

Jackie Kennedy
The White House

May 26, 1962

Dear Jackie,

Your letter made me so happy. Very little does right now, so I am glad. I am having a rough time with <u>Something's Got to Give</u>. Some of it isn't that terrible, though. Today I did a nude scene, and didn't look bad for thirty six either. Also had to do a scene with a Swedish accent, and imitated our friend Greta!

But back to the birthday party—lots of people have been very kind and friendly to me about my song—but I still feel kind of strange that the President hasn't said anything nice to me about it. It would be lovely if you could ask him to call me, just for a second, so he could tell me what he really thought, now that he has had the time to think about it. Perhaps if you are there when he calls, we can talk afterwards.

I guess another thing you could do, if you want, is to tell him that you advised me to act so sexy onstage. But if you did, you would have to tell him all about our letters, then maybe he would want to read them, and I don't remember everything I wrote, so perhaps that isn't a good idea.

But when he calls me, everything will work out anyway.

Love,
Marilyn

WESTERN UNION TELEGRAM

MARILYN MONROE
12305 Fifth Helena Drive
Brentwood, California

Jackie Kennedy
The White House

May 29, 1962

Dear Jackie,

He still didn't call. You must have told him to call, but he hasn't. Will he ever forgive me? Please try and explain to him that I did what I did because you told me to. Please don't let him put me in prison for a crime I didn't commit. Please tell him that I love and honor my President and my country more than ever.

Love,
Marilyn

MARILYN MONROE
12305 Fifth Helena Drive
Brentwood, California

Jackie Kennedy
The White House

May 31, 1962

Dear Jackie,
   Please call the moment you get my letter, and get Jack to as well. I must know that things are OK between us all or I'll go crazy. I love you both.

Marilyn

WESTERN UNION TELEGRAM

MARILYN MONROE
12305 Fifth Helena Drive
Brentwood, California

Jackie Kennedy
The White House

June 1, 1962

Jackie,
I can't take it anymore. Make Jack call me, please.

WESTERN UNION TELEGRAM

MARILYN MONROE
12305 Fifth Helena Drive
Brentwood, California

Jackie Kennedy
The White House

June 2, 1962

To Jacqueline Kennedy, The White House

Dear Mrs. President,

I am writing this to you and I hope that you will read it so you know. My heart is broken with a hammer, I stutter and I stammer every time I think of Mr. G, you know. Over, over, over, help me, Jackie, help me, I'm going crazy, purple is still crazy, and blue, very blue, blue eyes, the bluest in the world, teeth white, starlight, starbright, dark night, night, twinkle twinkle twinkle, Mr. Wonderful, Mr. G, H, I, J, K, over, over, over, letters are a girl's best friend, help, help, help, please, help

WESTERN UNION TELEGRAM

MARILYN MONROE
12305 Fifth Helena Drive
Brentwood, California

June 3, 1962

Dear Jackie,
Thank you for sending me a good angel. Thank you for saving my life.

Love, forever,
Marilyn

June 7, 1962

Dear Marilyn,

I was delighted to learn from your last cable that you are feeling better.

I am sorry not to be able to write to you at great length this time, but am presently preparing for the summer vacation (am leaving for Europe on August 7 with Lee, and am taking a series of small trips before then).

Do take care of yourself and write to me once *Something's Got to Give* is completed and you have time.

Love, as always,
Jackie

Jackie wrote in her diary, "Have decided to distance myself from MM for a while. Not because of Jack—because I am convinced that is over. I put paid to it, and I'm not sorry I did. However, strangely enough, I still care about her and wish her well. I just need time before I forgive and, maybe, forget. After all, knowing Jack, she is probably merely one of hundreds. Sometimes I could just strangle him."

MARILYN MONROE
12305 Fifth Helena Drive
Brentwood
California

Jackie Kennedy
1095 North Ocean Boulevard
Palm Beach, Florida

July 9, 1962

Dear Jackie,

I know you said you were getting ready for Europe and traveling, but when I phoned the compound, they said you would be back by now and I need to write you so badly.

My whole life has changed and I owe it all to you. I am happier than I have ever been, ever. Except for just one thing—knowing in my heart that I have not been honest with you, the kindest, best person I have ever known. Whenever I remember what I have done, everything is spoiled, feels dirty, and I don't want to feel that way anymore. I want to be happy without any more shadows or any more guilt.

They say confession is good for the soul. Well, sometimes I wonder whether I even have one. I know I am an actress—and acting is telling lies, lies someone else writes for you that you are passing on—but I hate lying when I am not acting. I owe you the whole truth at last, because although I lost Mr. G, because of you, I found Mr. X and I am in heaven!

The only reason I can write this letter—apart from the reason I said—is that my whole world has changed. It is as if there has been an earthquake in my heart. Mr. G has finally been eklipsed [sic] by another man—Mr. X. X as in exciting, exhillerating [sic], exceptional, sexy, and extra special. I can't promise never to see Mr. G again, but I don't think I will ever see him again in the way in which I have always seen him.

All through the years, you never asked who Mr. G was. Nor did you try to find out. Many times, when you were kind and caring toward me, I longed to tell you the truth. But I knew that if I did, he'd kill me. But now I don't care anymore about him. I just care about you, and not feeling guilty or dirty ever again in my life.

There is no easy way to say this. Or any easy time. I am telling you now, I think, because I believe that once you know how much in love I am with Mr. X, you will realize that you are safe. Safe from me. Safe because Mr. G's real name is Jack Kennedy and I don't love him anymore. Please don't stop reading. In some ways, I hope that you suspected all along. You might have, which is probably why you suggested I sing "Happy Birthday" the way I sang it. You probably knew Jack would hate it. You must have guessed that he would despise me for it. But I didn't. I had no idea. You see, I know the private Jack real well, but the public Jack is completely aliun [sic] to me.

Maybe, if I tell you how Jack and I ever happened—and remember, I promise from the very bottom of my heart that it won't ever happen again—it won't seem quite so bad, and then—so long as you forgive me—we can go on and still be friends like before.

This, as they say in the movies, is how the story began. I read somewhere that a man called Charles Bartlett first introduced you to Jack. Life is so strange. A man called Charles also first introduced me to Jack as well. My Charles was Charles Feldman, the agent whom we all had dinner with in 1954. Long before that, though, I had already met Jack at Charlie's. I met him there in 1951, on May 15.

I nearly fainted when I read that you first met Jack just twelve days before I did, on May 3, 1951.

I read that that first night, you played charades with Jack and beat him—he would have been impressed, but deep down, somewhere, probably didn't really like it. But you were a debutante, a prizewinner—*Vogue*'s *Prix de Paris*, I think—and rich and beautiful, so I suppose Jack decided to take it, and you.

I once read a Victorian novel where the author said something like that the good luck and the bad luck of life all depend on who you meet when. I agree with that. But I want to add something. It also depends on who you meet *where* and how. Because, looking back, if I had met Jack in another place, he might have thought of me differently and then things might have turned out differently as well.

In those days—1951—I was hanging around Charlie Feldman's house. Charlie handled some big stars—in every which way . . . including Gene Teirney [sic]. Johnny Hyde used to take me to Charlie's with him and because I was Johnny's girl, Charlie treated me with respekt [sic]. I liked that.

But once Johnny died, Charlie was all over me like paper over a fly. I suppose I should have married Johnny—he asked me—but I didn't love him. Everyone told me I was being real dumb—because I would have been a very rich widow. But I didn't care. Still don't. To me, money is like the tide, it comes in and then it goes out. You have it, and then you don't. Then you do again.

That night at Charlie's, the night I met Jack, I was feeling scared and alone. My husband, Jim, and I were over, I'd had a fling with Elia Kazan—most of the time, all he could do was talk about Arthur Miller. Isn't life funny, that I ended up marrying Arthur. . . .

I knew Charlie was going to make his move on me that night. I suppose you could say that in those days, I was easy. But that wouldn't be right. I wasn't easy. It's just that sex was easy—for me, that is. But I still didn't

237

really want to go to bed with Charlie. Sure, he was powerful and clever, but there was a coldness to him. I couldn't imagine ever being able to love Charlie.

But I took one look at Jack and couldn't imagine ever being able to love anyone else. Now, of course, I do—Mr. X. But looking back on how it all began with me and Jack, I see Jack as he was that first night. Even now, though, I still wish I hadn't met him there, at Charlie's, because I know he still sees me as I was then. No matter how famous I am, no matter how many men desire me, marry me, love me, no matter how many awards I win, how many acting lessons I take, to Jack, I will always be that easy little 24-year-old starlet whom he met that night at Charlie's. Which is what that Victorian novelist I mentioned before meant. The bad luck of who you meet when. Or rather, _who_ you are when you meet them.

My first impression of Jack was that he was very young and very thin. Just a boy, really. That night, he had a bag of fudge in his pocket, which he kept popping into his mouth. A long time later, he told me that he always gorged himself on fudge when he was bored. After that first night, he never ate fudge around me again.

The thing I most remember about Jack from that very first time is his eyes. When Jack focused those eyes on you, you really felt it. He had a special way of staring at you—his secret trick. Years later, he explained it to me—but I still can't get it right—first he stared at your left eye, then your right. Each eye at a time, never together.

The first time he looked at me, I felt like he was raping me with his eyes. Not the kind of rape that hurts you. The other kind. When he looked at me like that—that very first night—I blushed from head to foot. A red flush. All over my body.

We had sex that same evening, at a bungalow he rented for us at the Beverly Hills Hotel. I am sure you don't want to know any of the details. But Jack had magic on me. That night and always. Since then no one else—not Joe, and not even Frank—ever had that kind of magic on me. Only Jack—and now Mr. X.

Jack was just a Congressman then. I didn't know much about what he did. Just that he was a cute guy who set me on fire and that when I woke up in his arms, I felt safer, more special than I ever had before. I've had so many men, stronger, sexier, taller, and bigger than Jack. But no one ever reached into my heart, body, and soul like he did. Until Mr. X, that is.

Jack made me want to be good for him, to be special for him. He made me want to improve myself. So that summer, because of Jack—and because I wanted to—I took an art history class at UCLA. I also did a lot of reading: the classics, Freud. I was hoping Freud could give me a clue to solving the mystery of Jack's magic over me, and break the spell, but there was nothing he wrote that explained it. If I had had a father, then Freud might have said that Jack had magic on me because he reminded me of him. But I didn't. So Jack couldn't. Nor was he the father whom I dreamed of having. Gable was that. If anything, Jack reminded me of myself.

In March 1952, when the calendar came out with me photographed in the nude on red velvet, I was petrified that he would despise me for it. But he didn't. He just laughed and asked me to send him some copies. Then he said, "Don't deny you did it. Tell them how you're an orphan, that you were broke. Be Cinderella. Everyone loves Cinderella, Marilyn. Cinderella sells." I remembered that. I remember everything Jack ever said to me, because when I am with him I am like a great big sponge. So when the press asked me why I'd posed for the calendar, I used Jack's concept. I gave them a Cinderella story, just like Jack said, and it worked.

The day after the calendar came out, I met Joe. I really went out with Joe only as a stunt, to kill any negative publicity that might have arisen from the calendar. More than that, I hoped that by dating someone as famous as Joe, I might make Jack forget how he first saw me and even make him jealous. It did a bit, but not enough to make him want to marry me. By that time, I knew that the higher Jack climbed in politics, the less chance there would be of him marrying a mere actress. I did think, though, that if I could one day do some theater, which, of course, I eventually did, I might make a suitable wife for Jack. I did want to marry him, but he didn't want to marry me, so I married Joe instead, for want of being able to marry Jack. A rebound marriage. I tried to be happy with Joe, to be a good wife to him, but he wasn't Jack. He didn't talk about politics or books or ideas. He just watched TV and played ball.

When I read about you and Jack getting engaged, I felt as if I could die. He didn't even warn me. I bought every newspaper and magazine featuring articles about you. I wanted to know all about you and what he saw in you. Seeing your picture made me want to die. I think I would have killed myself, only my career was on such a high. Just two days after the engagement announcement, Jane Russell and I did our footprints in the cement at Grauman's, and Gentlemen Prefer Blondes was released three weeks afterwards. The studio loved me in it, I was doing great, but not in the way I wanted. I wanted Jack.

He called and invited me to your wedding. He said he wanted me to come because his father had invited Marion Daveis [sic], and he wanted to win points over him by inviting me, because I was an even bigger star than she ever was. Typical of Jack, so set on competing with his father that he forgot all about me and how I would feel, standing there at your wedding, watching him promise to be faithful and to love you forever. It would have been hell for me. When the invitation arrived, I was surprised to see that it came from Jack's father's office, and not from Jack's. Then Jack explained that, at the last minute, he was afraid you might suspect something, so he made his father invite me instead. He said that he thought the invitation might have the dual effect of making you think I was his father's mistress as well. At first, that hurt me, nearly as much as the fact that he was getting married, because I felt as if he was throwing me away. Then I thought about it more and realized that it was a compliment, apart from which it showed that Jack still wanted to carry on with me, even though he was marrying you. Otherwise, he wouldn't have cared so much what you thought. Anyway, even though I pretended to be mad at him for insinuating that about his father and me, inside, I wouldn't have cared if Jack said I was fucking King Kong, just as long as he still wanted me.

Jack had some nerve, though. He told me he really wanted me to come to the wedding, but for once, I told him exactly what I thought of him. No way. Of course, I turned the invitation down. Now and again, though, I fantasised [sic] about coming to the wedding and when they asked if there was anyone present who knew any reason why the marriage shouldn't take place, shouting out, "Yes, me! I love him and he loves me." But of course I didn't do that.

Instead, I sent you that wedding present. Part of me, the good part, the part that I want to be me—all of me—really did want to wish you and Jack luck. But another part of me—the dark part—the person within me that scares and terrifies me, wanted to put a curse on your marriage to Jack. Like the bad witch in <u>Sleeping Beauty</u>.

So I sent you the music box that played "Falling in Love Again" instead. Jack always said I should do a remake of <u>Blue Angel</u>—and I thought he might hear the music and think of me. I held the music box before I sent it to you. Rubbed my hands all over it. Half imagining that I was rubbing Jack's body. Half hoping that he would feel my hands, smell my scent, when he touched it. I used to picture it in your house, in the living room in Georgetown, the tune playing, reminding Jack of me.

So I wrote to you, Jackie, and you wrote back. At the beginning, getting your letters was almost like getting a piece of Jack. But I didn't keep writing to you because of Jack. Maybe at first, but then I grew to love your letters, Jackie, looked forward to them, used to lie awake at night anticipating what you would write to me and what I would write back.

When I was on the set, or out on a date, I would think, "I must tell Jackie that."

The good part of me did all that. The bad part kept writing to you about other men, hoping you would tell Jack, get him hot and jealous. That part of me thought of you as my secret weapon in my battle to get to Jack. To get Jack. What to do with him if I ever got him, I didn't quite know. I just always felt as if there was a hand pushing me, more and more, faster and faster, toward him.

So the bad part of me kept writing to you, Jackie, sending messages to Jack through you, staying close to the scene of the crime like a murderer stays close to his victim. The bad part of me wanted to come to the White House when you sent me formal invitations to events there. The good part knew I shouldn't. The good part knew that it would have been wrong to look into your eyes while all the time, deep inside, I was lusting after Jack and still seeing him secretly. The good side won and I never came to the White House.

Not when you were there, Jackie. But once, late one night—you were in Paris—Jack smuggled me in.* I wore a black wig and when I saw myself in the mirror, I looked like you. That felt strange, and wrong.

I never wanted you to know the truth. Never. But when I was sick in the hospital and under the influence of drugs, the painkillers they gave me, plus the ones I brought with me and they didn't know about, I wrote to you about Mr. G. The next day, I wished I hadn't, and tried to get you not to read the letter, but it was too late. In a way, I suppose I secretly really did want you to know about Mr. G and was confessing—and you are the one who is Catholic—to you. Dr. Greenson says that in my unconscious, by telling you all about Mr. G in my letters, I was having a ménage à trois with you and Jack, and that it was you—not Jack—whom I really desired!

---

*"Jack had Marilyn Monroe up at the White House absolutely," Senator George Smathers said (see Heymann). "I know because I saw Marilyn at the White House. She was there."

But I don't want to think about that. Sometimes I think that analysis can damage your soul—and your heart as well. The heart shouldn't be torn apart in analysis. The heart should just be allowed to beat with love.

I never wished you harm, Jackie. I just wanted to be you. I wanted to be in Jack's bed instead of you. But I never really worked out how I would get there. I just let life and him—his arrangements for me—sweep me along. Sometimes, though, Jack and I were so happy together that I used to wish for a magic wand and that you would be happy with someone else, so that I could be happy with him and he could be happy with me. He comes from another world from me, but there are things—were things—between us that only God or fate or mystery can explain.

Now, though, it is over. I have finally found the true love of my life, the only love, the last love. I don't want to tell you about him in this letter. There is too much to tell.

Just write and say that you forgive me. More than anything, I want to stay your friend. I know I sound a little confused—the Nembutal, which I take because I'm having real trouble sleeping, is kicking in—but I am very clear about wanting to be your friend forever.

Please don't give up on me. Write and tell me I still mean something to you.

Love,
Marilyn

P.S. I think my telephone is being tapped.

———————

According to Patty Renoir, Marilyn was in a pensive mood when she asked her to mail this letter to Jackie. "She was quiet at first, but I saw something in her eyes that I knew meant she was all drugged up. Suddenly, she grabbed my hand and said, 'Hug me, Patty, hug me.' I did, then she pulled away and said, 'Patty, I've taken a gamble, a really big one. Just couldn't help myself. A fucking big one.' Then she starts laughing, a high, tinkling laugh, like the sound of glass breaking. 'Put all my cards on the table, every single fucking one of them. So wish me luck, Patty.' I said I did, although I didn't know what the hell she meant."

Marilyn Monroe
12305 Fifth Helena Drive
Brentwood, California

July 12, 1962

Dear Marilyn,

DON'T BE ALARMED—THIS IS A FRIENDLY LETTER!

I am grateful for your honesty in telling me the truth about you and Jack at last. In a strange way, it has come as an intense relief to me. Now, at last, I am no longer tortured by suspicions. For (as far as I am concerned) knowing is preferable to not knowing. Now that I hold all the cards, I can react accordingly.

On reflection, dear Marilyn, I bear you no animosity, for no woman alive is more aware than I regarding the potent nature of Jack's special magic and the spell his presence weaves. Only a corpse could resist the full force of Jack's charm, his seductive cleverness, his charisma.

Perhaps I always knew about you and Jack, but I was never sure. Maybe I didn't want to confront the truth, until you made that flimsy excuse about Gramble Bear. On a subconscious level (as your Dr. Greenson would say) I suppose I was hurt by you and angry with you and deeply threatened by the thought that you and Jack could be lovers. Consequently, and to my everlasting shame (for I blame Jack for seducing you, not vice versa), I set you up to sing "Happy Birthday" in such an overt manner. In retrospect, I think I did so not merely in order to damage Jack's feelings for you but also to punish you for having lied to me. That emotion was unworthy of me, and I am sorry. You always were, and remain, very dear to me, Marilyn.

As soon as I received your last letter, I wanted to telephone you, but as you told me of your fears that the phone was tapped, I restrained myself. "Restrained" reminds me of Jack, of how it all went wrong between us, and why—despite your misgivings—I truly can cope (employing a certain amount of equanimity) with all that you have told me.

I shall explain the "restrained" reference later. First of all, I want to tell you that you have lost nothing through your letter. Least of all, our friendship. Quite the reverse, because now I, too, can tell you the truth.

When you first wrote to us, after my wedding to Jack, I was surprised. I suppose I had my suspicions, but I tried to block them out (one of my more useful talents is my capacity for blocking out unpleasantness). But had I known conclusively that you and Jack were lovers, I would probably have been almost fascinated. Nearly glad. To understand my meaning, you would have to comprehend my entire state of mind upon marrying Jack.

When I met him, I was fully aware of his playboy past— and present. I knew that he was an inveterate womanizer, just like every other Kennedy male. I was aware that if I married him, he would probably cheat on me. Although I have to confess that a part of me was vain enough to think I might be able to prevent him from doing so. On another level, I wanted to prove that I could handle my cheating husband far better than my mother had handled my cheating father.

I wanted to prove that I was superior to her. To prove that she had been wrong in not accepting my father's infidelity. I thought that if she had just turned the other cheek, or pretended not to notice, they might have lived a long and fruitful life together. All in all, that was my challenge—to prove her wrong, to rewrite history, and I used Jack to do it.

From the moment we married, I goaded him into cheating on me.

I told him the story of how my father cheated on my mother during their honeymoon. Then, when we were on our honeymoon, I joked to Jack that I was waiting for him to cheat on me, just like my father did on my mother. I kept on teasing him that way. Till he did. He cheated on me during our honeymoon. I felt such a sense of triumph and control. First, because I had engineered the whole thing. Second, that I was ready for him. I had been prepared for his infidelity. Then I ignored it, even joked about it. In short, by cheating on me, Jack played right into my hands.

I think he was slightly unnerved by the nonchalant way in which I virtually ignored his infidelity. In the end, I think my attitude probably caused him to feel unloved. More than likely, he would probably have relished me making jealous scenes. Maybe even a catfight (I have always believed that men love pitting women against one another. Divide and conquer . . .).

For a long time, I got a thrill every time I thought Jack was cheating on me. I didn't blame myself, nor did I blame him. In some ways, I virtually guaranteed that he would cheat on me. Ever since my childhood, I have had a propensity for mocking other people. Either behind their backs or—whenever possible—in front of them. When it came to Jack, I indulged that propensity. He hated it when I did things like mimic his Boston accent, the way he says "foah moah yeahs." Once, when he was being photographed by an important publication, I sneaked up behind him and threw a wreath over his head, so he looked like a prize pony. He was livid.

I suppose I was making a mistake when I treated him that way, but I just couldn't help it. It's my nature. Jack would never admit it to me, but I think he must loathe it when I diminish him (especially in front of other people). Because no matter how spoiled and feted and powerful Jack is, inside he remains that small, frail, lonely little boy whose mother kept sailing away to Europe and leaving him and whose father constantly pushed him to emulate his dead brother. I think I reminded him of all of that when I made fun of him. In retrospect, I think that drove him to other women—women like you, who would never dream of trying to diminish him.

Part of Jack's and my problem, however, is not exclusively my fault. During a rare attempt to play the wise mama, my mother once said, "Bad sex ruins a marriage. Good sex doesn't make one." Which, I suppose, is what you once wrote me regarding your marriage to Joe—that if sex were all, you would have been blissfully happy.

It all started to go wrong on our wedding night at the Waldorf when Jack indicated that I should perform a certain sex act on him. I attempted to, but was less than enthusiastic in my execution. The very thought of that act demeans me in all sorts of ways. Apart from the fact that (and it is far too late in our relationship for me to be coy with you), quite simply, I cannot conceive of the manner in which one is supposed to do it.

That first year, Jack and I did have intercourse, which I began to almost enjoy. But even that went awry. We were in Manhattan, staying at the Westbury. My father went to live there after he divorced my mother, and I used to visit him there. I was happy with Jack, that night at the Westbury, remembering. We went to bed and, for the first time in our marriage, I reached fulfillment. Whereupon Jack slapped my face and said, "You bitch!"

Without a word, I got up and started dressing. I was about to leave when Jack (who finds it congenitally impossible to apologize), for the first time in his life, did. I demanded to know why he had spoken to me in such an insulting manner. I had never seen Jack search for words before, but now he was genuinely unable to articulate. He seemed at a loss regarding his own motives. Finally, he said, "I just hate it when you are unrestrained." I never permitted myself to reach fulfillment with him again.

Funnily enough, when you sent the music box as our wedding present, I was far more disturbed by the song which it played than by the fact that you sent it. "Falling in Love Again," of course, is Marlene Dietrich's theme song. I know that she had made herself available sexually to Joe K and I believed Jack wanted her as well (Kennedy men all pass their women from one to the other as if the women were like a plate of angel cakes). Strangely enough (until Judy), I was always more threatened by the women whom Jack desired than by the women he was having. I know that once he has a woman, she immediately begins to bore him. You, of course, were clearly the exception. But you know that. . . .

So you and I began our correspondence. Then we met (in 1954, with Joe DiMaggio) and I felt relief because you seemed so in love with Joe. I don't know, even today, whether or not you were acting. Because you really are a very good actress, Marilyn. But when I saw Joe's jealous rage and the way in which you pandered to him, I knew that the ice was very thin between you and it was only a matter of time before it cracked irrevocably and you would be free again. I was afraid that when you were free, you might crave Jack.

I understand why you always craved him, Marilyn, because even I do, now and again. As I wrote that, I remembered something Simone Signoret said about you in a newspaper last year, that she understood your being in love with Yves because she was. By the way, were you really in love with Yves, or was he just a smokescreen to hide your deep emotions for Jack?

Until last November, when you made that slip about Gramble Bear, I was never really completely sure whether or not you and Jack were lovers. But by mentioning Gramble Bear, you virtually announced to me that you were. You see, only Jack, Caroline, John, and I knew that he told her bedtime stories about a bear called Gramble. I certainly hadn't mentioned Gramble to you, so I suspected Jack had. I just couldn't work out where or when, or why. You concocted that story about asking Jack about bedtime stories when you met him at that fund-raiser in L.A. However, I didn't for one moment believe it. I think far too highly of your intelligence, your passion for politics and civil rights, to believe that you would waste a rare meeting with the President of the United States by prattling about bedtime stories. Not unless you were meeting him privately as well and often. Lately, I have wondered whether you made your Freudian slip because you subconsciously wanted me to know about you and Jack. Did you?

Once I knew the truth about you and Jack, I was devastated. In a way, it was worse, it being you rather than any other of the others. Not just because we were friends, but because I knew that you were not one of Jack's usual floozies. Uncannily enough, you sometimes reminded me of him. The way you thought, your perceptions, your sense of humor, your quickness, and your lust for life.

My suspicions caused me to inveigle you into singing the birthday song in a suggestive way which I knew would alienate Jack forever. You see, I instinctively understood that Jack would end his relationship with you, wouldn't risk it anymore, because in full view of the entire world, you proclaimed your affair with him so blatantly. He knew then that through you he could lose the world. No woman, not even you, could compensate him for that. For he is Jack Kennedy, bred to be President, not the Duke of Windsor, merely born to be King.

Despite that, there were times when I worried that your relationship with Jack would cause our marriage to end. You may ask me why I would have cared. First, because of Jack's place in history—and, of course, my own. For although there is a lot of animosity and bitterness between us, both of us still relish the opportunities the Presidency offers us.

There is also my pride. I have no intention of failing at my marriage like my mother did. Or like Lee, living out her life among tawdry Europeans, traveling from fashionable resort to fashionable resort, following the social season like dirty water swilling around in an enclosed basin.

Then, of course, there are the children. The ones we lost and the ones we have. Caroline is a sensitive, loving little girl, sometimes wounded by all the public attention, other times unaffected and happy. I would hate her to be the victim of divorce, as I was. Or to grow up infused with an abiding father hunger, as I was (and still am). As for John—he is only a baby, but already his tiny face lights up at the sound of his father's voice. I would not wish to be responsible for depriving him of that joy.

All of which is another way of saying, Marilyn, that I am delighted that you have fallen in love with Mr. X and out of love, at last, with Jack. If you hadn't—I would have survived (I am inordinately stoic), but I am glad things are ending this way. Write and tell me about your mysterious Mr. X. I can't wait!

Now that we have both come clean, as they say in the movies, on another front, there is something else. Tell me, if you will, what, if anything, Jack ever said to you about me. Did you ever tell him we are secret pen pals? Did you show him my letters? If that is the case, what did he say? I am also curious where, when, and how you and Jack ever managed to conduct your trysts.

There is also something else which I should like to know. I am not altogether sure how to phrase this request. . . . Just to say that it would amuse me greatly to learn exactly what Jack was like with you. In a sexual sense. Tell me everything. If I blush, then so be it.

Love,

J

"Jackie was not threatened," Clare Booth Luce said. "Not even by Marilyn Monroe. But if somehow word had gotten out, it would have upset her terribly. She could not bear the thought of being publicly humiliated" (see Bradford).

MARILYN MONROE
12305 Fifth Helena Drive
Brentwood, California

Jackie Kennedy
The White House

July 22, 1962

Dear Jackie,

My phone probably isn't tapped after all, but I am glad that I thought it was and told you. This way, I can read your letter over and over again. If it had been a telephone call, I couldn't have.

Thank you for not making me feel bad for telling you. I never wanted you to know about Jack and me while it was still going on. I didn't make that Freudian slip on purpose. It was an accident. I never wanted to hurt you or Caroline or John. I am not saying that I was pure—hardly . . . because I also was afraid that if you knew the truth, Jack would find out you did and stop seeing me. Or you would tell him to. Either way.

To answer your questions: I never once showed your letters to Jack, and I never would have. But sometimes I used to fantasise [sic] that you knew about Jack and me, that you didn't mind, that you were giving us your blessing. Other times I was afraid that you knew and that Jack knew you knew and that you talked about me together and laughed at me. I couldn't have borne that. I know that wasn't true, was it?

How, where, and when did Jack and I manage to meet? Some nights, when I can't sleep, I count all the hotel suites where Jack and I had what he used to call our "interludes." That sounds romantic, doesn't it? But it didn't always feel that way. Sometimes it was short and cold, with me being smuggled up to the suite in a service elevator, like a hamburger, then bundled out afterwards, like dirty laundry. There was also the guilt, particularly that time when you lost the baby. I was in London with Sir Olivier, Jack called, asked me to fly to Paris to meet him, and I did. That weekend, you lost the baby. Jack didn't even know. He was too busy having fun with me. When you wrote and told me, I knew God would punish me one day for my wickedness.

Other times, though, it was glamorous—like in Chicago when Jack was there campaigning. We met in his suite at the Ambassador, he was elated with success and already had the smell of power all over him. I liked that smell, I liked his power. I also liked him powerless as well. In the hospital, when he was close to death and just lay there, looking at me, helpless. So helpless that it was easy for me to make him happy. I loved making Jack happy. I lived to make him happy because when he was happy, so was I.

I think I should also tell you another secret—or how else are you ever going to trust in me again and tell me things the way you used to? Now and again—not too often, probably about ten times through all the years—I wrote to you and put something in that I hoped would make him jealous. Part of me was always hoping that you would show Jack the letter so that he would call me. Did you ever do that? If you did, I would have been glad. Other times, when I missed him desperately but hadn't heard from him, I thought he might want to see me if he found out from you that I was blue. On the other hand, I would rather he only ever saw me because he wanted to, not because I was blue and he felt sorry for me. On second thought, I am sure he never did. Men only ever like happy girls.

I meant to say that I feel sad that you put up with Jack's cheating because of wanting to best your mother. It seems more self-destructive than I ever expected you to be. But nobody, not even you, can always stop themselves from stabbing themselves in the heart.

You say you got a thrill sometimes about Jack cheating. Did you ever ask him about other women in bed? I don't know how you would have liked it if he did tell you about other women in bed. I've had plenty of men who think that hearing about other women in bed will arouse me. I like to hear about other women's sexual tricks—in case I can learn anything—but I don't want to hear how much the man I'm with cared about them, or how beautiful they were. The only aspect that sometimes titillates me is if, before I go to bed with a man, he tells me about a sex fantasy he acted out with another woman. That way, the woman doesn't seem real, but I get to hear about the fantasy.

I don't know whether you really hurt Jack by making fun of him. There is a side of him that needs a woman who diminishes him. Not me, of course. He doesn't see me that way. I think it is sad, though, that he put you down when you had an orgasm. I discussed the situation with Dr. Greenson—disguising you and calling you "Geraldine," saying you lived in Wisconsin and were a friend of mine needing help—and he said, "The man in question has a Madonna/whore complex. To him, Geraldine, his wife, is the Madonna. She is pure and innocent, elevated on a pedestel [sic], rather like a superior mother figure. But if she exhibits an enjoyment of sex, she topples from that pedestel [sic] and becomes a woman. Just like his mother."

Dr. Greenson says that the man in question probably had incestuous fantasies about his mother and that he can't enjoy sex with a woman whom he equates with his mother. He can only have sex with a woman who is diametrically opposed to his mother. That way, he doesn't feel like he is having sex with her (his mother). "So I am just the whore?" I asked Dr. Greenson, forgetting this wasn't supposed to be about me. "No, Marilyn," he said, "you are not a whore. Men know you are not. It just arouses them to *fantasise [sic] like that.*" I didn't buy it, but I hope it explains something about Jack to you.

He talks about you a lot. Sometimes I think it is just to stop himself from getting swept away. To remind himself that he is married. Or because he feels that by talking about you, he is somehow including you in us and that way, he won't feel too guilty. I don't know if he does feel guilty, though. I know he pretends to. I'd like to think that he felt guilty about seeing me but just couldn't help himself. But I don't think that is the truth.

When he talks about you, he always refers to you as "my wife." Never as Jackie or Jacqueline. In one way, calling you "my wife" is a way of making sure I never forget he is married—why would I? In another, it is a way of putting you up on that pedestel [sic] again, so you aren't sexy and he doesn't have to feel like he's fucking his mother.

I think you could break him of all that if one day, when you were alone with him, you did something really wild or outrageous. Like Jean Arthur did in A Foreign Affair. I remember you said you'd seen it, when she gets—I can't remember the name of the actor—I'll ask Billy Wilder if ever I talk to him again—drunk and lures him back from Marlene. There goes that name again! Sorry. Perhaps she pops into my mind because Marlene and Marilyn are very close. In name only.

I've left your last, most difficult question to the end. What is Jack like in bed with me? I don't know if he is any different with me than he is with you. Except that I suppose I do fellatio—I call it "head"—and that pleases him, so maybe he tries a little harder, in return, to please me. In any case, I am not difficult to please.

Jack is brilliant at getting me hot. He doesn't do it with presents or compliments. Mostly by talking about sex, which excites me, telling me beforehand what he wants to do to me, and what he wants me to do to him—although I know that already.

No matter how many women a man goes to bed with, he usually wants the same thing from every woman, has the same desires, the same triggers, the same needs, with all of them. In fact, I sometimes think it would be easier for us if men carried printed instructions around with them (a do-it-yourself kit) so you know how to assemble them. Or, rather, get them hot and then satisfy them.

Jack adores getting head. Of course, he is useless at giving it, but I don't really care. Every man loves getting head. Only Joe wasn't wild about it—although he was very proud of his prick—it was enormous, but not as big as Frank's—Frank is really genetically gifted. Sometimes, though, I would rather look at Frank than have him inside of me. Looking at a really big prick is very appealing. Having it inside of you can sometimes be painful.

I suppose I have given head to more men than I care to remember. The first time I did it, I was eight years old. The man—and I never knew his name—said, "Suck it like a lollipop." I said, "But I don't suck lollipops. I bite them." But he wasn't afraid. Sometimes I am amazed that men aren't. If I had a prick—and I often wish I did—they are so powerful, so beautiful, so useful—I'd think twice about putting it in just anyone's mouth. I'd be afraid of being bitten.

Anyway, when I married Joe, I didn't do it to him much. He was very athletic and into performing, which was nice, only sometimes I got bored with all the positions. I felt like I was in the circus. Like a performing pretzel.

Older men want it more. Johnny Hyde begged me to do it. Even went down on his knees! Funny, that, because generally it's me who goes down on her knees. I don't mind being in that position.

Some men want you to mind giving them head, though, because for them it is a kick to think they are forcing you to do it. I don't like doing it to a man who has those kinds of thoughts.

I don't think there is anything demeening [sic] about doing it to a man.

Joe Schenk and Harry Cohn made it feel like work, though. They each gave me a fixed appointment every day, then expected me to turn up and do it. If I was one minute late, they would start yelling. I hated that. Perhaps that's why, these days, now that I don't need them anymore—although poor Joe is dead and I couldn't need him anyway, even if I wanted to—I love being as late for appointments as I want.

With Joe and Harry I used to do each of them in eight minutes, max. Sometimes quicker, if I could. With Jack, though, I want to take as long as I can. I sometimes tease Jack that he has brainwashed me into wanting to spend so long giving him head. The power of suggestion, you know, because he once told me about a $1,500-a-night hooker he had—that was before your time, I think. I asked him what she did for all that money. He knew I would ask. He said that she made head last for what seemed like forever, which is why I said afterward that he brainwashed me. But it wasn't that story that made me want to do it to him for ages. The way I feel about Jack did.

You see, I don't feel powerless when I give head. Nor do I feel particularly powerful either. But perhaps it would help you if you looked at doing it as a way of having power over a man. I suppose, when you really think about it, a man is completely defenseless when you do it to him, vulnerable. Especially if he wants it as much as Jack does. So you could look at it in terms of the power it gives you. I know most women think of it as just something you do before having sex, but I don't feel that way. I don't think of it like you think of a cocktail before dinner, but as dinner itself. When I do it, I always let the man know how much I love doing it to him—I don't just give a quick lick and wait for him to do all the rest—I give him head as if it is the only thing in the world I want to do—as if his prick is the only thing in the world I want at that moment. I'm not faking when I do that, either, I really mean it, because I really do want to please the man I'm doing it to.

Mostly when I give head—and most of all with Jack—I feel as if I am giving a man something very special. So when I do it, I somehow feel as if I am getting it done to me as well. I can't really explain it, only that with Jack, I love doing it more than I've ever done it with anyone else. He always goes on about how well I do it, as if I am going through a routine. But that isn't true. I do it to Jack differently than I've ever done it to any other man. Of course, I still breath the same—Constance Collier taught me how to breathe for acting—I just took what she taught and applied it elsewhere. . . . But giving great head isn't technique. Saying that it is is the same thing as saying that if you do finger exercises at the piano, you are playing music. But that isn't true. The exercises become music only when you add passion.

I have such passion when I give Jack head. Part of the reason is that I know how much it means to him. Jack finds it so hard to switch off his mind. He never can, not even in his sleep—I've slept with him and he tosses and talks, and once even walked in his sleep. But when I give him head, I know that he can switch his mind off at last. Being able to do that for him is ecstasy for me. Sure, he does things to me, and I love it—kissing me, touching me, talking dirty to me—but if—before I met Mr. X—someone had told me I would never have sex with Jack again except one last time, I would want to give him head. I hope I haven't made you blush, but I wanted to be truthful.

Now that I have been, I can tell you about Mr. X at last. After I do, I really hope you will wish me luck, plus give me a little advise. You will be able to give me advise, Jackie, because—guess what? You know Mr. X really, really well.

By now, you have probably realized who I mean. You are so clever. But if you haven't yet, when you do, you will be thrilled. First, because you hate his wife. Second, because I know that you are rooting for him to be happy. And I am going to make him happy, for always.

He says he wants to marry me and I know he means it. Up till now, we have only ever met in California—he lives back East. But although I haven't been to his home yet—or met his children, he has shown me photos of them all—I am ahead of the game because I know his family. I know his brother real well, and his sister-in-law. I know her real, real well. In fact, we are quite close. No, more than that: we talk all the time. By letter, that is.

Oh, Jackie! Me and Bobby! Bobby and me! No director, no writer, could have ever thought of anything more perfect. He is Jack, only more innocent. Jack, only more loving. Jack, only not married to you. So I don't feel guilty. And I can go ahead, get him away from her, and marry him. He is already in my heart and I am in his, he says. More than any other woman in his entire life. I owe it all to you, Jackie, because you sent him to me in my hour of need and he saved me. I owe you Bobby, Jackie, so I owe you everything.

Write and say that you are glad.

Love,
Marilyn

July 28, 1962

Martha,

This is the last letter I shall ever write to you. Our correspondence is over. I have retrieved all your letters from Miss S and am herewith returning them to you.

Josephine

On the afternoon of her birthday, after mailing this letter, Jackie wrote in her diary, "Out of all the men in the universe, she had to pick Bobby. . . . I could cope with Jack, but not with him. Never him. He was pure, and now she's sullied him. I could murder her."

The ultimate flowering of Jackie's passion for Bobby, which allegedly occurred after Jack's assassination, was detailed by Heymann in his biography of Bobby Kennedy, *RFK: A Candid Biography of Robert F. Kennedy* (New York: Dutton, 1998).

MARILYN MONROE
12305 Fifth Helena Drive
Brentwood, California

Jackie Kennedy
The White House

August 4, 1962

Dear Jackie,
Part of me is shocked by your letter. Part of me is not. I was never worthy
of you, Jackie. I have no integrity. I have no soul. I am no one and nothing.
I don't deserve to live. But I probably am not even good enough to die either.
No one—not even you—can hate me as much as I do. I am so ashamed.
I only wish I knew which words I wrote that tore everything apart. I've
tried guessing, but I suppose I will die without ever knowing.
Your letters meant so much to me, Jackie. They made me feel like a per-
son, not just a bit of celluloid floating from movie to movie. I never told
you—not even in the last letters, when I thought I could tell you everything,
and did—how excited I used to get when the phone rang and it was Patty
telling me that a letter had arrived from Josephine. I was always sorry if I
wasn't there when the letter popped through the mailbox like a cascade of
good-luck charms.
Your letters were my lucky charms. I felt that nothing bad could ever
happen to me, no one could ever hurt me, while you were writing to me. I
felt special. Like a person, every time you wrote to me. That feeling didn't
go away. It lasted from letter to letter.

I even liked writing back to you. I used to write letters to you in my head, notice things through the day, and say, "I must tell Josephine." Sometimes, I couldn't wait to get home and start writing to you. Of course, I knew that my letters weren't as educated as yours, but I felt you didn't care, didn't look down on me, and I learned from your letters as well.

I don't know what my life will be like from now on, without you and your letters in it. I don't think it will be worth living, not really, not anymore. Kiss Bobby for me, and John and Caroline. Be kind to Jack, because in his heart, Jackie, he really does love you. And do as much good to yourself as you have always done for me.

Love,
Marilyn

Sometime in the late evening of August 4, 1962, Marilyn wrote this letter to Jackie. She never mailed it.

3 A.M., August 5, 1962

Dearest Marilyn,

I am writing this letter to you this early in the morning because, as soon as I have finished it, I plan to ring for the steward and, despite the early hour, instruct him to send it to you by special courier as soon as humanly possible. I am desperate that this letter reach you at once. For I am consumed by a burning guilt and wish only that I could turn back the clock and curb the insane rashness which caused me to send my last cruel and unkind letter to you and to return to you your cherished letters as well.

There are many explanations for my hotheaded and unworthy behavior—most best made in person, or over the telephone. However, without wishing to unduly alarm you with the following information, I am not altogether sure whether you are entirely wrong about your telephone being tapped. In the last few days, there have been meetings in the Oval Office between Bobby and Jack and Hoover, and during one of them, I chanced to hear mention of 'Marilyn.' I may be jumping to an erroneous conclusion, but just in case, take care, as you always do.

Had we spoken on the telephone, I would have asked you how you could ever forgive me. More to the point, how can I ever forgive myself? If I could turn back the clock (and which of us can?), I would never have sent that stupid, self-indulgent, misguided note.

How can I fully explain my state of mind when I wrote my last letter to you? How will you ever begin to understand my callous act of cruelty? I am not sure, but I shall strive to explain myself to you. Of course, if after you have read my explanation, you no longer wish to correspond with me, I will understand utterly and completely. For I have behaved unconscionably.

Since coming to my senses, I have imagined your reaction to my brutal note and felt like a monster. You are always so open, so direct, wear your heart on your sleeve, as I never would, never could. In this case, however, I owe you the truth. I sent that letter, Marilyn, not because of Jack, but because of Bobby.

When I received your cry for help after the birthday party, my first instinct was to turn to Bobby—who was then in California—and ask him to rush to your side and endeavor to help you. I never dreamed that a romantic relationship would ensue. When you told me that it had, for a mad, irrational, unforgivable moment, I was overwhelmed by jealousy and fear. For although I have hitherto hidden the truth from everyone, even myself, Bobby has always been close to my heart. The sweet-natured, pure-spirited younger brother, the boy who represented everything that is good, innocent, and worth loving in Jack. When Jack was false to me, absent, or cruel, it was Bobby about whom I fantasized. Your admission that you love Bobby and that he loves you shocked me to the very core. For however much I always knew that Bobby and I have no future, the thought that I might lose him to you was, for a moment, unbearable.

There is more to say, Marilyn, much more, but I will save it all till September, when I understand you will be in Washington for the Josh Logan opening. I fervently hope that now that the air between us has completely cleared, we shall finally meet and talk at last. We have so much in common, you and I. Not just Jack, but as our letters have always demonstrated, we share so much more. For while it might seem to outsiders that I merely wrote to you in order to nourish my rather infantile thirst for Hollywood gossip and my desire to burnish my image through your advice, and that you wrote to me because you viewed me as a conduit to Jack, we both know that isn't the truth.

Throwing all modesty aside, we two are the most famous women of our time, able to trust no one but each other with our confidences because we each have so much to lose. It also seems to me that both of us, in our own ways, are actresses, both simmering with a father hunger, both strong but vulnerable, weak but tough, and so much more.

As for Bobby, my irrational longing for him has subsided for reasons which will become clear to you. So that if Bobby is the one upon whom you have set your heart, you do, indeed, have my blessings. Write and tell me how I can help. I owe you so much.

Let me explain: Jack has just returned to his room, I am ecstatic, and I owe it all to you. When I first read your letter regarding Jack's sexuality, my only reaction was to focus on Bobby. I ignored all your perceptions regarding Jack and his needs, and focused only on the fact of you and Bobby being romantically involved.

It was only yesterday that I reread your letter, this time focusing on Jack. Since then, you have revolutionized not only my entire attitude toward Jack, but also my attitude to life, in general. I suppose I was always far too controlling. When it came to Jack, I exercised that control by refusing to give him everything he wanted from me. I resisted his drive to involve me in politics until he was close to power. Then I wanted power myself, almost as much as he did. So I helped him. Yet taunted him, secretly opposed him, and never gave him what he truly wanted.

I am not talking about one isolated sex act, but my entire attitude to love and loving. Reading your letters (the first and, more especially, the second, in which you talk about Jack in detail and your feelings for him), I realized that I never truly understood how to love. As a result, I never really loved Jack the way in which he deserved to be loved. Nor did I ever fully understand him. Not like you did. I didn't understand Jack, nor did I really love him.

Since your last letters, Marilyn, all that has changed. I have finally understood both Jack and myself. Consequently, our marriage will never be the same again. Apart from wanting the very best for you (because you are a good person with far more integrity within you than I shall ever muster), all I want is to grow old with Jack and the children. To live with him and love him. To see John's and Caroline's children grow up and to love them as much as I know Jack will. I pray that time and fate will grant me my dream. And you, yours, Marilyn. And you, yours.

With love and heartfelt thanks,
Jackie

Marilyn Monroe was found dead in bed early in the morning of August 5, 1962.

BIBLIOGRAPHY

In addition to the essays, articles, and reviews cited in the text, the following books were consulted.

JACKIE KENNEDY BOOKS

Abbott, James A., and Elaine M. Rice. *Designing Camelot: The Kennedy White House Restoration*. New York: Van Nostrand Reinhold, 1998.

Abramson, Rudy. *Spanning the Century: The Life of W. Averell Harriman*. New York: Morrow, 1992.

Adams, William Howard. *Atget's Gardens*. Garden City, N.Y.: Doubleday, 1979.

Alphand, Hervé. *L'etonement d'etre journal 1939–1973*. Paris: Fayard, 1977.

Alsop, Joseph W., with Adam Platt. *"I've Seen the Best of It": Memoirs*. New York: W. W. Norton, 1992.

Alsop, Susan Mary. *To Marietta from Paris, 1945–1960*. London: Weidenfeld and Nicholson, 1976.

Anderson, Christopher. *Jackie After Jack: Portrait of the Lady*. New York: William Morrow, 1998.

———. *Jack and Jackie*. New York: William Morrow, 1996.

Anthony, Carl Sferrazza. *First Ladies, Volume II: The Saga of the Presidents' Wives and Their Power, 1961–1990*. New York: Morrow, 1991.

Aronson, Steven M. L. *Hype*. New York: Morrow, 1983.

Baldrige, Letitia. *In the Kennedy Style: Magical Evenings in the Kennedy White House, with Recipes by White House Chef René Verdon*. New York: Doubleday, 1998.

Baldwin, Billy. *Billy Baldwin Remembers*. New York: Harcourt Brace Jovanovich, 1974.

Ball, George. *The Post Has Another Pattern: Memoirs*. New York: W. W. Norton, 1982.

Beale, Betty. *Power at Play: A Memoir of Parties, Politicians, and the Presidents in My Bedroom*. Washington, D.C.: Regnery Gateway, 1993.

Beard, Peter. *Longing for Darkness: Kamante's Tales from Out of Africa*. New York: Harcourt Brace Jovanovich, 1975.

Beevor, Anthony, and Artemis Cooper. *Paris After the Liberation, 1944–1949*. London: Hamish Hamilton, 1994.

Belle, John. *Grand Central: Gateway to a Million Lives*. New York: W. W. Norton, 1999.

Beschloss, Michael R. *Taking Charge: The Johnson White House Tapes, 1963–1964*. New York: Simon & Schuster, 1997.

Billings, Lem. *Jack Remembered*. Honolulu: Baynards Press, 1964.

Birmingham, Stephen. *Jacqueline Bouvier Kennedy Onassis*. London: Victor Gollancz, London: 1979.

Botherel, Jean. *Louise, ou la vie de Louise de Vilmorin*. Paris: Bernard Grasset, 1993.

Bouvier, Jacqueline and Lee. *One Special Summer*. New York: Delacorte Press, 1974.

Braden, Joan. *Just Enough Rope: An Intimate Memoir*. New York: Villard, 1989.

Bradford, Sarah. *America's Queen: A Life of Jacqueline Kennedy Onassis*. New York: Viking Press, 2000.

Bradlee, Benjamin C. *Conversations with Kennedy*. London: Quartet, 1975.

———. *A Good Life: Newspapering and Other Adventures*. New York: Touchstone, 1995.

Bryant, Traphes, and Frances Spatz Leighton. *Dog Days at the White House: The Outrageous Memoirs of the Presidential Kennel Keeper*. New York: Macmillan, 1975.

Buchan, John. *Memory Hold-the-Door (The Pilgrim's Way)*. London: Hodder and Stoughton, 1940.

Burleigh, Nina. *A Very Private Woman: The Life and Unsolved Murder of Presidential Mistress Mary Meyer*. New York: Bantam, 1998.

Burns, James McGregor. *John Kennedy: A Political Profile*. New York: Harcourt, Brace and World, 1961.

Cafarakis, Christian. *The Fabulous Onassis, His Life and Loves*. New York: Morrow, 1972.

Canfield, Cass. *Up and Down and Around*. London: Collins, 1972.

Capote, Truman. *Answered Prayers: The Unfinished Novel.* London: Hamish Hamilton, 1986.

Carpenter, Liz. *Ruffles and Flourishes.* College Station, Tex.: Texas A & M University Press, 1993.

Cassini, Igor, with Jeanne Molli. *I'd Do It All Over Again: The Life and Times of Igor Cassini.* New York: Putnam's Sons, 1977.

Cerf, Bennett. *At Random: The Reminiscences of Bennet Cerf.* New York: Random House, 1977.

Chellis, Marcia. *The Joan Kennedy Story: One Woman's Victory Over Infidelity, Politics and Privilege.* London: Sidgwick and Jackson, 1985.

Cheshire, Maxine. *Maxine Cheshire, Reporter.* Boston: Houghton Mifflin, 1978.

Churchill, Sarah. *Keep on Dancing: An Autobiography.* New York: Coward, McCann and Geoghegan, 1981.

Clarke, Gerald. *Capote: A Biography.* London: Hamish Hamilton, 1988.

Clifford, Clark, with Richard Holbrooke. *Counsel to the President: A Memoir.* New York: Random House, 1991.

Collier, Peter, and David Horowitz. *The Kennedys: An American Drama.* London: Pan, 1985.

Cooper, Diana. *The Rainbow Comes and Goes.* London: Rupert Hart-Davis, 1958.

Crick, Michael, and Jeffrey Archer. *Stranger than Fiction.* London: Hamish Hamilton, 1995.

Curtis, Charlotte. *First Lady.* New York: Pyramid, 1962.

Dallek, Robert. *Flawed Giant: Lyndon Johnson and His Times, 1961–1973.* New York: Oxford University Press, 1998.

Damore, Leo. *The Cape Cod Years of John Fitzgerald Kennedy.* Englewood Cliffs, N.J.: Prentice Hall, 1962.

———. *The Kennedys: Dynasty and Disaster.* London: Sidgwick and Jackson, 1985.

Davis, John H. *The Bouviers: From Waterloo to the Kennedys and Beyond.* Washington, D.C.: National Press, 1993.

———. *Jacqueline Bouvier: An Intimate Memoir.* New York: John Wiley and Sons, 1996.

Davis, Kenneth S. *The Politics of Honor: A Biography of Adlai E. Stevenson.* New York: Putnam's Sons, 1967.

Davis, Nancy, and Barbara Donahue. *Miss Porter's School: A History.* Farmington, Conn.: Miss Porters's School, 1992.

De Gaulle, Charles. *Memoires de'spor: Memoirs of Hope: Renewal 1958–62 and Endeavour: 1962.* London: Weidenfeld and Nicolson, 1971.

DeLoach, Cartha "Deke." *Hoover's FBI: The Inside Story by Hoover's Trusted Lieutenant.* Washington D.C.: Regnery, 1995.

Dempster, Nigel. *Heiress: The Story of Christina Onassis*. London: Weidenfeld and Nicolson, 1989.

Dickerson, Nancy. *Among Those Present: A Reporter's View of Twenty-five Years in Washington*. New York: Random House, 1976.

Doubleday, eds. *A Tribute to Jacqueline Kennedy Onassis*. New York: Doubleday, 1995.

Douglas Home, William. *Old Men Remember*. London: Collins and Brown, 1991.

DuBois, Diana. *In Her Sister's Shadow: An Intimate Biography of Lee Radziwill*. London: Little, Brown, 1995.

Duchin, Peter, with Charles Michener. *Ghost of a Chance, A Memoir*. New York: Random House, 1996.

Evans, Peter. *Ari: The Life and Times of Aristotle Socrates Onassis*. London: Jonathan Cape, 1986.

Exner, Judith, as told to Ovid Demaris. *My Story*. New York: Grove Press, 1977.

Fay, Paul B., Jr. *The Pleasure of His Company, Author's Edition*. USA, November 1982.

Freeman, Dr. Erika Padon. *Insights: Conversations with Theodor Reik*. Englewood Cliffs, N.J.: Prentice Hall, 1971.

Fursenko, Aleksandr, and Timothy Naftali. *"One Hell of a Gamble": Khrushchev, Castro and Kennedy, 1958–1964*. New York: W. W. Norton, 1997.

Galbraith, John Kenneth. *Ambassador's Journal: A Personal Account of the Kennedy Years*. London: Hamish Hamilton, 1969.

Galella, Ron. *Jacqueline*. New York: Sheed and Ward, 1974.

Galitzine, Irene. *Dalla Russia Alla Russia, Memorie di Irene Galitzine Raccolte da Cinzia Toni*. Milan: Longanesi and C., 1996.

Gallagher, Mary Barelli, ed. Frances Spatz Leighton. *My Life with Jacqueline Kennedy*. London: Michael Joseph, 1970.

Gilbert, Robert E. *The Mortal Presidency: Illness and Anguish in the White House*. New York: Basic Books, 1992.

Goodwin, Doris Kearns. *The Fitzgeralds and the Kennedys: An American Saga*. London: Weidenfeld and Nicolson, 1987.

Goodwin, Richard N. *Remembering America: A Voice from the Sixties*. Boston: Little, Brown, 1988.

Graham, Katharine. *Personal History*. New York: Knopf, 1997.

Gutham, Edwin. *We Band of Brothers: A Memoir of Robert F. Kennedy*. New York: Harper & Row, 1971.

Hackett, Pad, ed. *The Andy Warhol Diaries*. London: Simon & Schuster, 1989.

Halberstam, David. *The Best and the Brightest*. London: Narrie and Jenkins, 1972.

———. *The Fifties*. New York: Villard, 1993.

Hamilton, Edith. *The Great Age of Greek Literature*. London: W.W. Norton, 1942.

Hamilton, Nigel. *Life and Death of an American President, Volume One: Reckless Youth*. London: Random House, 1992.

Heymann, C. David. *RFK: A Candid Biography of Robert F. Kennedy*. New York: Dutton, 1998.

———. *A Woman Named Jackie: An Intimate Biography of Jacqueline Bouvier Kennedy Onassis, complete updated edition*. New York: Birch Lane Press, 1994.

Horne, Alistair. *Macmillan, 1957–1986*. London: Macmillan, 1989.

Horowitz, Helen Lefkowitz. *Alma Mater: Design and Experience in the Women's Colleges from Their Nineteenth-Century Beginnings to the 1930s*. New York: Knopf, 1984.

Hoving, Thomas. *Making the Mummies Dance: Inside the Metropolitan Museum of Art*. New York: Simon & Schuster, 1993.

Isaacson, Walter, and Evan Thomas. *The Wise Men, Six Friends and the World They Made: Acheson, Bohlen, Harriman, Kennan, Lovett, McCloy*. New York: Simon & Schuster, 1986.

Johnson, Lady Bird. *A White House Diary*. New York: Holt, Rinehart and Winston, 1970.

Kelly, Kitty. *Jackie Oh!* New York: Granada Publishing, 1978.

Kennedy, John F., ed. *As We Remember Joe*. Privately printed, 1945.

Kennedy, Rose Fitzgerald. *Time to Remember: An Autobiography*. London. Collins, 1974.

Kessler, Ronald. *The Sins of the Father: Joseph P. Kennedy and the Dynasty He Founded*. New York: Warner, 1996.

Klein, Edward. *All Too Human: The Love Story of Jack and Jackie Kennedy*. New York: Pocket Books, 1996.

———. *Just Jackie: Her Private Years*. New York: Ballantine, 1998.

Koestebaum, Wayne. *Jackie Under My Skin: Interpreting an Icon*. London: Fourth Estate, 1996.

Krock, Arthur. *Memoirs: Sixty Years on the Firing Line*. New York: Funk and Wagnalls, 1968.

Kunhardt, Philip B., Jr., ed. *Life in Camelot: The Kennedy Years*. Boston: Little, Brown, 1988.

Kuntz, Tom and Phil, eds. *The Sinatra Files: The Secret FBI Dossier*. New York: Three Rivers Press, 2000.

Lacuture, Jean, tr. Alan Sheridan. *De Gaulle, The Ruler (1945–1970)*. London: Harvill, 1991.

Landon, Angela. *"We Meet in Grief": The Relationship Between Jacqueline Kennedy and Lyndon Johnson*. Unpublished thesis.

Langley Hall, Gordon, and Ann Pinchot. *Jacqueline Kennedy: A Biography*. New York: Signet, 1966.

Lankford, Nelson D. *The Last American Aristocrat: The Biography of David K. E. Bruce, 1899–1977*. Boston: Little, Brown, 1996.

Lash, Joseph P. *Eleanor: The Years Alone*. London: Andre Deutsch, 1973.

Lawford, Patricia Seaton, with Ted Schwarz. *The Peter Lawford Story: Life with the Kennedys, Monroe and the Rat Pack*. New York: Carroll and Graf, 1988.

Leamer, Laurence. *The Kennedy Women: The Triumph and Tragedy of America's First Family*. London: Bantam, 1995.

L'Etang, Hugh. *Fit to Lead*. London: William Heinemann Medical Books, 1980.

Lilly, Doris. *Three Fabulous Greeks: Onassis, Niarchos and Livanos, Three of the World's Richest Men*. New York: Cowles Book Company, 1970.

Lincoln Anne H. *The Kennedy White House Parties*. New York: Viking, 1967.

Lincoln, Evelyn. *My Twelve Years with John F. Kennedy*. New York: David McKay, 1965.

Lowe, Jacques. *Jacqueline Kennedy Onassis: A Tribute*. New York: Jacques Lowe Visual Arts Project, 1995.

McTaggart, Lynne. *Kathleen Kennedy: Her Life and Times*. New York: Dial Press, 1983.

Macmillan, Harold. *At the End of the Day*. London: Macmillan, 1973.

———. *Pointing the Way*. London: Macmillan, 1972.

Mailer, Norman. *The Presidential Papers*. London: Andre Deutsch, 1964.

Malraux, André, tr. Irene Clephane. *Fallen Oaks: Conversations with de Gaulle*. London: Hamish Hamilton, 1972.

———. *La Corde et les Souris*. Paris: Gallimard, 1976.

Manchester, William. *Controversy and Other Essays in Journalism*. Boston: Little, Brown, 1976.

———. *The Death of a President: November 20–November 25, 1963*. New York: Harper & Row, 1967.

———. *The Glory and the Dream: A Narrative History of America, 1932–1972*. New York: Bantam, 1980.

Martin, John Bartlow. *Adlai Stevenson and the World: The Life of Adlai Stevenson*. Garden City, N.Y.: Doubleday, 1977.

Martin, Ralph G. *A Hero for Our Time: An Intimate Story of the Kennedy Years*. New York: Ballantine, 1983.

———. *Seeds of Destruction: Joe Kennedy and His Sons*. New York: Putnam's Sons, 1995.

May, Ernest R., and Philip D. Zelikow, eds. *The Kennedy Tapes: Inside the White House During the Cuban Missile Crisis*. Cambridge: Harvard University Press, 1997.

Morris, Sylvia Jukes. *Rage for Fame: The Ascent of Clare Booth Luce*. New York: Random House, 1997.

Mosley, Charlotte, ed. *The Letters of Nancy Mitford: Love from Nancy*. London: Hodder and Stoughton, 1993.

Moutsatsos, Kiki Feroudi, with Phyllis Karas. *The Onassis Women: An Eyewitness Account*. New York: Putnam's Sons, 1998.

O'Donnell, Kennth P., and David F. Powers with Joe McCarthy. *"Johnny, We Hardly Knew Ye": Memories of John Fitzgerald Kennedy*. Boston: Little, Brown, 1970.

Oppenheimer, Jerry. *The Other Mrs. Kennedy, Ethel Skakel Kennedy: An American Drama of Power, Privilege, and Politics*. New York: St. Martin's Press, 1994.

Paglia, Camille. *Sexual Personae: Art and Decadence from Nefertiti to Emily Dickinson*. London: Penguin Books, 1992.

Peyser, Joan. *Bernstein: A Biography*. New York: Morrow, 1987.

Plimpton, George. *Truman Capote*. London: Picador, 1998.

Potter, Jeffrey. *Men, Money and Magic: The Story of Dorothy Schiff*. New York: Coward, McCann and Geoghegan, 1976.

Powers, Richard. *President Kennedy, Profile of Power*. New York: Simon & Schuster, 1993.

Reeves, Thomas C. *A Question of Character: A Life of John F. Kennedy*. Rocklin, Calif.: Forum Prima Publishing, 1997.

Reich, Cary. *Financior: The Biography of Andre Meyer, A Story of Money, Power and the Reshaping of American Business*. New York: John Wiley and Sons, 1997.

Rhea, Mini. *I Was Jacqueline Kennedy's Dressmaker*. New York: Fleet, 1962.

Rostow, Walt W. *The Diffusion of Power: An Essay in Recent History*. New York: Macmillan, 1972.

Russell, Jan Jarboe. *Lady Bird: A Biography of Mrs. Johnson*. New York: Lisa Dew/Scribner, 1999.

Salinger, Pierre. *P.S.: A Memoir*. New York: St. Martin's Press, 1995.

———. *With Kennedy*. Garden City, N.Y.: Doubleday, 1996.

Seebohm, Caroline. *No Regrets: The Life of Marietta Tree*. New York: Simon & Schuster, 1997.

Sgubin, Marta, and Nancy Nicholas. *Cooking for Madam: Recipes and Reminiscences from the Home of Jacqueline Kennedy Onassis*. New York: Lisa Drew/Scribner, 1998.

Shapley, Deborah. *Promise and Power: The Life and Times of Robert McNamara*. Boston: Little, Brown, 1993.

Shaw, Mark. *The John F. Kennedys: A Family Album*. New York: Noonday Press, 1964.

Shaw, Maud. *White House Nannie: My Years with Caroline and John Kennedy, Jr.* New York: New American Library, 1966.

Shesol, Jeff. *Mutual Contempt: Lyndon Johnson, Robert Kennedy, and the Feud That Defined a Decade.* New York: W. W. Norton, 1997.

Smith, Sally Bedell. *Reflected Glory: The Life of Pamela Churchill Harriman.* New York: Simon & Schuster, 1996.

Sorensen, Theodore C. *Kennedy.* London: Hodder and Stoughton, 1965.

Stassinopoulos, Arianna. *Maria: Beyond the Callas Legend.* London: Weidenfeld and Nicolson, 1980.

Stein, Jean, and George Plimpton, eds. *American Journey: The Times of Robert Kennedy.* New York: Harcourt Brace Jovanovich, 1970.

Sulzberger, C. L. *The Last of the Giants.* London: Weidenfeld and Nicolson, 1972.

Sutherland, Robert. *Maria Callas: Diaries of a Friendship.* London: Constable, 1999.

Taki. *Princes, Playboys and High-Class Tarts.* New York: Karz-Cohl, 1984.

Tapert, Annette, and Diana Edkins. *The Power of Style: The Women Who Defined the Art of Living Well.* New York: Crown, 1994.

Thayer, Mary Van Rensselaer. *Jacqueline Kennedy: The White House Years.* Boston: Little, Brown, 1967.

Thomas, Helen. *Front Row at the White House: My Life and Times.* New York: Lisa Drew/Scribner, 1999.

Thompson, Lawrence, and R. H. Winnick. *Robert Frost: The Late Years, 1938–1963.* New York: Holt, Rinehart and Winston, 1976.

Truman, Margaret. *First Ladies.* New York: Random House, 1995.

Vanden Heuvel, William, and Milton Gwirtzman. *On His Own: RFK, 1964–1968.* Garden City, N.Y.: Doubleday, 1970.

Vidal, Gore. *Palimpsest: A Memoir.* London: Andre Deutsch, 1995.

Von Post, Gunilla, with Carl Johnes. *Love, Jack.* New York: Crown, 1997.

Vreeland, Diana, with eds. George Plimpton and Christopher Hemphill. *D.V.* New York: Da Capo Press, 1997.

West, J. F., with Mary Lynn Kotz. *Upstairs at the White House: My Life with the First Ladies.* London: W. H. Allen, 1994.

White, Theodore H. *The Making of the President, 1960.* London: Jonathan Cape, 1962.

————. *In Search of History: A Personal Adventure.* New York: Warner, 1978.

Wills, Gary. *The Kennedy Imprisonment: A Meditation on Power.* Boston: Little, Brown, 1981.

Wofford, Harris. *Of Kennedys and Kings.* New York: Farrar, Straus and Giroux, 1980.

Youngblood, Russ W. *Twenty Years in the Secret Service: My Life with Five Presidents.* New York: Simon & Schuster, 1973.

Ziegler, Philip. *Diana Cooper.* London: Hamish Hamilton, 1981.

MARILYN MONROE BOOKS

Adams, Cindy. *Lee Strasberg: The Imperfect Genius of the Actors Studio.* Garden City N.Y.: Doubleday, 1980.

Allen, Maury. *Where Have You Gone, Joe DiMaggio?* New York: Dutton, 1975.

Anderson, Janice. *Marilyn Monroe.* London: Hamlyn, 1983.

Arnold, Eve. *Marilyn Monroe: An Appreciation.* New York: Knopf, 1987.

Axelrod, George. *Will Success Spoil Rock Hunter?* New York: Samuel French, 1955.

Bacall, Lauren. *By Myself.* New York: Knopf, 1979.

Baker, Roger. *Marilyn Monroe: Photographs from UPI/Bettmann.* New York: Portland/Crescent, 1990.

Barris, George. *Marilyn: Her Life in Her Own Words.* New York: Birch Lane Press, 1995.

Belmont, Georges (interviewer). *Marilyn Monroe and the Camera.* Boston: Bulfinch, 1989.

Benny, Jack, with Joan Benny. *Sunday Nights at Seven.* New York: Warner, 1990.

Bentley, Eric, ed. *Thirty Years of Treason: Excerpts from Hearings Before the House Committee on Un-American Activities, 1938–1968.* New York: Viking, 1971.

Blair, Joan, and Clay, Jr. *The Search for J.F.K.* New York: Berkeley, 1976.

Bogdanovich, Peter. *Fritz Lang in America.* New York: Praeger, 1967.

Bosworth, Patricia. *Montgomery Clift: A Biography.* New York: Harcourt Brace Jovanovich, 1978.

Brown, David. *Let Me Entertain You.* New York: Morrow, 1990.

Brown, Peter, and Patte Barham. *Marilyn: The Last Take.* New York: Penguin, 1992.

Capell, Frank. *The Strange Death of Marilyn Monroe.* Staten Island, N.Y.: Herald of Freedom, 1964.

Carpozi, George, Jr. *Marilyn Monroe: Her Own Story.* New York: Belmont Books, 1961.

Chekhov, Michael. *To the Actor: On the Techniques of Acting.* New York: Harper & Row, 1953.

Clark, Colin. *The Prince, the Showgirl and Me.* New York: St. Martin's Press, 1996.

Conover, David. *Finding Marilyn.* New York: Grosset & Dunlap, 1981.

Cotton, Joseph. *Vanity Will Get You Somewhere.* London: Columbus Books, 1987.

Crivello, Kirk. *Fallen Angels*. Secaucus, N.J.: Citadel Press, 1988.

Crown, Lawrence. *Marilyn at Twentieth Century-Fox*. London: Comet/Planet, 1987.

Davis, Sammy, Jr. *Hollywood in a Suitcase*. New York: Morrow, 1980.

De Dienes, Andrew. *Marilyn Mon Amour*. New York: St. Martin's Press, 1985.

Doll, Susan. *Marilyn: Her Life and Legend*. New York: Beekman House, 1990.

Dougherty, James E. *The Secret Happiness of Marilyn Monroe*. Chicago: Playboy Press, 1976.

Edwards, Anne. *Judy Garland*. New York: Simon & Schuster, 1975.

Eells, George. *Robert Mitchum*. New York: Franklin Watts, 1984.

Eisner, Lotte H. *Fritz Lang*. London: Secker & Warburg, 1976.

Exner, Judith, and Ovid Demaris. *My Story*. New York: Grove, 1977.

Farber, Stephen, and Marc Green. *Hollywood on the Couch*. New York: Morrow, 1993.

Finler, Joel W. *The Hollywood Story*. London: Octopus, and New York: Crown, 1988.

Fowler, Will. *Reporters: Memoirs of a Young Newspaperman*. Santa Monica, Calif.: Roundtable Publications, 1991.

Franklin, Joe, and Laurie Palmer. *The Marilyn Monroe Story*. New York: Rudolph Field, 1953.

Freedland, Michael. *Gregory Peck*. New York: Morrow, 1980.

Freeman, Lucy. *Why Norma Jean Killed Marilyn Monroe*. Chicago: Global Rights, 1992.

Gates, Daryl F. *Chief: My Life in the L.A.P.D.* New York: Bantam, 1992.

Gentry, Curt. *J. Edgar Hoover: The Man and the Secrets*. New York: Penguin, 1991.

Gunther, Marc. *The House That Roone Built*. Boston: Little, Brown, 1994.

Golden, Even. *Platinum Girl: The Life and Legends of Jean Harlow*. New York: Abbeville Press, 1991.

Goode, James. *The Story of the Misfits*. Indianapolis: Bobbs-Merrill, 1961.

Goodman, Ezra. *The Fifty-Year Decline and Fall of Hollywood*. New York: Simon & Schuster, 1961.

Greenson, Ralph R. *The Technique and Practice of Psychoanalysis*. New York: International University Press, 1967.

Gregory, Adela, and Milo Speriglio. *Crypt 33*. Secaucus, N.J.: Carol, 1993.

Grobel, Lawrence. *The Hustons*. New York: Avon, 1989.

Guiles, Fred Lawrence. *Legend: The Life and Death of Marilyn Monroe*. New York: Stein and Day, 1984.

————. *Norma Jean: The Life of Marilyn Monroe*. New York: McGraw-Hill, 1969.

Hamblett, Charles. *Who Killed Marilyn Monroe?* London: Leslie Frewin, 1966.

Hamon, Herve, and Patrick Rotman. *Yves Montand: Tu vois, je n'ai pas oublie.* Paris: Seuil/Fayard, 1990.

Harris, Marlys J. *The Zanucks of Hollywood.* New York: Crown, 1989.

Haspiel, James. *Marilyn: The Ultimate Look at the Legend.* New York: Henry Holt, 1991.

Hersh, Seymour M. *The Dark Side of Camelot.* Boston: Little, Brown, 1997.

Howe, Irving, and Lewis Coser. *The American Communist Party.* Boston: Beacon, 1957.

Hoyt, Edwin P. *Marilyn: The Tragic Venus.* Philadelphia: Chilton, 1965.

Hudson, James A. *The Mysterious Death of Marilyn Monroe.* New York: Volitant, 1968.

Huston, John. *An Open Book.* New York: Knopf, 1980.

Hutchinson, Tom. *Marilyn Monroe.* New York: Exeter Books, 1982.

Johnson, Dorris, and Ellen Leventhal, eds. *The Letters of Nunnally Johnson.* New York: Knopf, 1981.

Kahn, Roger. *Joe & Marilyn: A Memory of Love.* New York: Morrow, 1986.

Kaminsky, Stuart. *John Huston: Maker of Magic.* Boston: Houghton Mifflin, 1978.

Kazan, Elia. *A Life.* New York: Knopf, 1988.

Kelly, Kitty. *His Way: The Unauthorized Biography of Frank Sinatra.* New York: Bantam Books, 1986.

Kessler, Ronald. *The Sins of the Father.* New York: Warner, 1996.

Kobal, John, ed. *Marilyn Monroe: A Life on Film.* London: Hamlyn, 1974.

————. *People Will Talk.* New York: Knopf, 1985.

Lambert, Gavin. *On Cukor.* New York: Putnam's Sons, 1972.

Lawford, Patricia Seaton, and Ted Schwarz. *The Peter Lawford Story.* New York: Carroll & Graf, 1988.

Leigh, Wendy. *Prince Charming: The John F. Kennedy, Jr., Story.* New York: Dutton, 1993.

Logan, Joshua. *Movie Stars, Real People and Me.* New York: Delacorte, 1978.

Luijiters, Guus. *Marilyn Monroe, In Her Own Words.* London: Omnibus, 1991.

McBride, Joseph. *Hawks on Hawks.* Berkeley: University of California Press, 1982.

McCann, Graham. *Marilyn Monroe.* New Brunswick, N.J.: Rutgers University Press, 1988.

Madsen, Axel. *John Huston.* Garden City, N.Y.: Doubleday, 1978.

Mailer, Norman. *Marilyn.* New York: Grosset & Dunlap, 1973.

————, with photographs by Milton H. Greene. *Of Women and Their Elegance.* New York: Simon & Schuster, 1980.

Mankiewicz, Joseph L. *More About All About Eve.* New York: Random House, 1972.

Masters, George, and Norma Lee Browning, *The Masters Way to Beauty*. New York: NAL/Signet, 1978.

Meaker, M. J. *Sudden Endings*. Garden City, N.Y.: Doubleday, 1964.

Mellen, Joan. *Marilyn Monroe*. New York: Pyramid, 1973.

Miller, Arthur. *After the Fall*. New York: Dramatists Play Service, 1964.

————. *Timebends*. New York: Grove Press, 1987.

Miracle, Berniece Baker, and Mona Rae Miracle. *My Sister Marilyn*. Chapel Hill, N.C.: Algonquin Books, 1994.

Molnar, Michael. *The Diary of Sigmund Freud*. New York: Robert Stewart/Charles Scribner's Sons, 1992.

Monroe, Marilyn. *My Story*. New York: Stein and Day, 1976.

Montand, Yves, with Herne Hamon and Patrick Rotman. *You See, I Haven't Forgotten*. New York: Knopf, 1992.

Moore, Robin, and Gene Schoor. *Marilyn & Joe DiMaggio*. New York: Manor Books, 1977.

Morphos, Evangeline, ed. *Lee Strasberg: A Dream of Passion*. Boston: Little, Brown, 1987.

Mosley, Leonard. *Zanuck*. Boston: Little, Brown, 1984.

Murray, Eunice. *Marilyn: The Last Months*. New York: Pyramid, 1975.

Negulesco, Jean. *Things I Did . . . and Things I Think I Did*. New York: Linden Press/Simon & Schuster, 1984.

Noguchi, Thomas T. *Coroner*. New York: Pocket, 1983.

Nolan, William F. *John Huston: King Rebel*. Los Angeles: Sherbourne Press, 1965.

Oliver, Laurence. *Confessions of an Actor*. New York: Simon & Schuster, 1982.

————. *On Acting*. New York: Touchstone/Simon & Schuster, 1986.

Oppenheimer, Jerry. *The Other Mrs. Kennedy*. New York: St. Martin's Press, 1994.

Otash, Fred. *Investigation Hollywood*. Chicago: Regnery, 1976.

Overholt, Alma. *The Catalina Story*. Los Angeles: n.p., 1962.

Palmer, Edwin O. *History of Hollywood*. New York: Garland Publishing, 1978.

Parsons, Louella O. *Tell It to Louella*. New York: Putnam's Sons, 1961.

Pepitone, Lena, and William Stadiem. *Marilyn Monroe Confidential*. New York: Simon & Schuster, 1979.

Pratley, Gerald. *The Cinema of John Huston*. Cranbury, N.J.: A. S. Barnes and Co., 1977.

Preminger, Otto. *Preminger: An Autobiography*. Garden City, N.Y.: Doubleday, 1977.

Rand, Christopher. *Los Angeles: The Ultimate City*. New York: Oxford University Press, 1967.

Rappleye, Charles, and Ed Becker. *All American Mafioso*. New York: Doubleday, 1991.

Ricci, Mark, and Michael Conway. *The Complete Films of Marilyn Monroe.* Secaucus, N.J.: Citadel, 1964.

Riese, Randall, and Neal Hitchens. *The Unabridged Marilyn: Her Life from A to Z.* New York: Congdon & Weed, 1987.

Robins, Natalie. *Alien Ink.* New York: Morrow, 1992.

Rollyson, Carl E., Jr. *Marilyn Monroe: A Life of the Actress.* Ann Arbor, Mich.: UMI Research Press, 1986.

Rose, Frank. *The Agency.* New York: HarperCollins, 1995.

Rosten, Norman. *Marilyn: An Untold Story.* New York: NAL/Signet, 1973.

Russell, Jane. *Jane Russell: My Paths and My Detours.* New York: Franklin Watts, 1985.

Scagnetti, Jack. *The Life and Loves of Gable.* Middle Village, N.Y.: Jonathan David, 1978.

Schlesinger, Arthur M., Jr. *Robert Kennedy and His Times.* Boston: Houghton Mifflin, 1978.

Shaw, Sam, and Norman Rosten. *Marilyn Among Friends.* London: Bloomsbury, 1987.

Shevey, Sandra. *The Marilyn Scandal.* New York: Morrow, 1988.

Signoret, Simone. *Nostalgia Isn't What It Used to Be.* New York: HarperCollins, 1978.

Skolsky, Sidney. *Don't Get Me Wrong—I Love Hollywood.* New York: Putnam's Sons, 1975.

———. *Marilyn.* New York: Dell, 1954.

Slatzer, Robert. *The Life and Curious Death of Marilyn Monroe.* New York: Pinnacle, 1974.

Smith, Ella. *Starring Miss Barbara Stanwyck.* New York: Crown, 1985.

Spada, James, and George Zeno. *Monroe: Her Life in Pictures.* Garden City, N.Y.: Doubleday, 1982.

Speriglio, Milo. *The Marilyn Conspiracy.* New York: Pocket Books, 1986.

Spoto, Donald. *Laurence Oliver: A Biography.* New York: HarperCollins, 1992.

———. *Marilyn Monroe: The Biography.* New York: HarperCollins, 1993.

Stack, Robert, with Mark Evans. *Straight Shooting.* New York: Macmillan, 1980.

Steinem, Gloria, with photographs by George Barris. *Marilyn.* New York: Henry Holt and Company, 1986.

Stempel, Tom. *Screenwriter: The Life and Times of Nunnally Johnson.* San Diego: A. S. Barnes, 1980.

Strasberg, Susan. *Bittersweet.* New York: Putnam's Sons, 1980.

———. *Marilyn and Me: Sisters, Rivals, Friends.* New York: Warner, 1992.

Sullivan, William C., and Bill Brown. *The Bureau: My Thirty Years in Hoover's FBI.* New York: Norton, 1979.

Summers, Anthony. *Goddess: The Secret Lives of Marilyn Monroe.* New York: Macmillan, 1985.

Swanson, Gloria. *Swanson on Swanson.* New York: Random House, 1980.

Taylor, Roger G. *Marilyn in Art.* Salem, N.H.: Salem House, 1984.

———. *Marilyn Monroe: In Her Own Words.* New York: Delilah/Putnam, 1985. (U.K.: *Marilyn on Marilyn.* London: Zachary Kwintner, 1983.)

Theoharis, Athan, editor. *From the Secret Files of J. Edgar Hoover.* Chicago: Dee, 1991.

Tierney, Gene, and Mickey Herskowitz. *Self-Portrait.* New York: Wydon, 1979.

Tornabene, Lyn. *Long Live the King.* New York: Putnam's Sons, 1976.

Trescott, Pamela. *Cary Grant: His Movies and His Life.* Washington, D.C.: Acropolis Books, 1987.

Tynan, Kenneth. *Profiles.* London: Nick Hern/Walker Books, 1989.

Victor, Adam. *The Marilyn Encyclopedia.* Woodstock, N.Y.: Overlook Press, 1999.

Vineberg, Steve. *Method Actors.* New York: Schirmer, 1991.

WPA. *Los Angeles: A Guide to the City and Its Environs.* New York: Hastings House, 1941.

Wagenknecht, Edward. *Marilyn Monroe: A Composite View.* Philadelphia: Chilton, 1969.

Walker, Alexander. *Vivien: The Life of Vivien Leigh.* New York: Grove, 1987.

Warren, Doug. *Betty Grable: The Reluctant Movie Queen.* New York: St. Martin's Press, 1981.

Whalen, Richard J. *The Founding Father: The Story of Joseph P. Kennedy.* New York: NAL World, 1964.

Williams, Jay. *Stage Left.* New York: Scribner, 1974.

Winters, Shelley. *Shelley II.* New York: Simon & Schuster, 1989.

Weatherby, W. J. *Conversations with Marilyn.* New York: Mason/Charter, 1976.

Wilson, Earl. *Show Business Laid Bare.* New York: Putnam's Sons, 1974.

———. *The Show Business Nobody Knows.* Chicago: Cowles Book Co., 1971.

Wood, Tom. *The Bright Side of Billy Wilder, Primarily.* Garden City, N.Y.: Doubleday, 1970.

Young-Bruehl, Elisabeth. *Anna Freud.* New York: Summit, 1988.

Zolotow, Maurice. *Billy Wilder in Hollywood.* New York: Putnam's Sons, 1977.

———. *Marilyn Monroe.* New York: Harcourt Brace, 1960.